The House of Silence

More Handheld Classics

Betty Bendell, *My Life And I. Confessions of an Unliberated Housewife, 1966–1980*
Henry Bartholomew (ed.), *The Living Stone. Stories of Uncanny Sculpture, 1858–1943*
Algernon Blackwood, *The Unknown. Weird Writings, 1900–1937*
Ernest Bramah, *What Might Have Been. The Story of a Social War* (1907)
D K Broster, *From the Abyss. Weird Fiction, 1907–1940*
John Buchan, *The Runagates Club* (1928)
John Buchan, *The Gap in the Curtain* (1932)
Melissa Edmundson (ed.), *Women's Weird. Strange Stories by Women, 1890–1940*
Melissa Edmundson (ed.), *Women's Weird 2. More Strange Stories by Women, 1891–1937*
Zelda Fitzgerald, *Save Me The Waltz* (1932)
Marjorie Grant, *Latchkey Ladies* (1921)
A P Herbert, *The Voluble Topsy, 1928–1947*
Inez Holden, *Blitz Writing. Night Shift & It Was Different At The Time* (1941 & 1943)
Inez Holden, *There's No Story There. Wartime Writing, 1944–1945*
Margaret Kennedy, *Where Stands A Wingèd Sentry* (1941)
Rose Macaulay, *Non-Combatants and Others. Writings Against War, 1916–1945*
Rose Macaulay, *Personal Pleasures. Essays on Enjoying Life* (1935)
Rose Macaulay, *Potterism. A Tragi-Farcical Tract* (1920)
Rose Macaulay, *What Not. A Prophetic Comedy* (1918)
James Machin (ed.) *British Weird. Selected Short Fiction, 1893–1937*
Vonda N McIntyre, *The Exile Waiting* (1975)
Elinor Mordaunt, *The Villa and The Vortex. Supernatural Stories, 1916–1924*
Jane Oliver and Ann Stafford, *Business as Usual* (1933)
John Llewelyn Rhys, *England Is My Village, and The World Owes Me A Living* (1939 & 1941)
John Llewelyn Rhys, *The Flying Shadow* (1936)
Malcolm Saville, *Jane's Country Year* (1946)
Helen de Guerry Simpson, *The Outcast and The Rite. Stories of Landscape and Fear, 1925–1938*
J Slauerhoff, *Adrift in the Middle Kingdom*, translated by David McKay (1934)
Ann Stafford, *Army Without Banners* (1942)
Rosemary Sutcliff, *Blue Remembered Hills* (1983)
Amara Thornton and Katy Soar (eds), *Strange Relics. Stories of Archaeology and the Supernatural, 1895–1954*
Elizabeth von Arnim, *The Caravaners* (1909)
Sylvia Townsend Warner, *Kingdoms of Elfin* (1977)
Sylvia Townsend Warner, *Of Cats and Elfins. Short Tales and Fantasies* (1927–1976)
Sylvia Townsend Warner, *T H White. A Biography* (1967)

The House of Silence

Ghost Stories, 1887–1920

By E Nesbit

Edited by Melissa Edmundson

Handheld Classic 38

This edition published in 2024 by Handheld Press
16 Peachfield Road, Malvern WR14 4AP, United Kingdom.
www.handheldpress.co.uk

ISBN 978-1-912766-82-6

1 2 3 4 5 6 7 8 9 0

Series design by Nadja Robinson and typeset in Adobe Caslon Pro and Open Sans.

Printed and bound in Great Britain by Short Run Press, Exeter.

Contents

Acknowledgements

My thanks to Kate Macdonald of Handheld Press, for commissioning me to curate the stories in this book. I also wish to thank Jeff Makala for his feedback on the introduction and for his editorial assistance. And my gratitude, as always, goes to Murray, Maggie, Sofie, Simone, and Remy for their furry support.

Melissa Edmundson is Senior Lecturer in British Literature and Women's Writing at Clemson University, South Carolina, and specializes in nineteenth and early twentieth-century British women writers, with a particular interest in women's supernatural fiction. She is the author of *Women's Ghost Literature in Nineteenth-Century Britain* (2013) and *Women's Colonial Gothic Writing, 1850–1930: Haunted Empire* (2018). Her critical editions include Alice Perrin's *East of Suez* (1901), published in 2011, *Avenging Angels: Ghost Stories by Victorian Women Writers*, published in 2018, and Charlotte Riddell's *The Uninhabited House* (1875), published in 2022.

She has edited these Handheld Press titles: *Women's Weird: Strange Stories by Women, 1890–1940* (2019), *Women's Weird 2: More Strange Stories by Women, 1891–1937* (2020), Elinor Mordaunt's *The Villa and The Vortex: Supernatural Stories, 1916–1924* (2021), Helen de Guerry Simpson's *The Outcast and The Rite: Stories of Landscape and Fear, 1925–1938* (2022), and D K Broster's *From the Abyss: Weird Fiction, 1907–1940* (2022).

Introduction

BY MELISSA EDMUNDSON

The name 'E Nesbit' most likely brings fond memories of the Bastable children in *The Story of the Treasure Seekers* (1899), the sand fairy in *Five Children and It* (1902), or of Bobbie, Peter and Phyllis in *The Railway Children* (1906). These books for children, which have never been out of print, were inspired by Nesbit's own childhood. Before she was the famed author 'E Nesbit', 'Daisy' Nesbit was an imaginative and precocious child who enjoyed exploring the outdoors with her brothers and who felt miserable and confined while at school. This zest for life, and a flair for disregarding convention, continued into her adulthood. Edith Nesbit refused to follow the cultural norms of the Victorian period. She campaigned for social reform to help improve the lives of others and chose to live her own life as freely and independently as possible. In private, she dealt with personal losses and domestic troubles. Throughout her life, she formed deep attachments and suffered great disappointments. Yet she had an irrepressible spirit that drew people to her. The many sides of Edith Nesbit's personality found their way into her fiction. Before becoming a bestselling author of children's literature, Nesbit was a pioneering writer of ghost stories. She began writing these stories in the 1880s, with the story that many consider to be her best, 'Man-size in Marble', published in 1887. Most of her supernatural and macabre fiction appears in the collections *Grim Tales* (1893), *Something Wrong* (1893), and *Fear* (1910). These three collections contain her most well-known stories, while other stories appeared regularly in popular literary magazines of the day, such as *The Strand*. She would continue to write supernatural fiction until the 1920s.

The House of Silence: Ghost Stories, 1887–1920 collects E Nesbit's best ghost stories spanning thirty-three years. Taken together, these stories showcase Nesbit's unique contributions to the genre. Her fiction reflects the dangers of romantic attachment – which often becomes romantic entanglement – that in turn leads to dire results. As a writer, E Nesbit was not afraid of an unhappy ending, and readers are frequently left just as unsettled as her protagonists. Her stories explore what is known as the unexplained supernatural, in which the ghosts are very much 'real' within the context of the stories, as well as the explained supernatural, where there is some sort of rational explanation behind the hauntings. Yet readers never feel cheated or dissatisfied with this latter kind of tale because of the unique way that Nesbit blends unexpected plot twists, dark comedy and occasionally the hand of fate in these narratives. Her troubled and sometimes flawed narrators are forever changed by their encounters with the supernatural, but this is only ever part of the story. Her characters are always hiding something, and their attempts to bury something from their past – whether it be a disappointment, a regret, a fear, a secret, or a crime – is often directly tied to the return of that past represented in the form of a ghost. Nesbit's ghost stories suggest that memories can betray us and no matter how much we try to escape from the past, it has a way of catching up with us. There are not only a wide variety of ghosts in these pages, but also just as many ways to be haunted.

✳

Edith Nesbit was born on 15 August 1858 to John Collis Nesbit, an agricultural chemist, and Sarah Green Alderton Nesbit. Edith's father owned the College of Agriculture and Chemistry in Kennington, south London, and the family lived in relative comfort until his death in 1862. After this Sarah Nesbit assumed the responsibilities of running the college for a short time, but she and her children were forced to move after Edith's sister Mary became increasingly ill with tuberculosis. They first moved to Brighton and then relocated to the south of France. During this period, Edith and her brothers were sent to various boarding schools. She later recalled feeling lonely while away from her mother and siblings. These periods were interspersed with happier times when the family, including Edith's older half-sister, Saretta, were together for the summers. Edith recalled one summer when her mother rented a farmhouse in La Haye, Brittany, a place where she and her brothers were allowed 'to run wild' (Nesbit 1966, 99). Ever the imaginative child, Edith enjoyed discovering different areas around their home. After Mary's death in 1871, Sarah and her children moved to Halstead in Kent (Fitzsimons 38). Edith, who was affectionately known in her family as 'Daisy', was happy to once again be in the countryside. A few years later, the family moved back to London and here Edith met Hubert Bland, who was working at a London bank. Edith left home in 1879, aged 21, and moved in with Alfred Knowles and his family. During this time, she was known as 'Edith Bland'. Nesbit and Bland were married in April 1880, by which time Edith was already pregnant with their first son Paul (Fitzsimons 52–53, 56).

Edith Nesbit became interested in socialist causes through her relationship with Hubert Bland, and they were among the founding members of the Fabian Society upon its creation in 1884. Nesbit was an active member of the Society from the beginning. The social reformer and fellow member Annie Besant remarked that 'Sidney Webb, G Bernard Shaw, Hubert and Mrs Bland, Graham Wallas – these were some of those who gave time, thought, incessant work to the popularising of Socialist thought, the spreading of sound economics, the effort to turn the workers' energy toward social rather than mere political thought' (quoted in Fitzsimons 81). Havelock Ellis described Nesbit as '[a] woman, young and beautiful it seemed to me, and certainly full of radiant vitality; she turned around and looked into one's face with a frank and direct gaze of warm sympathy which in a stranger I found singularly attractive so that I asked afterwards who she was' (quoted in Fitzsimons 85).

In 1884, Nesbit was elected to the Fabians' pamphlet committee. Two years later, she was elected to the Fabian Society Conference Committee. She also wrote for and helped edit the society's journal, *To-Day* (Fitzsimons 86). During this period, Nesbit became what she called an 'advanced' woman, spending time working in the

British Museum Reading Room with other female members of the society. She cut her hair short, wore more comfortable clothing, and smoked (Briggs 67–68). In an undated letter to her friend Ada Breakell, she wrote of her new appearance: 'It is *deliciously* comfortable [...] I have also taken to all-wool clothing which is also *deliciously* pleasant to wear' (quoted in Briggs 67).

While Nesbit was enjoying a newfound freedom and independence, she was at the same time dealing with Bland's numerous extramarital affairs. While he was courting Nesbit, Bland's relationship with Maggie Doran had already produced a child (Fitzsimons 50). In 1881, after opening a letter Doran had written to Bland, Nesbit discovered the affair. The letter revealed that Doran knew nothing of Bland's marriage to Nesbit or of Nesbit's two children with Bland (Fitzsimons 64).

Nesbit turned to writing in order to support her growing family, which now included Mary Iris, born in 1881, and a second son, Fabian, born in 1885. She also raised two of Bland's children by Alice Hoatson, a manuscript reader for the woman's magazine *Sylvia's Home Journal*, whom Nesbit had met and befriended in 1882. By 1886, Hoatson was having an affair with Bland, and she eventually moved in with the Blands as Nesbit's housekeeper and companion (Briggs 113). Accounts differ over the extent to which Nesbit approved of this situation. The unusual living arrangements were commented on by many of the Blands' friends and acquaintances. George Bernard Shaw, a friend of the Blands and for whom Nesbit had a romantic attachment, described Bland as a man 'who sported fashionable clothes, wore a monocle, and maintained simultaneously three wives, all of whom bore him children. Two of the wives lived in the same house. The legitimate one was E Nesbit' (quoted in Briggs 108). In 1886, Hoatson gave birth to a daughter, Rosamund, and in 1899, gave birth to a son, John. Hoatson's official role was 'aunt' to the children, who she referred to as her niece and nephew (Fitzsimons 114, 186, 325).

Nesbit and Bland wrote collaboratively under the pseudonym 'Fabian Bland'. In 1885, they published *The Prophet's Mantle* and the following year *Something Wrong*. In an April 1884 letter to Ada Breakell, Nesbit described their habitual process, saying, 'In all stories Hubert and I "go shares" – I am sure it is much better when we write together than when we write separately' (quoted in Briggs 61). Some of their co-written fiction had supernatural content. 'Psychical Research', published in the Christmas Number of *Longman's Magazine* in December 1884, incorporates new photographic technology with the possible sighting of a ghost in a graveyard. 'The Fabric of a Vision', published in the *Argosy* in March 1885, is a premonition story in which a woman sees a nightmarish vision of another woman being pushed to her death. Other stories, such as 'A Strange Experience', published in *Longman's Magazine* in March 1884 under Nesbit's own name, show her early interest in macabre narratives. Eleanor Fitzsimons suggests that the plot of this story, involving a young woman who refuses to be separated from the body of her deceased sister, was possibly inspired by the loss of Nesbit's sister Mary (36–37). Throughout her career, Nesbit's Gothic fiction ranged from horrific to comedic. In the 13 March 1895 issue of the *Sketch*, she, along with friend and fellow Fabian Society member Oswald Barron published 'Poor Basinghall's Chambers', a light-hearted tale of a man who is mistaken for a ghost.

Edith Nesbit also published poetry collections throughout her life. These include *Lays and Legends* (1886), *Leaves of Life* (1888), *A Pomander of Verse* (1895), *Songs of Love and Empire* (1898), *Garden Poems* (1909), and *Many Voices* (1922). Several of her poems incorporate the supernatural, and, as in her ghost stories, revolve around a lingering sense of loss and emotional distance. 'The Dead to the Living' focuses on the need to escape from life's troubles and the pain that comes from losing someone. Likewise, the mother in 'Haunted' worries that her child will be taken from her by the ghosts whose 'sad voices on the wind come thin and wild' (Nesbit 1898b, 124). The desire of the dead to reconnect with the living – and vice versa – is a recurring subject. The speaker in 'The Ghost' is tortured by the return of a lost love who remains forever out of reach: 'I hear the silken gown you wear / Sweep on the gallery floor, / Your step comes up the wide, dark stair / And passes at my door' (Nesbit 1895, 46). 'The Ghost Bereft', originally published in *The Yellow Book* in January 1897, describes a ghost's return to his home to find that his beloved has herself died. However, the woman has gone to heaven, 'where memories cease', and the couple remains apart (Nesbit 1898a, 53). A similar journey occurs in 'The Return', in which a woman's spirit journeys to her former home only to discover another woman in her place. She returns to her grave but cannot find rest, lamenting, 'I cannot sleep as I used to do' (Nesbit 1922b, 11). In these poems, the ghosts are unable to find peace because they cannot let go of their former lives, a theme that Nesbit would also explore in her stories. Other poems, such as 'Ghosts', tread a fine line between the ghostly and the real in their descriptions of troubled relationships. 'Fear' is even more enigmatic:

> If you were here,
> Hopes, dreams, ambitions, faith would disappear,
> Drowned in your eyes; and I should touch your hand,
> Forgetting all that now I understand.
> For you confuse my life with memories
> Of unrememberable ecstasies
> Which were, and are not, and can never be...
> Ah! keep the whole earth between you and me.
> (Nesbit 1922a, 78)

In these poems, fear, memory, and haunting are interconnected. They provide intriguing comparisons to Nesbit's short stories, and we can recognize hints of her fictional plots within the poetry.

By the 1890s, Nesbit was writing the works for children that would make her a bestselling author. These popular works include narratives about the adventures of the Bastable children which appear in *The Story of the Treasure Seekers* (1899), *The Wouldbegoods* (1901), and *The New Treasure Seekers* (1904). Nesbit often incorporated fantasy elements in her children's fiction, such as in the trilogy *Five Children and It* (1902), *The Phoenix and* the Carpet (1904), and The Story of the Amulet (1906). These fantasy elements can also be found in The Book of Dragons (1899), Nine Unlikely Tales for Children (1901), The Enchanted Castle (1907), and The Magic World (1912). The Railway Children (1906) became Nesbit's most popular book and was adapted into several films, including the 1970 version written and directed by Lionel Jeffries.

In 1899, Nesbit and her family moved to Well Hall in Eltham, a district south-east of London. She was happier in the countryside and found it a peaceful place to live and work. A profile of Nesbit in The Strand Magazine in September 1905 stated, 'she hates London with a deep and abiding hate, as she hates the interviewing, intellectualizing, hair-splitting world of literary London' (Anon 1905, 288). She enjoyed playing piano, dancing, and charades, as well as outdoor pursuits such as badminton, boating, swimming, and cycling. The author Berta Ruck, a frequent visitor to Well Hall along with other friends such as H G Wells, recalled Nesbit's schedule being balanced between work and play: 'she would write a chapter of three to five thousand words, send it to be typed, then head outdoors to do "some quite hefty gardening" or play "a hard game of badminton"' (Fitzsimons 228). The Blands often entertained their friends, and Nesbit enjoyed hosting dinner parties. The journalist Ada Chesterton described her as a larger-than-life personality during these gatherings:

> She was a very tall woman, built on the grand scale, and on festive occasions wore a trailing gown of peacock blue satin with strings of beads and Indian bangles from wrist to elbow. Madame, as she was always called, smoked incessantly, and her long cigarette holder became an indissoluble part of the picture she suggested – a raffish Rossetti, with a long full throat and dark luxuriant hair, smoothly parted. (quoted in Briggs 233; Fitzsimons 201)

Well Hall was also reputed to be haunted. Nesbit told the anthologist and novelist Andrew Lang that there was a ghost in the garden, and there were supposedly other ghosts in the house as well, with one having 'a disconcerting habit of standing behind her and sighing softly as she worked' (Fitzsimons 184).

While Nesbit was finding professional and financial success with her novels and stories for magazines, particularly her work for *The Strand*, she was undergoing private sorrows. Her son Fabian died unexpectedly during an operation in 1900, and Hubert died in April 1914 after years of declining health. During the First World War she took in boarders while she simultaneously struggled with illness related to a duodenal ulcer. She sold flowers and garden produce to local military hospitals, and sold freshly laid eggs from her own hens (Fitzsimons 302–303). It was during this time that Nesbit met Thomas Terry Tucker, a marine engineer who had lost his wife to illness in 1916. Tucker went into partnership with Nesbit in her horticultural and egg business, and in 1917, she and Tucker married (Fitzsimons 307–09, 311–12). Alice Hoatson had continued to manage the finances and the day-to-day running of the household since Hubert Bland's death, but after Nesbit's marriage she moved to Yorkshire to stay with her sister and eventually returned to London (Fitzsimons 306, 314).

Nesbit found happiness and contentment with Tucker, especially during the time they spent together at their home in Romney Marsh. In February 1917, she wrote to her brother Harry, 'I am very, very happy. I feel as though I had opened another volume of the book of life (the last volume) and it is full of beautiful stories and poetry' (quoted in Briggs 374; Fitzsimons 312).

Edith Nesbit died on 4 May 1924 and was buried in the churchyard of St Mary in the Marsh, near New Romney. Her obituary in the *Times* on 5 May 1924 describes her as a 'poet, novelist, and writer of children's books' (Anon 1924, 16).

※

While she was writing her stories for children, Nesbit was also creating what would become some of the finest supernatural and weird fiction of the late nineteenth and early twentieth centuries. From the 1880s–1920s, she published her ghost stories in leading magazines of the day, including *Temple Bar*, *Longman's Magazine*, *Black and White*, *Pearson's*, *Atlantic Monthly*, *Windsor Magazine*, and *The Strand*. *Grim Tales* (1893) contains seven tales that range from ghost stories to horror stories of unexplained premonitions. Nesbit considered these stories to be some of her best short fiction. As part of the series 'My Best Story and Why I Think So', which appeared in *The Grand Magazine* in November 1906, Nesbit chose 'John Charrington's Wedding' but admitted that she had difficulty choosing from among her other stories: 'If I consider *Grim Tales* my best stories it is because the late Sir Walter Besant said they were the best ghost stories he had ever read, and if I must choose one of them I would select "John Charrington's Wedding"' (517). *Something Wrong* (1893) is another collection of mostly non-supernatural macabre stories. *Fear* (1910) reprints some of Nesbit's previous stories while adding a few new ones. Other supernatural stories that had previously been serialized in magazines were collected in *Man and Maid* (1906) and *To the Adventurous* (1923).

Reviews of Nesbit's supernatural fiction show that the stories were well received, with several reviewers expressing surprise that 'E Nesbit', the celebrated children's author, could write such tales. In a May 1893 review, the *Bookman* commended the variety of the stories, saying, 'They are of ghosts and witches, and very uncanny sights and sounds and happenings. As creepy tales they are altogether successful' (Anon 1893, 58). The novelist James Stanley Little's review in *The Academy* praised Nesbit's ability to craft a good supernatural story: 'the author of these tales knows the secret of writing an effective "bogie-story" excellently well. She holds her *motif* well in hand, and treats it with judgment and finesse' (Little 502). Andrew Lang's review in *Longman's Magazine* in July 1893 stated that the stories 'deserve praise for really being grim' (Lang 281). Lang also appreciated Nesbit's use of the unexplained supernatural in many of the stories included in the collection, remarking that 'people who like a ghost, with no nonsense of explanation, will do well to purchase *Grim Tales*' (Lang 281).

Reviews of *Fear* were equally positive. In October 1910, the reviewer for the *Bookman*, after initially admitting the belief that 'it cannot be Mrs E Nesbit Bland who has done a book with this title', called the stories 'amazingly well written' (Anon 1910c, 60). The *Scotsman* stated that the volume 'may be warranted to banish sleep from the pillows of nervous subjects who devour it in a believing mood before going to bed' (Anon 1910a, 2). The reviewer appreciated the focus on 'the passion of fear' and how this feeling is brought about as a reaction to forces that are unknown, mysterious, or supernatural. This focus is elevated by the way in which the stories are written, as they contain 'much intellectual ingenuity in construction, as well as imaginative boldness in conception' (Anon 1910a, 2). *The Academy* found the stories reminiscent of Edgar Allan Poe in their 'weirdness of imagination' and, like the *Scotsman* reviewer, warned 'all highly nervous persons to leave them unread' (Anon 1910b, 85). Cecil Chesterton's review in the *Chronicle* likewise mentioned the stories' similarity to Poe's in their 'power of making the flesh creep' (1910, 5). He compared the stories favourably to other contemporary writers of the supernatural: 'I doubt whether anything more powerfully gruesome has been written in our time – even remembering Mr Kipling's "Mark of the Beast" and Mr Jacobs' "Monkey's Paw" [sic] – than some of the stories in this volume' (Chesterton 1910, 5). Even in Nesbit's later collections that contained only a few supernatural stories, reviewers tended to spotlight these tales. The *Bookman*, in its August 1906 review of *Man and Maid*, stated that in 'The House of Silence' Nesbit 'has written with restraint and skill a short story which gives us an entirely fresh insight to her capacities. "The Power of Darkness" is thrilling, but "The House of Silence" has an almost allegorical force' (Anon 1906, 187).

Edith Nesbit had encounters with the supernatural throughout her life, and many of her stories were inspired by her own fears. Nesbit's first biographer, Doris Langley Moore, traced a fragment of a story written during Nesbit's childhood that shows an early flair for the macabre. The story, written on College of Chemistry and Agriculture paper, features a 'wild' and 'very pretty' Roman girl who wanders into a passage where a statue reveals a secret flight of steps. The girl descends the steps to find a 'room with doors all around', and one door reveals 'a corridor lined with dead bodies' (quoted in Moore 50). Nesbit later recalled a childhood experience while staying at a house in Sutherland Gardens, writing, 'Consider the horror of having behind you, as you lie trembling in the chill linen of a strange bed, a dark space, from which, even now, in the black silence something might be stealthily creeping – something which would presently lean over you, in the dark – whose touch you would feel' (Nesbit 1966, 53).

While her family was staying in France, Nesbit and her brothers were exploring the area and discovered an abandoned château. On looking more closely into one of the rooms, they witnessed a pile of straw whirl up to the ceiling. The scared children were running away when a local woman called after them: 'I see, children, that you have seen the spinning lady' (Fitzsimons 24–25). During this time Nesbit began to have nightmares about being visited by her deceased father. In a series titled 'My School Days' that ran in the *Girls' Own Paper* from 1896–1897, she recalls one night in which she 'dreamed that my father's ghost came to me' (quoted in Briggs 13). She associated this troubling dream with fears of death and the supernatural: 'Then I woke, rigid with terror, and finally summoned courage to creep across the corridor to my mother's room and seek refuge in her arms. I am particular to mention this dream because it is the first remembrance I have of any terror of the dead, or of the supernatural' (quoted in Briggs 13). Nesbit and her older sisters later visited the mummies of Bordeaux, an event which she called 'the crowning horror of my childish life' (Nesbit 1966, 64). She described the startling appearance of the mummies in the underground crypt:

> Not white clean skeletons, hung on wires, like the one you see at the doctor's, but skeletons with the flesh hardened on their bones, with their long dry hair hanging on each

side of their brown faces, where the skin in drying had drawn itself back from their gleaming teeth and empty eye-sockets. Skeletons draped in mouldering shreds of shrouds and grave-clothes, their lean fingers still clothed with dry skin, seemed to reach out towards me. There they stood, men, women, and children, knee-deep in loose bones collected from the other vaults of the church, and heaped round them. (Nesbit 1966, 61)

These experiences had a lasting effect on Nesbit and provided the inspiration that would lead her to write ghost stories:

[I]t is to them, I think, more than to any other thing, that I owe nights and nights of anguish and horror, long years of bitterest fear and dread. All the other fears could have been effaced, but the shock of that sight branded it on my brain, and I never forgot it. For many years I could not bring myself to go about any house in the dark, and long after I was a grown woman I was tortured, in the dark watches, by imagination and memory, who rose strong and united, overpowering my will and my reason as utterly as in my baby days. (Nesbit 1966, 64)

Just as the protagonists of her ghost stories struggle – sometimes successfully and sometimes not – to overcome their fears, Nesbit resolved to overcome her personal fears after having children. According to her biographers, she kept a human skull and bones in her house so her children would be used to seeing such morbid objects (Fitzsimons 5). Nesbit later wrote, 'It was not till I had two little children of my own that I was able to conquer this mortal terror of darkness, and teach imagination her place, under the foot of reason and will' (Nesbit 1966, 64). This desire to rid herself of her fears seems to have been only partially successful. According to her biographer Julia Briggs, the process of writing ghost stories frightened Nesbit to the point that she was often afraid to go to bed (174).

Nesbit did not rely solely on traumatic events from her childhood as inspiration for her short fiction, however. The recurring themes of love and troubled relationships between women and men are at the heart of many of her narratives. This focus was no doubt heightened by her own complex, often troubled relationship with Hubert Bland. Elisabeth Galvin suggests that Nesbit's ghost stories 'reveal the mind of someone who wasn't in a happy place' and notes that '[m]any of the stories centre around the deep sadness of unrequited love between a man and a woman, a sadness that manifests itself in psychologically disturbing ways' (Galvin 79). Though we may not know the extent to which Nesbit based these stories on her own experiences, there is no doubt that she was an expert at exploring domestic tragedies through a supernatural lens. Her imaginative plots conjured ghosts from a wide variety of situations, but the capacity of these narratives to haunt the reader's imagination comes from their proximity to the everyday and the seemingly ordinary people whose lives are upended by spectral encounters. As M R James observed in the Preface to *More Ghost Stories of an Antiquary* (1911), the most effective ghost stories are the ones that could happen to us. Edith Nesbit well understood this, long before James put his words on paper.

✕

This collection is comprised of stories in which a ghost's presence – or the possibility of a ghost's presence – is central to both plot and character development. These ghosts reflect the often-blurred lines between reality and illusion, the explained and unexplained, as well as notions of guilt, regret, loss, and individual and collective fears. Nesbit's supernatural fiction frequently explores the nebulous borders of the ghost story. 'Man-size in Marble' opens with: 'Although every word of this story is true, I do not expect people to believe it. Nowadays a "rational explanation" is required before belief is possible' (1). Likewise, 'The Shadow' begins: 'This is not an artistically rounded off ghost story, and nothing is explained in it, and there seems to be no reason why any of it should have happened. But that is no reason why it should not be told. You must have noticed that all the real ghost stories you have ever come close to, are like this in these respects – no explanation, no logical coherence' (122). Both 'Man-size in Marble' and 'The Shadow' are two of Nesbit's most frequently anthologized stories, and they are included here because they represent her most effective explorations of what a ghost story can do. The lack of explanation for the events and the shocking endings makes these two stories possibly her most unsettling. Each story has a supernatural 'return' of some kind, but the seeming randomness of this return and its fatal effect on apparently innocent victims stays with the reader long after these stories are concluded.

Many of the stories deal with dynamics between women and men and the lengths people will go to in order to attain – and keep – a loved one. Love from beyond the grave is the central concern in 'John Charrington's Wedding'. In this version of the demon lover trope, Nesbit showcases a traditional love story about a couple who are devoted to one another but then upends the story by exploring how such love can quickly become overpowering and harmful. Women are possessed and possessing in these stories. In 'The Ebony Frame', a woman returns from the past to reconnect with a lost love. As with many Nesbit stories, the ending is far from comforting, and the main character must live out a form of death-in-life. As in 'John Charrington's Wedding', an encounter with a ghost leaves a lasting impression that continues to affect the living long after the ghost is gone. In 'From the Dead', a husband's vanity causes a rift between him and his wife that leads to fatal aftereffects. When he has a chance to reunite with her, the man once again makes a decision that has irrevocable consequences. This is another classic E Nesbit ending. What is revealed in the final lines of the story is another twist of the knife to already shaken readers who are often left just as haunted and unsettled as the narrators.

'Uncle Abraham's Romance' is one of Nesbit's most touching ghost stories and is notable for its sympathetic treatment of a disabled main character. The narrator, an older man who has been physically impaired since boyhood and who was shunned and teased by his peers, finds love and acceptance with the spirit of a woman who was likewise ostracized by her community. Nesbit's ghost stories often focus on the loneliness and isolation of the living who must continue without those they have loved and lost. As one character in 'The Detective' says to his ghostly companion, 'They talk about death being cold. It's life that's the cold thing' (245). Written towards the end of her life, 'The Detective' is one of Nesbit's most somber, contemplative stories. The couple in 'Hurst of Hurstcote' are likewise inseparable, even from beyond the grave. Much like Ida Helmont in 'From the Dead', the wife in this story is tied to her earthly body longer than she would perhaps like to be. It is the love between these respective couples that causes the women emotional turmoil as they both struggle to let go of their physical bodies.

Ghosts are often used as devices to keep people apart, but sometimes a ghostly presence brings people together. 'The White Lady', a 'lost' Nesbit story recently rediscovered by the editor and anthologist Johnny Mains, is a much more light-hearted tale, one that playfully disrupts our expectations of what a ghost story is or should be. In the story, the ghostly White Lady represents an obstacle to be overcome on the path to marriage. Various generations of women who marry into an aristocratic family must assume a ghostly persona in order to secure a marriage on their own terms, and handing down the white satin costume of the ghost becomes just as important – or perhaps even more so – than a wedding dress. This secret kept by generations of women puts them, rather than the men, solidly in control of their own future. It allows the women to choose, or, as Lady Cary says to her future daughter-in-law, to 'pronounce your own blessing on your own engagement' (78). Another comical tale, 'The Haunted Inheritance', is a clever reversal of a common supernatural trope. Instead of the ghost causing someone to vacate a property, the spectral presence is used by one of the protagonists to attain a property, as well as a love interest. 'Number 17' spotlights Nesbit's skill at writing dark comedy. A group staying at a hotel is treated to a ghost story, but by the story's end they are more directly involved in the haunting than they thought they were. The humorous twist at the end is tempered by the lingering presence of the ghastly and gruesome spirit who haunts Number 17, as well as the minds of those who hear his story.

Nesbit's science fiction tales, such as 'The Third Drug' and 'The Five Senses', are deeply invested in what it means to be human and the danger involved when boundaries are challenged. In these stories, there are attempts to become superhuman and go beyond the natural limits of what humans can (or should) be. There are hints of science fiction in her ghost stories as well. In 'The Haunted House', the main character is manipulated into staying at a supposedly haunted residence in the hopes of seeing its ghost. However, he falls victim to a much more real danger as the unknowing subject of a scientific experiment. The 'ghost' in the story proves to be more helpful – and powerful – as it intercedes to save the man's life. The story simultaneously explores the many sides of a person. The 'mad scientist' becomes a vampire through his diabolical experiments, and his victims utilize their ghostly place in the household to resist the scientist's power over those he entraps.

An encounter with the supernatural also has lasting effects on the main characters in 'The Pavilion'. Much like 'The Haunted House', the narrative begins as a ghost story but turns into something else, possibly even more disturbing. Once again, the narrative blends the ghostly with the vampiric and the Weird. This is one of Nesbit's most unforgiving stories in the ways in which it critiques gender expectations and how social norms – and the breaking of such norms – can haunt a person throughout their life. A different kind of haunting occurs in 'The Violet Car'. In this story, considered to be the first to feature a supernatural automobile, a past crime is reenacted over and over again. As in other stories in this collection, the narrator goes from skeptic to reluctant acceptance and then to confirmed believer through their interaction with the ghostly presence. Questions are raised along with apparitions in this narrative. New innovations can move us into the future, but what happens when that very technology takes away such futures?

As some titles in this collection suggest, fear of the dark takes a central place. 'In the Dark' concerns a shocking confession made by one man to his close friend. Once again, the ghostly return is central to the thematic force of the narrative. This return is not only a ghost, however. Other things come back, too – or never go away. Insistent memories of past actions and the struggle with personal guilt haunt one of the characters just as much, or even more than, the ghost itself. 'The Power of Darkness', no doubt inspired by Nesbit's earlier experience with the mummies of Bordeaux, is an expertly paced exploration of fear and whether it is better to accept or deny such emotions. The story is likewise about the power of the imagination and how it can turn on us. Nesbit's detailed descriptions of the figures in a wax museum perfectly capture their uncanniness. As one character remarks, 'They're like life – but they're much more like death' (112). In these stories, Nesbit establishes a fine line between the explained and unexplained supernatural as she explores the sometimes equally fine line between life and death.

Ideas of life and (re)animation are a central focus of 'The Marble Child'. This little-known story provides a fascinating counterpoint to 'Man-size in Marble', while also providing a rare instance of a Nesbit ghost story that bridges her supernatural writing for adults with her fiction written for children. The narrator, a young boy who lives with his aunts and yearns for the companionship of someone his own age, becomes attached to a marble statue in a local church. When the statue comes to life and starts communicating with the boy, even to the point of meeting him in the nearby woods, the boy must choose between his world and the world of the marble child. Yet Nesbit leaves much to the reader's imagination, including what the true motives of this supernatural spirit might be. As with Nesbit's best stories, there remains much that is unexplained.

What is the true nature of the marble child? Is it a deceased child's spirit, or simply a projection of a lonely little boy? And if it is all in the mind of the boy, how do we explain the ending?

The haunting in 'The House of Silence' is similarly less defined but is just as unsettling because of the unseen yet almost tangible presence that takes the form of an oppressive silence in the house. A paradise of riches becomes a nightmare when a thief becomes trapped in the house he is burgling. Nesbit leaves it up to the reader to decide whether there is something menacing within the walls of the house, or if it is all in the main character's mind. The horrific discovery the thief makes in the garden seems to point to something more sinister. The story, told from the thief's perspective, runs the gamut of emotions, from anticipation and excitement to claustrophobia, confusion, and terror. The story ends where it begins, but both protagonist and reader are left unsettled by the unexplained occurrences we encounter in the house as well as the unexpected sites found outside the house. The story is a tour de force in creating an ominous atmosphere and represents one of Nesbit's most haunting tales.

In the January 1903 issue of *Harper's Bazaar*, Edith Nesbit's lifelong friend, Marshall Steele, praised Nesbit's ability to craft an effective narrative. He notes her success in 'the difficult task of writing in the first person' and finds 'there is art of the best in the little subtle touches with which she reveals the idiosyncrasies of the narrator' (Steele 79). Steele then describes Nesbit's effectiveness at capturing a defining moment in these narrators' lives:

> [S]he has an artist's conception of the short story; she never overloads it, she rigidly excludes from it all that is unnecessary, and she chooses for its theme one episode, not a series of episodes, which would provide material for a novel of the old three-decker dimensions. In the short story she finds room for the display of her rarer powers, her fertile imagination, her delightful gift of humor, her insight, and her tenderness. (Steele 79)

This perfectly encapsulates what makes Nesbit such a gifted creator of supernatural fiction. These stories showcase her attention to detail, her ability to develop memorable narrators, and the ease with which she alternates between extreme fear and witty humor. The eighteen stories in *The House of Silence* represent the most comprehensive picture to date of Edith Nesbit's work as a writer of ghost stories. Taken together, the stories showcase the impressively wide range of meanings that a literary ghost can embody. In an era in which many writers specialized in ghostly fiction, E Nesbit was unique. Her spectres are ominous and threatening, yet at times comical and sympathetic. For years, Nesbit has been recognized as a pioneering writer of juvenile literature, and her books for children influenced generations of subsequent authors. Yet Nesbit should also be widely acknowledged for her innovative work with supernatural fiction across three decades. This volume will hopefully draw even greater attention to the pivotal role her short fiction plays in the ghost story's development. Nesbit was always an imaginative, versatile writer, but that imagination could go in vastly different directions. Her books for children opened magical new worlds. Her ghost stories explore different, nightmarish possibilities.

Works cited

Anon, Review of *Grim Tales*, *The Bookman* (May 1893), 58.

—, 'Mrs Hubert Bland ("E Nesbit")', *The Strand Magazine* (September 1905), 287–288.

—, Review of *Man and Maid*, *The Bookman* (August 1906), 187.

—, Review of *Fear*, *The Scotsman* (21 July 1910a), 2.

—, Review of *Fear*, *The Academy* (23 July 1910b), 85.

—, Review of *Fear*, *The Bookman* (October 1910c), 60.

—, 'E Nesbit', *The Times* (5 May 1924), 16.

Briggs, Julia, *A Woman of Passion: The Life of E Nesbit, 1858–1924* (New Amsterdam Books, 1987).

Chesterton, Cecil, 'Tales of Terror', *The Chronicle* (10 September 1910), 5.

Fitzsimons, Eleanor. *The Life and Loves of E Nesbit: Victorian Iconoclast, Children's Author, and Creator of* The Railway Children (Abrams Press, 2019).

Galvin, Elisabeth. *The Extraordinary Life of E Nesbit: Author of* Five Children and It *and* The Railway Children (Pen & Sword History, 2018).

Lang, Andrew, 'At the Sign of the Ship', *Longman's Magazine* (July 1893), 281.

Little, James Stanley, Review of *Grim Tales*, *The Academy* (10 June 1893), 502.

Moore, Doris Langley, *E Nesbit: A Biography* (Chilton Books, 1966).

Nesbit, E, 'The Ghost', *A Pomander of Verse* (John Lane, 1895), 46.

—, 'The Ghost Bereft', *Songs of Love and Empire* (Archibald Constable & Co, 1898a), 50–54.

—, 'Haunted', *Songs of Love and Empire* (Archibald Constable & Co, 1898b), 123–124.

—, 'My Best Story and Why I Think So', *The Grand Magazine* (November 1906), 517–522.

—, 'Fear', *Many Voices* (Hutchinson, 1922a), 78.

—, 'The Return', *Many Voices* (Hutchinson, 1922b), 9–11.

—, *Long Ago When I Was Young* (Ronald Whiting & Wheaton, 1966).

Steele, Marshall, 'E Nesbit: An Appreciation', *Harper's Bazaar* (January 1903), 78–79.

Bibliographical details

'Man-size in Marble' was published in *Home Chimes* in December 1887. It was later collected in *Grim Tales* (A D Innes and Co, 1893) and *Fear* (Stanley Paul & Co, 1910). The present text is based on the 1910 publication.

'John Charrington's Wedding' was published in the September 1891 issue of *Temple Bar* and later collected in *Grim Tales* and *Fear*. The present text is based on the 1910 publication.

'Uncle Abraham's Romance' was published in the 26 September 1891 issue of the *Illustrated London News*. It was later collected in *Grim Tales* and *Fear*. The present text is based on the 1910 publication.

'The Ebony Frame' was published in the October 1891 issue of *Longman's Magazine* and was later included in *Grim Tales* and *Fear*. The present text is based on the 1910 publication.

'From the Dead' was published in *Grim Tales* and later collected in *Fear*. The present text is based on the 1910 publication.

'Hurst of Hurstcote' was published in *Temple Bar* in June 1893 and was later collected in *Something Wrong* (A D Innes and Co, 1893) and *Fear*. The present text is based on the 1910 publication.

'The White Lady' was published in the 23 December 1893 Christmas Number of *Black and White*, with illustrations by G Grenville Manton.

'The Haunted Inheritance' was published in the 17 February 1900 issue of *The Saturday Evening Post* and was later published in December 1900 in *Pearson's Magazine*. It was collected as the leading story in *Man and Maid* (T Fisher Unwin, 1906). The present text is based on the 1906 publication.

'The Power of Darkness' was published in *The Strand Magazine* in April 1905 and was collected in *Man and Maid*. The present text is based on the 1906 publication.

'The Shadow' was originally published as 'The Portent of the Shadow' in *Black and White* in December 1905 and was republished in *The Index* (Pittsburgh) in January 1906. The story was later included as 'The Shadow' in *Fear*. The current text is based on the 1910 publication.

'The House of Silence' was published in *The Windsor Magazine* in March 1906 and was collected in *Man and Maid*. The present text is based on the 1906 publication.

'Number 17' was published in *The Strand Magazine* in June 1910 under the name 'E Bland' and with illustrations by F Carter.

'In the Dark' was published in *Fear*.

'The Violet Car' was published in *Fear*.

'The Marble Child' was published in the *Atlantic Monthly* in November 1910.

'The Haunted House' was published in *The Strand Magazine* in December 1913 under the name 'E Bland' and with illustrations by Graham Simmons.

'The Pavilion' was published in *The Strand Magazine* in November 1915 with illustrations by James Durden. It was later collected in *To the Adventurous* (Hutchinson and Co, 1923). The present text is based on the 1923 publication.

'The Detective' first appeared in *The Christmas Spirit* in 1920 and was later collected as the title story in *To the Adventurous*. The present text is based on the 1923 publication but retains the original title.

1 Man-size in Marble

Although every word of this story is true, I do not expect people to believe it. Nowadays a 'rational explanation' is required before belief is possible. Let me, at once, offer the 'rational explanation' which finds most favour among those who have heard the tale of my life's tragedy. It is held that we were 'under a delusion,' she and I, on that 31st of October; and that this supposition places the whole matter on a satisfactory and believable basis. The reader can judge, when he, too, has heard my story, how far this is an 'explanation,' and in what sense it is 'rational.' There were three who took part in this: Laura and I and another man. The other man lives still, and can speak to the truth of the least credible part of my story.

✕

I never knew in my life what it was to have as much money as would supply the most ordinary needs of life — good colours, canvasses, brushes, books, and cab-fares — and when we were married, we knew quite well that we should only be able to live at all by 'strict punctuality and attention to business.' I used to paint in those days, and Laura used to write, and we felt sure we could keep the pot at least simmering. Living in London was out of the question, so we went to look for a cottage in the country, which should be at once sanitary and picturesque. So rarely do these two qualities meet in one cottage that our search was for some time quite fruitless. We tried advertisements, but most of the desirable rural residences which we did look at proved to be lacking in both essentials, and when a cottage chanced to have drains, it always had stucco as well and was shaped like a tea-caddy. And if we found a vine or rose-covered porch, corruption invariably lurked within. Our minds got so befogged by the eloquence of house-agents and the rival disadvantages of the fever-traps and outrages to beauty which we had seen and scorned, that I very much doubt whether either of us, on our wedding morning, knew the difference between a house and a haystack. But when we got away from friends and house-agents on our honeymoon, our wits grew clear again, and we knew a pretty cottage when at last we saw one. It was at Brenzett — a little village set on a hill over against the southern marshes. We had gone there from the little fishing village where we were staying, to see the church, and two fields from the church we found this cottage. It stood quite by itself about two miles from Brenzett village. It was a low building with rooms sticking out in unexpected places. There was a bit of stonework — ivy-covered and moss-grown, just two old rooms, all that was left of a big house that once stood there — and round this stonework the house had grown up. Stripped of its roses and jasmine it would have been hideous. As it stood it was charming, and after a brief examination, enthusiasm usurped the place of discretion and we took it. It was absurdly cheap. The rest of our honeymoon we spent in grubbing about in second-hand shops in Ashford, picking up bits of old oak and Chippendale chairs for our furnishing. We wound up with a run up to town and a visit to Liberty's, and soon the low, oak-beamed, lattice-windowed rooms began to be home. There was a jolly old-fashioned garden, with grass paths and no end of hollyhocks, and sunflowers, and big lilies, and roses with thousands of small sweet flowers. From the window you could see the marsh-pastures, and beyond them the blue, thin line of the sea. We were as happy as the summer was glorious, and settled down into work sooner than we ourselves expected. I was never tired of sketching the view and the wonderful cloud effects from the open lattice, and Laura would sit at the table and write verses about them, in which I mostly played the part of foreground.

We got a tall, old peasant woman to do for us. Her face and figure were good, though her cooking was of the homeliest; but she understood all about gardening, and told us all the old names of the coppices and cornfields, and the stories of the smugglers and the highwaymen, and, better still, of the 'things that walked,' and of the 'sights' which met one in lonely lanes of a starlight night. She was a great comfort to us, because Laura hated housekeeping as much as I loved folklore, and we soon came to leave all the domestic business to Mrs Dorman, and to use her legends in little magazine stories which brought in guineas.

We had three months of married happiness. We did not have a single quarrel. And then it happened. One October evening I had been down to smoke a pipe with the doctor — our only neighbour — a pleasant young Irishman. Laura had stayed at home to finish a comic sketch of a village episode for the *Monthly Marplot*. I left her laughing over her own jokes, and came in to see her a crumpled heap of pale muslin, weeping on the window seat.

'Good heavens, my darling, what's the matter?' I cried, taking her in my arms. She leaned her head against my shoulder and went on crying. I had never seen her cry before — we had always been so happy, you see — and I felt sure some frightful misfortune had happened.

'What *is* the matter? Do speak!'

'It's Mrs Dorman,' she sobbed.

'What has she done?' I inquired, immensely relieved.

'She says she must go before the end of the month, and she says her niece is ill; she's gone down to see her now, but I don't believe that's the reason, because her niece is always ill. I believe someone has been setting her against us. Her manner was so queer —'

'Never mind, Pussy,' I said. 'Whatever you do, don't cry, or I shall have to cry, too, to keep you in countenance, and then you'll never respect your man again.'

She dried her eyes obediently on my handkerchief, and even smiled faintly.

'But, you see,' she went on, 'it is really serious, because these village people are so sheepy; and if one won't do a thing, you may be quite sure none of the others will. And I shall have to cook the dinners and wash up all the hateful, greasy plates; and you'll have to carry cans of water about, and clean the boots and knives — and we shall never have any time for work, or earn any money or anything. We shall have to work all day, and only be able to rest when we are waiting for the kettle to boil!'

I represented to her that even if we had to perform these duties, the day would still present some margin for other toils and recreations. But she refused to see the matter in any but the greyest light. She was very unreasonable, and I told her so, but in my heart … well, who wants a woman to be reasonable?

'I'll speak to Mrs Dorman when she comes back, and see if I can't come to terms with her,' I said. 'Perhaps she wants a rise in her screw. It will be all right. Let's walk up to the church.'

The church was a large and lonely one, and we loved to go there, especially upon bright nights. The path skirted a wood, cut through it once, and ran along the crest of the hill through two meadows and round the churchyard wall, over which the old yews loomed in black masses of shadow. This path, which was partly paved, was called the 'bier-balk,' for it had long been the way by which the corpses had been carried to burial. The churchyard was richly treed, and was shaded by great elms which stood just outside and stretched their kind arms out over the dead. A large, low porch let one into the building by a Norman doorway and a heavy oak door studded with iron. Inside, the arches rose into darkness, and between them shone the reticulated windows, which stood out white in the moonlight. In the chancel, the windows were of rich glass, which showed in faint light their noble colouring and made the black oak of the choir pews hardly more solid than the shadows. But on each side of the altar lay a grey marble figure of a knight in full armour, lying upon a low slab, with hands held up in everlasting prayer, and these figures, oddly enough, were always to be seen if there was any glimmer of light in the church. Their names were lost, but the peasants told of them that they had been fierce and wicked men, marauders by land and sea, who had been the scourge of their time, and had been guilty of deeds so foul that the house they had lived in — the big house, by the way, that had stood on the site of our cottage — had been stricken by lightning and the vengeance of Heaven. But for all that, the gold of their heirs had bought them a place in the church. Looking at the bad, hard faces reproduced in the marble, this story was easily believed.

The church looked at its best on that night, for the shadows of the yew trees fell through the windows upon the floor of the nave and touched the pillars with tattered shadow. We sat down together without speaking, and watched the solemn beauty of the old church with some of that awe which inspired its early builders. We walked to the chancel and looked at the sleeping warriors. Then we rested on the stone seat in the porch, looking out over the stretch of quiet, moonlit meadows, feeling in every fibre of our being the peace of the night and of our happy love; and came away at last with a sense that even scrubbing and black-leading were, at their worst, but small troubles.

Mrs Dorman had come back from the village, and I at once invited her to a *tête-à-tête*.

'Now, Mrs Dorman,' I said, when I had got her into my painting-room, 'what's all this about your not staying with us?'

'I should be glad to get away, sir, before the end of the month,' she answered, with her usual placid dignity.

'Have you any fault to find, Mrs Dorman?'

'None at all, sir; you and your lady have always been most kind, I'm sure —'

'Well, what is it? Are your wages not high enough?'

'No, sir, I gets quite enough.'

'Then why not stay?'

'I'd rather not,' with some hesitation. 'My niece is ill.'

'But your niece has been ill ever since we came.'

No answer. There was a long and awkward silence. I broke it.

'Can't you stay for another month?' I asked.

'No, sir. I'm bound to go on Thursday.'

And this was Monday.

'Well, I must say, I think you might have let us know before. There's no time now to get anyone else, and your mistress is not fit to do heavy housework. Can't you stay till next week?'

'I might be able to come back next week.'

I was now convinced that all she wanted was a brief holiday, which we should have been willing enough to let her have, as soon as we could get a substitute.

'But why must you go this week?' I persisted. 'Come, out with it.'

Mrs Dorman drew the little shawl, which she always wore, tightly across her bosom, as though she were cold. Then she said, with a sort of effort:

'They say, sir, as this was a big house in Catholic times, and there was a many deeds done here.'

The nature of the 'deeds' might be vaguely inferred from the inflection of Mrs Dorman's voice, which was enough to make one's blood run cold. I was glad that Laura was not in the room. She was always nervous, as highly strung natures are, and I felt that these tales about our house, told by this old peasant woman with her impressive manner and contagious credulity, might have made our home less dear to my wife.

'Tell me all about it, Mrs Dorman,' I said. 'You needn't mind about telling me. I'm not like the young people who make fun of such things.'

Which was partly true.

'Well, sir,' she sank her voice, 'you may have seen in the church, beside the altar, two shapes —'

'You mean the effigies of the knights in armour?' I said cheerfully.

'I mean them two bodies drawed out man-size in marble,' she returned, and I had to admit that her description was a thousand times more graphic than mine.

'They do say as on All Saints' Eve them two bodies sits up on their slabs and gets off of them, and then walks down the aisle *in their marble*' — (another good phrase Mrs Dorman) — 'and as the church clock strikes eleven, they walks out of the church door, and over the graves, and along the bier-balk, and if it's a wet night there's the marks of their feet in the morning.'

'And where do they go?' I asked, rather fascinated.

'They comes back to their old home, sir, and if anyone meets them —'

'Well, what then?' I asked.

But no, not another word could I get from her, save that her niece was ill and that she must go. After what I had heard I scorned to discuss the niece, and tried to get from Mrs Dorman more details of the legend. I could get nothing but warnings.

'Whatever you do, sir, lock the door early on All Saints' Eve, and make the blessed cross-sign over the doorstep and on the windows.'

'But has anyone ever seen these things?' I persisted.

'That's not for me to say. I know what I know.'

'Well, who was here last year?'

'No one, sir. The lady as owned the house only stayed here in the summer, and she always went to London a full month afore *the* night. And I'm sorry to inconvenience you and your lady, but my niece is ill, and I must go on Thursday.'

I could have shaken her for her reiteration of that obvious fiction.

She was determined to go, nor could our united entreaties move her in the least.

I did not tell Laura the legend of the shapes that 'walked in their marble,' partly because a legend concerning our house might perhaps trouble my wife, and partly, I think, for some more occult reason. This was not quite the same to me as any other story, and I did not want to talk about it till the day was over. I had very soon almost ceased to think of the legend, however. I was painting a portrait of Laura, against the lattice window, and I could not think of much else. I had got a splendid background of yellow and grey sunset, and was working away with enthusiasm at her face. On Thursday Mrs Dorman went. She relented, at parting, so far as to say:

'Don't you put yourselves about too much, ma'am, and if there's any little thing I can do next week, I'm sure I shan't mind.'

From which I inferred that she wished to come back to us after Hallowe'en. Up to the last she adhered to the fiction of the niece.

Thursday passed off pretty well. Laura showed marked ability in the matter of steak and potatoes, and I confess that my knives, and the plates, which I insisted upon washing, were better done than I had dared to expect. It was all so good, so simple, so pleasant. As I write of it, I almost forget what came after. But now I must remember, and tell.

Friday came. It is about what happened on that Friday that this is written. I wonder if I should have believed it if anyone had told it to me. I will write the story of it as quickly and plainly as I can. Everything that happened on that day is burnt into my brain. I shall not forget anything, nor leave anything out.

I got up early, I remember, and lighted the kitchen fire, and had just achieved a smoky success, when my wife came running down, as sunny and sweet as the clear October morning itself. We prepared breakfast together, and found it very good fun. The housework was soon done, and when brushes and brooms and pails were quiet again, the house was still indeed. It is wonderful what a difference one makes in a house. We really missed Mrs Dorman, quite apart from considerations of pots and pans. We spent the day in dusting our books and putting them straight, and dined gaily on cold steak and coffee. Laura was, if possible, brighter and gayer and sweeter than usual, and I began to think that a little domestic toil was really good for her. We had never been so merry since we were married, and the walk we had that afternoon was, I think, the happiest time of all my life. When we had watched the deep scarlet clouds slowly pale into leaden grey against a pale-green sky, and saw the white mists curl up along the hedgerows in the distant marsh, we came back to the house, silently, hand in hand.

'You are sad, Pussy,' I said half-jestingly, as we sat down together in our little parlour. I expected a disclaimer, for my own silence had been the silence of complete happiness. To my surprise, she said:

'Yes, I think I am sad, or rather I am uneasy. I hope I am not going to be ill. I have shivered three or four times since we came in, and it's not really cold, is it?'

'No,' I said, and hoped it was not a chill caught from the treacherous mists that roll up from the marshes in the dying light. No, she said, she did not think so. Then, after a silence, she spoke suddenly:

'Do you ever have presentiments of evil?'

'No,' I said, smiling, 'and I shouldn't believe in them if I had.'

'I do,' she went on; 'the night my father died I knew it, though he was right away in the north of Scotland.' I did not answer in words.

She sat looking at the fire in silence for some time, gently stroking my hand. At last she sprang up, came behind me, and drawing my head back, kissed me.

'There, it's over now,' she said. 'What a baby I am. Come, light the candles, and we'll have some of these new Rubinstein duets.'

And we spent a happy hour or two at the piano.

At about half-past ten, I began to fill the good-night pipe, but Laura looked so white that I felt that it would be brutal of me to fill our sitting-room with the fumes of strong cavendish.

'I'll take my pipe outside,' I said.

'Let me come too.'

'No, sweetheart, not tonight; you're much too tired. I shan't be long. Get to bed, or I shall have an invalid to nurse tomorrow, as well as the boots to clean.'

I kissed her and was turning to go, when she flung her arms round my neck and held me very closely. I stroked her hair.

'Come, Pussy, you're over-tired. The housework has been too much for you.'

She loosened her clasp a little and drew a deep breath.

'No. We've been very happy today, Jack, haven't we? Don't stay out too long.'

'I won't, Puss cat,' I said.

I strolled out of the front door, leaving it unlatched. What a night it was! The jagged masses of heavy, dark cloud were rolling at intervals from horizon to horizon, and thin, white wreaths covered the stars. Through all the rush of the cloud river, the moon swam, breasting the waves and disappearing again in the darkness. When, now and again, her light reached the woodlands, they seemed to be slowly and noiselessly waving in time to the clouds above them. There was a strange grey light over all the earth; the fields had that shadowy bloom over them which only comes from the marriage of dew and moonshine, or frost and starlight.

I walked up and down, drinking in the beauty of the quiet earth and changing sky. The night was absolutely silent. Nothing seemed to be abroad. There was no skurrying of rabbits, or twitter of half-asleep birds. And though the clouds went sailing across the sky, the wind that drove them never came low enough to rustle the dead leaves in the woodland paths. Across the meadow, I could see the church tower standing out black and grey against the sky. I walked there, thinking over our three months of happiness, and of my wife — her dear eyes, her pretty ways. Oh, my girl! my own little girl; what a vision came to me then of a long, glad life for you and me together!

I heard a bell-beat from the church. Eleven already! I turned to go in, but the night held me. I could not go back into our little warm rooms yet. I would go right on up to the church. I felt vaguely that it would be good to carry my love and thankfulness to the sanctuary, whither so many loads of sorrow and gladness had been borne by men and women dead long since.

I looked in at the low window as I went by. Laura was half lying on her chair in front of the fire. I could not see her face, only her head showed dark against the pale blue wall. She was quite still. Asleep, no doubt. My heart reached out to her, as I went on. There must be a God, I thought, and a God that was good. How otherwise could anything so sweet and dear as she ever have been imagined?

I walked slowly along the edge of the wood. A sound broke the stillness of the night. I stopped and listened. The sound stopped too. I went on, and now distinctly I heard another step than mine answer mine like an echo. It was a poacher or a wood-stealer, most likely, for these were not unknown in our Arcadia. But, whoever it was, he was a fool not to step more lightly. I turned into the wood, and now the footstep seemed to come from the path I had just left. It must be an echo, I thought. The wood lay lovely in the moonlight. The large, dying ferns and the brushwood showed where, through thinning foliage, the pale light came down. The tree trunks stood up like Gothic columns all around me. They reminded me of the church, and I turned into the bier-balk and passed through the corpse-gate between the graves to the low porch. I paused for a moment on the stone seat where Laura and I had last night watched the fading landscape. Then I noticed that the door of the church was open, and I blamed myself for having left it unlatched the other night. We were the only people who ever cared to come to the church except on Sundays, and I was vexed to think that through our carelessness the damp autumn airs had had a chance of getting in and injuring the old fabric. I went in. It will seem strange perhaps that I should have gone half-way up the aisle before I remembered — with a sudden chill, followed by as sudden a rush of self-contempt — that this was the very day and hour when, according to tradition, the 'shapes drawed out man-size in marble' began to walk.

Having thus remembered the legend, and remembered it with a shiver of which I was ashamed, I could not do otherwise than walk up towards the altar, just to look at the figures — as I said to myself; really what I wanted was to assure myself, first, that I did not believe the legend, and, secondly, that it was not true. I was rather glad that I had come. I thought that now I could tell Mrs Dorman how vain her fancies were, and how peacefully the marble figures slept on through the ghostly hour. With my hands in my pockets, I passed up the aisle. In the grey, dim light, the eastern end of the church looked larger than usual, and the arches above the tombs looked larger too. The moon came out and showed me the reason. I stopped short, my heart gave a great leap that nearly choked me, and then sank sickeningly.

The 'bodies drawed out man-size' *were gone*, and their marble slabs lay wide and bare in the vague moonlight that slanted through the west window.

Were they really gone? or was I mad? Clenching my nerves, I stooped and passed my hand over the smooth slabs and felt their flat unbroken surface. Had someone taken the things away? Was it some vile practical joke? I would make sure, anyway. In an instant I had made a torch of a newspaper which happened to be in my pocket, and lighting it held it high above my head. Its yellow glare illumined the dark arches and those slabs. The figures *were* gone. And I was alone in the church; or was I alone?

And then a horror seized me, a horror indefinable and indescribable — an overwhelming certainty of supreme and accomplished calamity. I flung down the torch and tore along the aisle and out through the door, biting my lips as I ran to keep myself from shrieking aloud. Was I mad — or what was this that possessed me? I leaped the churchyard wall and took the straight cut across the fields, led by the light from our windows. Just as I got over the first stile, a dark figure seemed to spring out of the ground. Mad still with that certainty of misfortune, I made for the thing that stood in my path, shouting, 'Get out of the way, can't you?'

But my push met with a very vigorous resistance. My arms were caught just above the elbow and held as in a vice, and the raw-boned Irish doctor actually shook me.

'Would ye?' he cried in his own unmistakable accents — 'would ye, then?'

'Let me go, you fool,' I gasped. 'The marble figures have gone from the church; I tell you they've gone.'

He broke into a ringing laugh. 'I'll have to give ye a draught tomorrow, I see. Ye've been smoking too much and listening to old wives' tales.'

'I'll tell you I've seen the bare slabs.'

'Well, come back with me. I'm going up to old Palmer's — his daughter's ill — its only hysteria, but it's as bad as it can be; we'll look in at the church and let *me* see the bare slabs.'

'You go if you like,' I said, a little less frantic for his laughter, 'I'm going home to my wife.'

'Rubbish, man,' said he. 'D'ye think I'll permit of that? Are ye to go saying all yer life that ye've seen solid marble endowed with vitality, and me to go all me life saying ye were a coward? No, sir — ye shan't do ut!'

The quiet night — a human voice — and I think also the physical contact with this six feet of solid common sense, brought me back a little to my ordinary self, and the word 'coward' was a shower-bath.

'Come on, then,' I said sullenly, 'perhaps you're right.'

He still held my arm tightly. We got over the stile and back to the church. All was still as death. The place smelt very damp and earthy. We walked up the aisle. I am not ashamed to confess that I shut my eyes; I knew the figures would not be there. I heard Kelly strike a match.

'Here they are, ye see, right enough; ye've been dreaming or drinking, asking yer pardon for the imputation.'

I opened my eyes. By Kelly's expiring vesta I saw two shapes lying 'in their marble' on their slabs. I drew a deep breath and caught his hand.

'I'm awfully indebted to you,' I said. 'It must have been some trick of light, or I have been working rather hard, perhaps that's it. Do you know, I was quite convinced they were gone.'

'I'm aware of that,' he answered rather grimly; 'ye'll have to be careful of that brain of yours, my friend, I assure ye.'

He was leaning over and looking at the right-hand figure, whose stony face was the most villainous and deadly in expression. He struck another match.

'By Jove,' he said, 'something has been going on here — this hand is broken.'

And so it was. I was certain that it had been perfect the last time Laura and I had been there.

'Perhaps someone had *tried* to remove them,' said the young doctor.

'That won't account for my impression,' I objected.

'Too much painting and tobacco will account for what you call your impression,' he said.

'Come along,' I said, 'or my wife will be getting anxious. You'll come in and have a drop of whisky and drink confusion to ghosts and better sense to me.'

'I ought to go up to Palmer's, but it's so late now, I'd best leave it till the morning,' he replied. 'I was kept late at the Union, and I've had to see a lot of people since. All right, I'll come back with ye.'

I think he fancied I needed him more than did Palmer's girl, so, discussing how such an illusion could have been possible, and deducing from this experience large generalities concerning ghostly apparitions, we saw, as we walked up the garden path, that bright light streamed out of the front door, and presently saw that the parlour door was open too. Had she gone out?

'Come in,' I said, and Dr Kelly followed me into the parlour. It was all ablaze with candles, not only the wax ones, but at least a dozen guttering, glaring, tallow dips, stuck in vases and ornaments in unlikely places. Light, I knew, was Laura's remedy for nervousness. Poor child! Why had I left her? Brute that I was.

We glanced round the room, and at first we did not see her. The window was open and the draught set all the candles flaring one way. Her chair was empty, and her handkerchief and book lay on the floor. I turned to the window. There, in the recess of the window, I saw her. Oh, my child, my love, had she gone to that window to watch for me? And what had come into the room behind her? To what had she turned with that look of frantic fear and horror? Had she thought that it was my step she heard and turned to meet — what?

She had fallen back against a table in the window, and her body lay half on it and half on the window-seat, and her head hung down over the table, the brown hair loosened and fallen to the carpet. Her lips were drawn back and her eyes wide, wide open. They saw nothing now. What had they last seen?

The doctor moved towards her. But I pushed him aside and sprang to her; caught her in my arms and cried —

'It's all right, Laura! I've got you safe, dear!'

She fell into my arms in a heap. I clasped her and kissed her, and called her by all her pet names, but I think I knew all the time that she was dead. Her hands were tightly clenched. In one of them she held something fast. When I was quite sure that she was dead, and that nothing mattered at all anymore, I let him open her hand to see what she held.

It was a grey marble finger.

2 John Charrington's Wedding

No one ever thought that May Forster would marry John Charrington; but he thought differently, and things which John Charrington intended should happen had a way of happening. He asked her to marry him before he went up to Oxford. She laughed and refused him. He asked her again next time he came home. Again she laughed, tossed her blonde head, and again refused. A third time he asked her; she said it was becoming a confirmed habit, and laughed at him more than ever.

John was not the only man who wanted to marry her; she was the belle of our village, and we were all in love with her more or less; it was a sort of fashion, like heliotrope ties or Inverness capes. Therefore we were as much annoyed as surprised when John Charrington walked into our little local club — we held it in a loft over the saddler's, I remember — and invited us all to his wedding.

'Your wedding?'

'You don't mean it?'

'Who's the happy fair? When's it to be?'

John Charrington filled his pipe and lighted it before he replied. Then he said:

'I'm sorry to deprive you fellows of your only joke — but Miss Forster and I are to be married in September.'

'You don't mean it?'

'He's got the mitten again, and it's turned his head.'

'No,' I said, rising, 'I see it's true. Lend me a pistol someone — or a first-class fare to the other end of Nowhere. Charrington has bewitched the only pretty girl in our twenty-mile radius. Was it mesmerism, or a love-potion, Jack?'

'Neither, sir, but a gift you'll never have — perseverance — and the best luck a man ever had in this world.'

There was something in his voice that silenced me, and all chaff of the other fellows failed to draw him further.

The queer thing about it was that, when we congratulated Miss Forster, she blushed, and smiled, and dimpled, for all the world as though she were in love with him and had been in love with him all the time. Upon my word, I think she had. Women are strange creatures.

We were all asked to the wedding. In Brixham, everyone who was anybody knew everybody else who was anyone. My sisters were, I truly believe, more interested in the *trousseau* than the bride herself, and I was to be best man. The coming marriage was much canvassed at afternoon tea-tables, and at our little club over the saddler's, and the question was always asked: 'Does she care for him?'

I used to ask that question myself in the early days of their engagement, but after a certain evening in August I never asked it again. I was coming home from the club through the churchyard. Our church is on a thyme-grown hill, and the turf about it is so thick and soft that one's footsteps are noiseless.

I made no sound as I vaulted the low wall and threaded my way between the tombstones. It was at the same instant that I heard John Charrington's voice and saw her. May was sitting on a low, flat gravestone, her face turned towards the full splendour of the setting sun. Its expression ended, at once and forever, any question of love for him; it was transfigured to a beauty I should not have believed possible, even to that beautiful little face.

John lay at her feet, and it was his voice that broke the stillness of the golden August evening.

'My dear, I believe I should come back to you from the dead, if you wanted me!'

I coughed at once to indicate my presence, and passed on into the shadow fully enlightened.

The wedding was to be early in September. Two days before, I had to run up to town on business. The train was late, of course, for we were on the South-Eastern, and as I stood grumbling with my watch in my hand, whom should I see but John Charrington and May Forster. They were walking up and down the unfrequented end of the platform, arm in arm, looking into each other's eyes, careless of the sympathetic interest of the porters.

Of course I knew better than to hesitate a moment before burying myself in the booking-office, and it was not till the train drew up at the platform that I obtrusively passed the pair with my Gladstone, and took the corner in a first-class smoking-carriage. I did this with as good an air of not seeing them as I could assume. I pride myself on my discretion, but if John were travelling alone, I wanted his company. I had it.

'Hullo, old man,' came his cheery voice as he swung his bag into my carriage, 'here's luck. I was expecting a dull journey.'

'Where are you off to?' I asked, discretion still bidding me turn my eyes away, though I saw, without looking, that hers were red-rimmed.

'To old Branbridge's,' he answered, shutting the door, and leaning out for a last word with his sweetheart.

'Oh, I wish you wouldn't go, John,' she was saying in a low, earnest voice. 'I feel certain something will happen.'

'Do you think I should let anything happen to keep me, and the day after tomorrow our wedding day?'

'Don't go,' she answered, with a pleading intensity that would have sent my Gladstone on to the platform, and me after it. But she wasn't speaking to me. John Charrington was made differently — he rarely changed his opinions, never his resolutions.

He just touched the ungloved hands that lay on the carriage door.

'I must, May. The old boy has been awfully good to me, and

now he's dying I must go and see him, but I shall come home in time —' The rest of the parting was lost in a whisper and in the rattling lurch of the starting train.

'You're sure to come?' she spoke, as the train moved.

'Nothing shall keep me,' he answered, and we steamed out. After he had seen the last of the little figure on the platform, he leaned back in his corner and kept silence for a minute.

When he spoke it was to explain to me that his godfather, whose heir he was, lay dying at Peasemarsh Place, some fifty miles away, and he had sent for John, and John had felt bound to go.

'I shall be surely back tomorrow,' he said, 'or, if not, the day after, in heaps of time. Thank Heaven, one hasn't to get up in the middle of the night to get married nowadays!'

'And suppose Mr Branbridge dies?'

'Alive or dead, I mean to be married on Thursday!' John answered, lighting a cigar and unfolding the *Times*.

At Peasemarsh station we said 'goodbye,' and he got out, and I saw him ride off. I went on to London, where I stayed the night.

When I got home the next afternoon, a very wet one, by the way, my sister greeted me with:

'Where's Mr Charrington?'

'Goodness knows,' I answered testily. Every man since Cain has resented that kind of question.

'I thought you might have heard from him,' she went on, 'as you're to give him away tomorrow.'

'Isn't he back?' I asked, for I had confidently expected to find him at home.

'No, Geoffrey,' — my sister always had a way of jumping to conclusions, especially such conclusions as were least favourable to her fellow creatures — 'he has not returned, and, what is more, you may depend upon it, he won't. You mark my words, there'll be no wedding tomorrow.'

My sister Fanny has a power of annoying me which no other human being possesses.

'You mark my words,' I retorted with asperity, 'you had better give up making such a thundering idiot of yourself. There'll be more wedding tomorrow than ever you'll take first part in.' A prophecy which, by the way, came true.

But though I could snarl confidently to my sister, I did not feel so comfortable when, late that night, I, standing on the doorstep of John's house, heard that he had not returned. I went home gloomily through the rain. Next morning brought a brilliant blue sky, gold sun, and all such softness of air and beauty of cloud as go to make a perfect day. I woke with a vague feeling of having gone to bed anxious, and of being rather averse to facing that anxiety in the light of full wakefulness.

With my shaving-water came a letter from John which relieved my mind and sent me up to the Forsters with a light heart.

May was in the garden. I saw her blue gown among the hollyhocks as the lodge gates swung to behind me. So I did not go up to the house, but turned aside down the turfed path.

'He's written to you too,' she said, without preliminary greeting, when I reached her side.

'Yes, I'm to meet him at the station at three, and come straight on to the church.'

Her face looked pale, but there was a brightness in her eyes and a softness about the mouth that spoke of renewed happiness.

'Mr Branbridge begged him so to stay another night that he had not the heart to refuse,' she went on. 'He is so kind, but ... I wish he hadn't stayed.'

I was at the station at half-past two. I felt rather annoyed with John. It seemed a sort of slight to the beautiful girl who loved him, that he should come as it were out of breath, and with the dust of travel upon him, to take her hand, which some of us would have given the best years of our lives to take.

But when the three o'clock train glided in and glided out again, having brought no passengers to our little station, I was more than annoyed. There was no other train for thirty-five minutes; I calculated that, with much hurry, we might just get to the church in time for the ceremony; but, oh, what a fool to miss that first train! What other man would have done it?

That thirty-five minutes seemed a year, as I wandered round the station reading the advertisements and the time-tables and the company's bye-laws, and getting more and more angry with John Charrington. This confidence in his own power of getting everything he wanted the minute he wanted it was leading him too far.

I hate waiting. Everyone hates waiting, but I believe I hate it more than anyone else does. The three-thirty-five was late too, of course.

I ground my pipe between my teeth and stamped with impatience as I watched the signals. Click. The signal went down. Five minutes later I flung myself into the carriage that I had brought for John.

'Drive to the church!' I said, as someone shut the door. 'Mr Charrington hasn't come by this train.'

Anxiety now replaced anger. What had become of this man? Could he have been taken suddenly ill? I had never known him have a day's illness in his life. And even so he might have telegraphed. Some awful accident must have happened to him. The thought that he had played her false never, no, not for a moment, entered my head. Yes, something terrible had happened to him, and on me lay the task of telling his bride. I almost wished the carriage would upset and break my head, so that someone else might tell her.

It was five minutes to four as we drew up at the churchyard. A double row of eager onlookers lined the path from lychgate to porch. I sprang from the carriage and passed up between them. Our gardener had a good front place near the door. I stopped.

'Are they still waiting, Byles?' I asked, simply to gain time, for of course I knew they were by the waiting crowd's attentive attitude.

'Waiting, sir? No, no, sir; why, it must be over by now.'

'Over! Then Mr Charrington's come?'

'To the minute, sir; must have missed you somehow, and I say, sir,' lowering his voice, 'I never see Mr John the least bit so afore, but my opinion is he's 'ad more than a drop; I wouldn't be going too far if I said he's been drinking pretty free. His clothes was all dusty and his face like a sheet. I tell you I didn't like the looks of him at all, and the folks inside are saying all sorts of things. You'll see, something's gone very wrong with Mr John, and he's tried liquor. He looked like a ghost, and he went in with his eyes straight before him, with never a look or a word for none of us; him that was always such a gentleman.'

I had never heard Byles make so long a speech. The crowd in the churchyard were talking in whispers and getting ready rice and slippers to throw at the bride and bridegroom. The ringers were ready with their hands on the ropes, to ring out the merry peal as the bride and bridegroom should come out.

A murmur from the church announced them; out they came. Byles was right. John Charrington did not look himself. There was dust on his coat, his hair was disarranged. He seemed to have been in some row, for there was a black mark above his eyebrow. He was deathly pale. But his pallor was not greater than that of the bride, who might have been carved in ivory — dress, veil, orange blossoms, face and all.

As they passed out, the ringers stooped — there were six

of them — and then, on the ears expecting the gay wedding peal, came the slow tolling of the passing bell.

A thrill of horror at so foolish a jest from the ringers passed through us all. But the ringers themselves dropped the ropes and fled like rabbits out into the sunlight. The bride shuddered, and grey shadows came about her mouth, but the bridegroom led her on down the path where the people stood with the handfuls of rice; but the handfuls were never thrown, and the wedding bells never rang. In vain the ringers were urged to remedy their mistake; they protested, with many whispered expletives, that they had not rung that bell; that they would see themselves further before they'd ring anything more that day.

In a hush, like the hush in the chamber of death, the bridal pair passed into their carriage, and its door slammed behind them.

Then the tongues were loosed. A babel of anger, wonder, conjecture from the guests and the spectators.

'If I'd seen his condition, sir,' said old Forster to me as we drove off, 'I would have stretched him on the floor of the church, sir, by Heaven I would, before I'd have let him marry my daughter!'

Then he put his head out of the window.

'Drive like hell,' he cried to the coachman; 'don't spare the horses.'

We passed the bride's carriage. I forebore to look at it, and old Forster turned his head away and swore.

We stood in the hall doorway, in the blazing afternoon sun, and in about half a minute we heard wheels crunching the gravel. When the carriage stopped in front of the steps, old Forster and I ran down.

'Great Heaven, the carriage is empty! And yet —'

I had the door open in a minute, and this is what I saw —

No sign of John Charrington; and of May, his wife, only a huddled heap of white satin, lying half on the floor of the carriage and half on the seat.

'I drove straight here, sir,' said the coachman, as the bride's father lifted her out, 'and I'll swear no one got out of the carriage.'

We carried her into the house in her bridal dress and drew back her veil. I saw her face. Shall I ever forget it? White, white, and drawn with agony and horror, bearing such a look of terror as I have never seen since, except in dreams. And her hair, her radiant blonde hair, I tell you it was white like snow.

As we stood, her father and I, half mad with the horror and mystery of it, a boy came up the avenue — a telegraph boy. They brought the orange envelope to me. I tore it open.

'John Charrington was thrown from the dogcart on his way to the station at half-past one. Killed on the spot.' — Branbridge, Peasemarsh Place.'

And he was married to May Forster in our parish church at *half-past three*, in presence of half the parish!

'I shall be married on Thursday dead or alive!'

What had passed in that carriage on the homeward drive? No one knows — no one will ever know.

Before a week was over they laid her beside her husband in the churchyard where they had kept their love-trysts.

This is the true story of John Charrington's wedding.

3 Uncle Abraham's Romance

'No, my dear,' my Uncle Abraham answered me, 'no —
nothing romantic ever happened to me — unless — but no;
that wasn't romantic either —'

I was. To me, I being eighteen, romance was the world.
My Uncle Abraham was old and lame. I followed the gaze
of his faded eyes, and my own rested on a miniature that
hung at his elbow-chair's right hand, a portrait of a woman,
whose loveliness even the miniature-painter's art had been
powerless to disguise — a woman with large eyes that shone,
and face of that alluring oval which one hardly sees nowadays.

I rose to look at it. I had looked at it a hundred times. Often
enough in my baby days I had asked, 'Who's that, uncle?' and
always the answer was the same: 'A lady who died long ago,
my dear.'

As I looked again at the picture, I asked, 'Was she like this?'
'Who?'
'Your — your romance!'

Uncle Abraham looked hard at me. 'Yes,' he said at last.
'Very — very like.'

I sat down on the floor by him. 'Won't you tell me about
her?'

'There's nothing to tell,' he said. 'I think it was fancy mostly,
and folly; but it's the realest thing in my life, my dear.'

A long pause. I kept silent. You should always give people
time, especially old people.

'I remember,' he said in the dreamy tone always promising
so well to the ear that loves a story — 'I remember, when
I was a young man, I was very lonely indeed. I never had a
sweetheart. I was always lame, my dear, from quite a boy;
and the girls used to laugh at me.'

Silence again. Presently he went on —

'And so I got into the way of mooning off by myself in lonely places, and one of my favourite walks was up through our churchyard, which was set on a hill in the middle of the marsh country. I liked that because I never met anyone there. It's all over, years ago. I was a silly lad; but I couldn't bear of a summer evening to hear a rustle and a whisper from the other side of the hedge, or maybe a kiss, as I went by.

'Well, I used to go and sit all by myself in the churchyard, which was always sweet with the thyme, and quite light (on account of its being so high) long after the marshes were dark. I used to watch the bats flitting about in the red light, and wonder why God didn't make everyone's legs straight and strong, and wicked follies like that. But by the time the light was gone I had always worked it off, so to speak, and could go home quietly, and say my prayers without bitterness.

'Well, one hot night in August, when I had watched the sunset fade and the crescent moon grow golden, I was just stepping over the low stone wall of the churchyard when I heard a rustle behind me. I turned round, expecting it to be a rabbit or a bird. It was a woman.'

He looked at the portrait. So did I.

'Yes,' he said, 'that was her very face. I was a bit scared and said something — I don't know what — she laughed and said, did I think she was a ghost? and I answered back; and I stayed talking to her over the churchyard wall till 'twas quite dark, and the glowworms were out in the wet grass all along the way home.

'Next night, I saw her again; and the next, and the next. Always at twilight time; and if I passed any lovers leaning on the stiles in the marshes it was nothing to me now.'

Again my uncle paused. 'It was very long ago,' he said shyly, 'and I'm an old man; but I know what youth means, and happiness, though I was always lame, and the girls used to laugh at me. I don't know how long it went on — you don't

THE HOUSE OF SILENCE

measure time in dreams — but at last your grandfather said I looked as if I had one foot in the grave, and he would be sending me to stay with our kin at Bath, and take the waters. I had to go. I could not tell my father why I would rather die than go.'

'What was her name, uncle?' I asked.

'She never would tell me her name, and why should she? I had names enough in my heart to call her by. Marriage? My dear, even then I knew marriage was not for me. But I met her night after night, always in our churchyard where the yew-trees were, and the old crooked gravestones so thick in the grass. It was there we always met and always parted. The last time was the night before I went away. She was very sad, and dearer than life itself. And she said:

"If you come back before the new moon, I shall meet you here just as usual. But if the new moon shines on this grave and you are not here — you will never see me again anymore."

'She laid her hand on the tomb against which we had been leaning. It was an old, lichened, weather-worn stone, and its inscription was just:

SUSANNAH KINGSNORTH,
Ob. 1723.

"I shall be here", I said.

"I mean it", she said, very seriously and slowly, "it is no fancy. You will be here when the new moon shines?"

'I promised, and after a while we parted.

'I had been with my kinsfolk at Bath for nearly a month. I was to go home on the next day when, turning over a case in the parlour, I came upon that miniature. I could not speak for a minute. At last I said, with dry tongue, and heart beating to the tune of heaven and hell:

"Who is this?"

"That?" said my aunt. "Oh! she was betrothed to one of our family years ago, but she died before the wedding. They say she was a bit of a witch. A handsome one, wasn't she?"

'I looked again at the face, the lips, the eyes of my dear lovely love, whom I was to meet tomorrow night when the new moon shone on that tomb in our churchyard.

"Did you say she was dead?" I asked, and I hardly knew my own voice.

"Years and years ago! Her name's on the back, and her date —"

'I took the portrait out from its case — I remember just the colour of its faded, red-velvet bed, and read on the back — "Susannah Kingsnorth, *Ob.* 1723".

'That was in 1823.' My uncle stopped short.

'What happened?' I asked breathlessly.

'I believe I had a fit,' my uncle answered slowly; 'at any rate, I was very ill.'

'And you missed the new moon on the grave?'

'I missed the new moon on the grave.'

'And you never saw her again?'

'I never saw her again —'

'But, uncle, do you really believe? — Can the dead — was she — did you —'

My uncle took out his pipe and filled it.

'It's a long time ago,' he said, 'a many, many years. Old man's tales, my dear! Old man's tales. Don't you take any notice of them.'

He lighted the pipe, and puffed silently a moment or two before he said: 'But I know what youth means, and love and happiness, though I was always lame, and the girls used to laugh at me.'

4 The Ebony Frame

To be rich is a luxurious sensation — the more so when you have plumbed the depths of hard-up-ness as a Fleet Street hack, a picker-up of unconsidered pars, a reporter, an unappreciated journalist; all callings utterly inconsistent with one's family feeling and one's direct descent from the Dukes of Picardy.

When my Aunt Dorcas died and left me seven hundred a year and a furnished house in Chelsea, I felt that life had nothing left to offer except immediate possession of the legacy. Even Mildred Mayhew, whom I had hitherto regarded as my life's light, became less luminous. I was not engaged to Mildred, but I lodged with her mother, and I sang duets with Mildred and gave her gloves when it would run to it, which was seldom. She was a dear, good girl, and I meant to marry her some day. It is very nice to feel that a good little woman is thinking of you — it helps you in your work — and it is pleasant to know she will say 'Yes' when you say, 'Will you?'

But my legacy almost put Mildred out of my head, especially as she was staying with friends in the country.

Before the gloss was off my new mourning, I was seated in my aunt's armchair in front of the fire in the drawing-room of my own house. My own house! It was grand, but rather lonely. I *did* think of Mildred just then.

The room was comfortably furnished with rosewood and damask. On the walls hung a few fairly good oil paintings, but the space above the mantelpiece was disfigured by an exceedingly bad print, 'The Trial of Lord William Russell,' framed in a dark frame. I got up to look at it. I had visited my aunt with dutiful regularity, but I never remembered seeing this frame before. It was not intended for a print, but for an oil painting. It was of fine ebony, beautifully and curiously carved.

I looked at it with growing interest, and when my aunt's housemaid — I had retained her modest staff of servants — came in with the lamp, I asked her how long the print had been there.

'Mistress only bought it two days afore she was took ill,' she said; 'but the frame — she didn't want to buy a new one — so she got this out of the attic. There's lots of curious old things there, sir.'

'Had my aunt had this frame long?'

'Oh, yes, sir! It must have come long before I did, and I've been here seven years come Christmas. There was a picture in it. That's upstairs too — but it's that black and ugly it might as well be a chimney-back.'

I felt a desire to see this picture. What if it were some priceless old master, in which my aunt's eyes had only seen rubbish?

Directly after breakfast next morning, I paid a visit to the attic.

It was crammed with old furniture enough to stock a curiosity shop. All the house was furnished solidly in the Mid-Victorian style, and in this room everything not in keeping with the drawing-room-suite ideal was stowed away. Tables of papier-mâché and mother-of-pearl, straight-backed chairs with twisted feet and faded needlework cushions, fire-screens of gilded carving and beaded banners, oak bureaux with brass handles, a little work-table with its faded, moth-eaten, silk flutings hanging in disconsolate shreds: on these, and the dust that covered them, blazed the full daylight as I pulled up the blinds. I promised myself a good time in re-enshrining these household gods in my parlour, and promoting the Victorian suite to the attic. But at present my business was to find the picture as 'black as the chimney-back'; and presently, behind a heap of fenders and boxes, I found it.

Jane, the housemaid, identified it at once. I took it downstairs carefully and examined it. Neither subject nor colour was distinguishable. There was a splodge of a darker tint in the middle, but whether it was figure, or tree, or house, no man could have told. It seemed to be painted on a very thick panel bound with leather. I decided to send it to one of those persons who pour on rotting family portraits the water of eternal youth; but even as I did so, I thought — why not try my own restorative hand at a corner of it.

My bath-sponge soap and nail-brush, vigorously applied for a few seconds, showed me that there was no picture to clean. Bare oak presented itself to my persevering brush. I tried the other side, Jane watching me with indulgent interest. The same result. Then the truth dawned on me. Why was the panel so thick? I tore off the leather binding, and the panel divided and fell to the ground in a cloud of dust. There were two pictures — they had been nailed face to face. I leaned them against the wall, and the next moment I was leaning against it myself.

For one of the pictures was myself — a perfect portrait — no shade of expression or turn of feature wanting. Myself — in the dress men wore when James the First was King. When had this been done? And how, without my knowledge? Was this some whim of my aunt's?

'Lor,' sir!' the shrill surprise of Jane at my elbow; 'what a lovely photo it is! Was it a fancy ball, sir?'

'Yes,' I stammered. 'I — I don't think I want anything more now. You can go.'

She went; and I turned, still with my heart beating violently, to the other picture. This was a beautiful woman's picture — very beautiful she was. I noted all her beauties — straight nose, low brows, full lips, thin hands, large, deep, luminous eyes. She wore a black velvet gown. It was a three-quarter-length portrait. Her arms rested on a table beside her, and her head on her hands; but her face was turned full forward, and her eyes met those of the spectator bewilderingly. On the table by her were compasses and shining instruments whose uses I did not know, books, a goblet, and a heap of papers and pens. I saw all this afterwards. I believe it was a quarter of an hour before I could turn my eyes from hers. I have never seen any other eyes like hers; they appealed, as a child's or a dog's do; they commanded, as might those of an empress.

'Shall I sweep up the dust, sir?' Curiosity had brought Jane back. I acceded. I turned from her my portrait. I kept between her and the woman in the black velvet. When I was alone again I tore down 'The Trial of Lord William Russell', and I put the picture of the woman in its strong ebony frame.

Then I wrote to a frame-maker for a frame for my portrait. It had so long lived face to face with this beautiful witch that I had not the heart to banish it from her presence; I suppose I *am* sentimental — if it be sentimental to think such things as that.

The new frame came home, and I hung it opposite the fireplace. An exhaustive search among my aunt's papers showed no explanation of the portrait of myself, no history of the portrait of the woman with the wonderful eyes. I only learned that all the old furniture together had come to my aunt at the death of my great-uncle, the head of the family; and I should have concluded that the resemblance was only a family one, if everyone who came in had not exclaimed at the 'speaking likeness'. I adopted Jane's 'fancy ball' explanation.

And there, one might suppose, the matter of the portraits ended. One might suppose it, that is, if there were not evidently a good deal more written here about it. However, to me then the matter seemed ended.

I went to see Mildred; I invited her and her mother to come and stay with me. I rather avoided glancing at the picture in the ebony frame. I could not forget, nor remember without singular emotion, the look in the eyes of that woman when mine first met them. I shrank from meeting that look again.

I reorganised the house somewhat, preparing for Mildred's visit. I brought down much of the old-fashioned furniture, and after a long day of arranging and re-arranging, I sat down before the fire, and lying back in a pleasant languor, I idly raised my eyes to the picture of the woman. I met her dark, deep, hazel eyes, and once more my gaze was held fixed as by strong magic — the kind of fascination that keeps one sometimes staring for whole minutes into one's own eyes in the glass. I gazed into her eyes, and felt my own dilate, pricked with a smart like the smart of tears.

'I wish,' I said, 'oh, how I wish you were a woman and not a picture! Come down! Ah, come down!'

I laughed at myself as I spoke; but even as I laughed, I held out my arms.

I was not sleepy; I was not drunk. I was as wide awake and as sober as ever was a man in this world. And yet, as I held out my arms, I saw the eyes of the picture dilate, her lips tremble — if I were to be hanged for saying it, it is true.

Her hands moved slightly, and a sort of flicker of a smile passed over her face.

I sprang to my feet. 'This won't do,' I said aloud. 'Firelight does play strange tricks. I'll have the lamp.'

I made for the bell. My hand was on it, when I heard a sound behind me, and turned — the bell still unrung. The fire had burned low and the corners of the room were deeply shadowed; but surely, there — behind the tall worked chair — was something darker than a shadow.

'I must face this out,' I said, 'or I shall never be able to face myself again.' I left the bell, I seized the poker, and battered the dull coals to a blaze. Then I stepped back resolutely, and looked up at the picture. The ebony frame was empty! From the shadow of the worked chair came a soft rustle, and out of the shadow the woman of the picture was coming — coming towards me.

I hope I shall never again know a moment of terror so blank and absolute. I could not have moved or spoken to save my life. Either all the known laws of nature were nothing, or I was mad. I stood trembling, but, I am thankful to remember, I stood still, while the black velvet gown swept across the hearthrug towards me.

Next moment a hand touched me — a hand, soft, warm, and human — and a low voice said, 'You called me. I am here.'

At that touch and that voice, the world seemed to give a sort of bewildering half-turn. I hardly know how to express it, but at once it seemed not awful, not even unusual, for portraits to become flesh — only most natural, most right, most unspeakably fortunate.

I laid my hand on hers. I looked from her to my portrait. I could not see it in the firelight.

'We are not strangers,' I said.

'Oh, no, not strangers.' Those luminous eyes were looking up into mine, those red lips were near me. With a passionate cry, a sense of having recovered life's one great good, that had seemed wholly lost, I clasped her in my arms. She was no ghost, she was a woman, the only woman in the world.

'How long,' I said, 'how long is it since I lost you?'

She leaned back, hanging her full weight on the hands that were clasped behind my head.

'How can I tell how long? There is no time in hell,' she answered.

It was not a dream. Ah! no — there are no such dreams. I wish to God there could be. When in dreams do I see her eyes, hear her voice, feel her lips against my cheek, hold her hands to my lips, as I did that night, the supreme night of my life! At first we hardly spoke. It seemed enough

> … after long grief and pain,
> To feel the arms of my true love,
> Round me once again.

※

It is very difficult to tell my story. There are no words to express the sense of glad reunion, the complete realisation of every hope and dream of a life, that came upon me as I sat with my hand in hers and looked into her eyes.

How could it have been a dream, when I left her sitting in the straight-backed chair, and went down to the kitchen to tell the maids I should want nothing more — that I was busy, and did not wish to be disturbed; when I fetched wood for the fire with my own hands, and, bringing it in, found her still sitting there — saw the little brown head turn as I entered, saw the love in her dear eyes; when I threw myself at her feet and blessed the day I was born, since life had given me this?

Not a thought of Mildred; all the other things in my life were a dream — this, its one splendid reality.

'I am wondering,' she said, after a while, when we had made such cheer, each of the other, as true lovers may after long parting — 'I am wondering how much you remember of our past?'

'I remember nothing but that I love you — that I have loved you all my life.'

'You remember nothing — really nothing?'

'Only that I am truly yours; that we have both suffered; that — tell me, my mistress dear, all that you remember. Explain it all to me. Make me understand. And yet — No, I don't want to understand. It is enough that we are together.'

If it was a dream, why have I never dreamed it again?

She leaned down towards me, her arm lay on my neck, and drew my head till it rested on her shoulder. 'I am a ghost, I suppose,' she said, laughing softly; and her laughter stirred memories which I just grasped at and just missed. 'But you and I know better, don't we? I will tell you everything you have forgotten. We loved each other — ah! no, you have not forgotten that — and when you came back from the wars, we were to be married. Our pictures were painted before you went away. You know I was more learned than women of that day. Dear one, when you were gone, they said I was a witch. They tried me. They said I should be burned. Just because I had looked at the stars and gained more knowledge than other women, they must needs bind me to a stake and let me be eaten by the fire. And you far away!'

Her whole body trembled and shrank. Oh love, what dream would have told me that my kisses would soothe even that memory?

'The night before,' she went on, 'the devil did come to me. I was innocent before — you know it, don't you? And even then my sin was for you — for you — because of the exceeding love I bore you. The devil came, and I sold my soul to eternal flame. But I got a good price. I got the right to come back through my picture (if anyone, looking at it, wished for me), as long as my picture stayed in its ebony frame. That frame was not carved by man's hand. I got the right to come back to you, oh, my heart's heart. And another thing I won, which you shall hear anon. They burned me for a witch, they made me suffer hell on earth. Those faces, all crowding round, the crackling wood and the choking smell of the smoke —'

'Oh, love, no more, no more!'

'When my mother sat that night before my picture, she wept and cried, 'Come back, my poor, lost child!' And I went to her with glad leaps of heart. Dear, she shrank from me, she fled, she shrieked and moaned of ghosts. She had our pictures covered from sight and put again in the ebony frame. She had promised me my picture should stay always there. Ah, through all these years your face was against mine.'

She paused.

'But the man you loved?'

'You came home. My picture was gone. They lied to you, and you married another woman; but some day I knew you would walk the world again and that I should find you.'

'The other gain?' I asked.

'The other gain,' she said slowly, 'I gave my soul for. It is this. If you also will give up your hopes of heaven, I can remain a woman, I can remain in your world — I can be your wife. Oh my dear, after all these years, at last — at last!'

'If I sacrifice my soul,' I said slowly, and the words did not seem an imbecility, 'if I sacrifice my soul I win you? Why, love, it's a contradiction in terms. You *are* my soul.'

Her eyes looked straight into mine. Whatever might happen, whatever did happen, whatever may happen, our two souls in that moment met and became one.

'Then you choose, you deliberately choose, to give up your hopes of heaven for me, as I gave up mine for you?'

'I will not,' I said, 'give up my hope of heaven on any terms. Tell me what I must do that you and I may make our heaven here, as now.'

'I will tell you tomorrow,' she said. 'Be alone here tomorrow night — twelve is ghost's time, isn't it? — and then I will come out of the picture and never go back to it. I shall live with you, and die, and be buried, and there will be an end of me. But we shall live first, my heart's heart.'

I laid my head on her knee. A strange drowsiness overcame me. Holding her hand against my cheek, I lost consciousness. When I awoke the grey November dawn was glimmering, ghost-like, through the uncurtained window. My head was pillowed on my arm, which rested — I raised my head quickly — ah! not on my lady's knee, but on the needleworked cushion of the straight-backed chair. I sprang to my feet. I was stiff with cold and dazed with dreams, but I turned my eyes on the picture. There she sat, my lady, my dear love. I held out my arms, but the passionate cry I would have uttered died on my lips. She had said twelve o'clock. Her lightest word was my law. So I only stood in front of the picture and gazed into those grey-green eyes till tears of passionate happiness filled my own.

'Oh! my dear, my dear, how shall I pass the hours till I hold you again?'

No thought, then, of my whole life's completion and consummation being a dream.

I staggered up to my room, fell across my bed, and slept heavily and dreamlessly. When I awoke it was high noon. Mildred and her mother were coming to lunch.

I remembered, at one o'clock, Mildred's coming and her existence.

Now, indeed, the dream began.

With a penetrating sense of the futility of any action apart from *her*, I gave the necessary orders for the reception of my guests. When Mildred and her mother came I received them with cordiality; but my genial phrases all seemed to be someone else's. My voice sounded like an echo; my heart was not there.

Still, the situation was not intolerable, until the hour when afternoon tea was served in the drawing-room. Mildred and her mother kept the conversational pot boiling with a profusion of genteel commonplaces, and I bore it, as one in sight of heaven can bear mild purgatory. I looked up at my sweetheart in the ebony frame, and I felt that anything which might happen, any irresponsible imbecility, any bathos of boredom, was nothing, if, after all, *she* came to me again.

And yet, when Mildred, too, looked at the portrait, and said: 'Doesn't she think a lot of herself? Theatrical character, I suppose? One of your flames, Mr Devigne?' I had a sickening sense of impotent irritation which became absolute torture when Mildred — how could I ever have admired that chocolate-box barmaid style of prettiness? — threw herself into the high-backed chair, covering the needlework with ridiculous flounces, and added, 'Silence gives consent! Who is it, Mr Devigne? Tell us all about her: I am sure she has a story.'

Poor little Mildred, sitting there smiling, serene in her confidence that her every word charmed me — sitting there with her rather pinched waist, her rather tight boots, her rather vulgar voice — sitting in the chair where my dear lady had sat when she told me her story! I could not bear it.

'Don't sit there,' I said, 'it's not comfortable!'

But the girl would not be warned. With a laugh that set every nerve in my body vibrating with annoyance, she said, 'Oh, dear! mustn't I even sit in the same chair as your black-velvet woman?'

I looked at the chair in the picture. It *was* the same, and in her chair Mildred was sitting. Then a horrible sense of the reality of Mildred came upon me. Was all this a reality after all? But for fortunate chance, might Mildred have occupied, not only her chair, but her place in my life? I rose.

'I hope you won't think me very rude,' I said, 'but I am obliged to go out.'

I forget what appointment I alleged. The lie came readily enough.

I faced Mildred's pouts with the hope that she and her mother would not wait dinner for me. I fled. In another minute I was safe, alone, under the chill, cloudy, autumn sky — free to think, think, think of my dear lady.

I walked for hours along streets and squares; I lived over and over again every look, word, and hand-touch — every kiss; I was completely, unspeakably happy.

Mildred was utterly forgotten; my lady of the ebony frame filled my heart, and soul, and spirit.

As I heard eleven boom through the fog, I turned and went home.

When I got to my street, I found a crowd surging through it, a strong red light filling the air.

A house was on fire. Mine!

I elbowed my way through the crowd.

The picture of my lady — that, at least, I could save.

As I sprang up the steps, I saw, as in a dream — yes, all this was *really* dream-like — I saw Mildred leaning out of the first-floor window, wringing her hands.

'Come back, sir,' cried a fireman; 'we'll get the young lady out right enough.'

But *my* lady? The stairs were cracking, smoking, and as hot as hell. I went up to the room where her picture was. Strange to say, I only felt that the picture was a thing we should like to look on through the long, glad, wedded life that was to be ours. I never thought of it as being one with her.

As I reached the first floor I felt arms about my neck. The smoke was too thick for me to distinguish features.

'Save me,' a voice whispered. I clasped a figure in my arms and bore it with a strange dis-ease, down the shaking stairs and out into safety. It was Mildred. I knew *that* directly I clasped her.

'Stand back,' cried the crowd.

'Everyone's safe,' cried a fireman.

The flames leaped from every window. The sky grew redder and redder. I sprang from the hands that would have held me. I leaped up the steps. I crawled up the stairs. Suddenly the whole horror came to me. *'As long as my picture remains in the ebony frame.*' What if picture and frame perished together?

I fought with the fire and with my own choking inability to fight with it. I pushed on. I must save my picture. I reached the drawing-room.

As I sprang in, I saw my lady, I swear it, through the smoke and the flames, hold out her arms to me — to me — who came too late to save her, and to save my own life's joy. I never saw her again.

Before I could reach her, or cry out to her, I felt the floor yield beneath my feet, and I fell into the flames below.

✕

How did they save me? What does that matter? They saved me somehow — curse them. Every stick of my aunt's furniture was destroyed. My friends pointed out that, as the furniture was heavily insured, the carelessness of a nightly-studious housemaid had done me no harm.

No harm!

That was how I won and lost my only love.

I deny, with all my soul in the denial, that it was a dream. There are no such dreams. Dreams of longing and pain there are in plenty; but dreams of complete, of unspeakable happiness — ah, no — it is the rest of life that is the dream.

But, if I think that, why have I married Mildred and grown stout, and dull, and prosperous?

I tell you, it is all *this* that is the dream; my dear lady only is the reality. And what does it matter what one does in a dream?

5 From the Dead

I

'But true or not true, your brother is a scoundrel. No man — no decent man — tells such things.'

'He did not tell me. How dare you suppose it? I found the letter in his desk; and since she was my friend and your sweetheart, I never thought there could be any harm in my reading anything she might write to my brother. Give me back the letter. I was a fool to tell you.'

Ida Helmont held out her hand for the letter.

'Not yet,' I said, and I went to the window. The dull red of a London sunset burned on the paper, as I read in the pretty handwriting I knew so well, and had kissed so often:

> Dear, I do — I do love you; but it's impossible. I must marry Arthur. My honour is engaged. If he would only set me free — but he never will. He loves me foolishly. But as for me — it is you I love — body, soul, and spirit. There is no one in my heart but you. I think of you all day, and dream of you all night. And we must part. Goodbye —
> Yours, yours, yours,
>
> ELVIRA

I had seen the handwriting, indeed, often enough. But the passion written there was new to me. That I had not seen.

I turned from the window. My sitting-room looked strange to me. There were my books, my reading-lamp, my untasted dinner still on the table, as I had left it when I rose to dissemble my surprise at Ida Helmont's visit — Ida Helmont, who now sat looking at me quietly.

'Well — do you give me no thanks?'

'You put a knife in my heart, and then ask for thanks?'

'Pardon me,' she said, throwing up her chin. 'I have done nothing but show you the truth. For that one should expect no gratitude — may I ask, out of mere curiosity, what you intend to do?'

'Your brother will tell you —'

She rose suddenly, very pale, and her eyes haggard.

'You will not tell my brother?' she began.

She came towards me — her gold hair flaming in the sunset light.

'Why are you so angry with me?' she said. 'Be reasonable. What else could I do?'

'I don't know.'

'Would it have been right not to tell you?'

'I don't know. I only know that you've put the sun out, and I haven't got used to the dark yet.'

'Believe me,' she said, coming still nearer to me, and laying her hands in the lightest touch on my shoulders, 'believe me, she never loved you.'

There was a softness in her tone that irritated and stimulated me. I moved gently back, and her hands fell by her sides.

'I beg your pardon,' I said. 'I have behaved very badly. You were quite right to come, and I am not ungrateful. Will you post a letter for me?'

I sat down and wrote:

I give you back your freedom. The only gift of mine that can please you now.

Arthur

I held the sheet out to Miss Helmont, but she would not look at it. I folded, sealed, stamped, and addressed it.

'Goodbye,' I said then, and gave her the letter. As the door closed behind her, I sank into my chair, and cried like a child, or a fool, over my lost plaything — the little, dark-haired woman who loved someone else with 'body, soul, and spirit'.

I did not hear the door open or any foot on the floor, and therefore I started when a voice behind me said:

'Are you so very unhappy? Oh, Arthur, don't think I am not sorry for you!'

'I don't want anyone to be sorry for me, Miss Helmont,' I said.

She was silent a moment. Then, with a quick, sudden, gentle movement she leaned down and kissed my forehead — and I heard the door softly close. Then I knew that the beautiful Miss Helmont loved me.

At first that thought only fleeted by — a light cloud against a grey sky — but the next day reason woke, and said:

'Was Miss Helmont speaking the truth? Was it possible that —?'

I determined to see Elvira, to know from her own lips whether by happy fortune this blow came, not from her, but from a woman in whom love might have killed honesty.

I walked from Hampstead to Gower Street. As I trod its long length, I saw a figure in pink come out of one of the houses. It was Elvira. She walked in front of me to the corner of Store Street. There she met Oscar Helmont. They turned and met me face to face, and I saw all I needed to see. They loved each other. Ida Helmont had spoken the truth. I bowed and passed on. Before six months were gone, they were married, and before a year was over, I had married Ida Helmont.

What did it, I don't know. Whether it was remorse for having, even for half a day, dreamed that she could be so base as to forge a lie to gain a lover, or whether it was her beauty, or the sweet flattery of the preference of a woman who had half her acquaintances at her feet, I don't know;

anyhow, my thoughts turned to her as to their natural home. My heart, too, took that road, and before very long I loved her as I never loved Elvira. Let no one doubt that I loved her — as I shall never love again — please God!

There never was anyone like her. She was brave and beautiful, witty and wise, and beyond all measure adorable. She was the only woman in the world. There was a frankness — a largeness of heart — about her that made all other women seem small and contemptible. She loved me and I worshipped her. I married her, I stayed with her for three golden weeks, and then I left her. Why?

Because she told me the truth. It was one night — late — we had sat all the evening in the verandah of our seaside lodging, watching the moonlight on the water, and listening to the soft sound of the sea on the sand. I have never been so happy; I never shall be happy anymore, I hope.

'My dear, my dear,' she said, leaning her gold head against my shoulder, 'how much do you love me?'

'How much?'

'Yes — how much? I want to know what place I hold in your heart. Am I more to you than anyone else?'

'My love!'

'More than yourself?'

'More than my life.'

'I believe you,' she said. Then she drew a long breath, and took my hands in hers. 'It can make no difference. Nothing in heaven or earth can come between us now.'

'Nothing,' I said. 'But, my dear one, what is it?'

For she was trembling, pale.

'I must tell you,' she said; 'I cannot hide anything now from you, because I am yours — body, soul, and spirit.'

The phrase was an echo that stung.

The moonlight shone on her gold hair, her soft, warm, gold hair, and on her pale face.

'Arthur,' she said, 'you remember my coming to Hampstead with that letter?'

'Yes, my sweet, and I remember how you —'

'Arthur!' she spoke fast and low — 'Arthur, that letter was a forgery. She never wrote it. I —'

She stopped, for I had risen and flung her hands from me, and stood looking at her. God help me! I thought it was anger at the lie I felt. I know now it was only wounded vanity that smarted in me. That *I* should have been tricked, that *I* should have been deceived, that *I* should have been led on to make a fool of myself! That *I* should have married the woman who had befooled me. At that moment she was no longer the wife I adored — she was only a woman who had forged a letter and tricked me into marrying her.

I spoke; I denounced her; I said I would never speak to her again. I felt it was rather creditable in me to be so angry. I said I would have no more to do with a liar and forger.

I don't know whether I expected her to creep to my knees and implore forgiveness. I think I had some vague idea that I could by-and-by consent with dignity to forgive and forget. I did not mean what I said. No, oh no, no; I did not mean a word of it. While I was saying it, I was longing for her to weep and fall at my feet, that I might raise her and hold her in my arms again.

But she did not fall at my feet; she stood quietly looking at me.

'Arthur,' she said, as I paused for breath, 'let me explain — she — I —'

'There is nothing to explain,' I said hotly, still with that foolish sense of there being something rather noble in my indignation, the kind of thing one feels when one calls one's self a miserable sinner. 'You are a liar and a forger, and that is enough for me. I will never speak to you again. You have wrecked my life —'

'Do you mean that?' she said, interrupting me, and leaning forward to look at me. Tears lay on her cheeks, but she was not crying now.

I hesitated. I longed to take her in my arms and say — 'What does all that old tale matter now? Lay your head here, my darling, and cry here, and know how I love you.'

But instead I said nothing.

'*Do* you mean it?' she persisted.

Then she put her hand on my arm. I longed to clasp it and draw her to me.

Instead, I shook it off, and said:

'Mean it? Yes — of course I mean it. Don't touch me, please. You have ruined my life.'

She turned away without a word, went into our room, and shut the door.

I longed to follow her, to tell her that if there was anything to forgive, I forgave it.

Instead, I went out on the beach, and walked away under the cliffs.

The moonlight and the solitude, however, presently brought me to a better mind. Whatever she had done had been done for love of me — I knew that. I would go home and tell her so — tell her that whatever she had done, she was my dearest life, my heart's one treasure. True, my ideal of her was shattered, at least I felt I ought to think that it was shattered, but, even as she was, what was the whole world of women compared to her? And to be loved like that ... was that not sweet food for vanity? To be loved more than faith and fair dealing, and all the traditions of honesty and honour? I hurried back, but in my resentment and evil temper I had walked far, and the way back was very long. I had been parted from her for three hours by the time I opened the door of the little house where we lodged. The house was dark and very still. I slipped off my shoes and crept up the narrow stairs and opened the door of our room quite softly. Perhaps she would have cried herself to sleep, and I would lean over her and waken her with my kisses and beg her to forgive me. Yes, it had come to that now.

I went into the room — I went towards the bed. She was not there. She was not in the room, as one glance showed me. She was not in the house, as I knew in two minutes. When I had wasted a precious hour in searching the town for her, I found a note on my pillow:

'Goodbye! Make the best of what is left of your life. I will spoil it no more.'

She was gone, utterly gone. I rushed to town by the earliest morning train, only to find that her people knew nothing of her. Advertisement failed. Only a tramp said he had seen a white lady on the cliff, and a fisherman brought me a handkerchief marked with her name which he had found on the beach.

I searched the country far and wide, but I had to go back to London at last, and the months went by. I won't say much about those months, because even the memory of that suffering turns me faint and sick at heart. The police and detectives and the Press failed me utterly. Her friends could not help me, and were, moreover, wildly indignant with me, especially her brother, now living very happily with my first love.

I don't know how I got through those long weeks and months. I tried to write; I tried to read; I tried to live the life of a reasonable human being. But it was impossible. I could not endure the companionship of my kind. Day and night I almost saw her face — almost heard her voice. I took long walks in the country, and her figure was always just round the next turn of the road — in the next glade of the wood. But I never quite saw her — never quite heard her. I believe I was not altogether sane at that time. At last, one morning, as I was setting out for one of those long walks that had no goal but weariness, I met a telegraph boy, and took the red envelope from his hand.

On the pink paper inside was written:

'Come to me at once. I am dying. You must come. — IDA — Apinshaw Farm, Mellor, Derbyshire.'

There was a train at twelve to Marple, the nearest station. I took it. I tell you there are some things that cannot be written about. My life for those long months was one of them, that journey was another. What had her life been for those months? That question troubled me, as one is troubled in every nerve by the sight of a surgical operation, or a wound inflicted on a being dear to one. But the overmastering sensation was joy — intense, unspeakable joy. She was alive. I should see her again. I took out the telegram and looked at it: 'I am dying.' I simply did not believe it. She could not die till she had seen me. And if she had lived all those months without me, she could live now, when I was with her again, when she knew of the hell I had endured apart from her, and the heaven of our meeting. She must live; I could not let her die.

There was a long drive over bleak hills. Dark, jolting, infinitely wearisome. At last we stopped before a long, low building, where one or two lights gleamed faintly. I sprang out.

The door opened. A blaze of light made me blink and draw back. A woman was standing in the doorway.

'Art thee Arthur Marsh?' she said.

'Yes.'

'Then th'art ower late. She's dead.'

II

I went into the house, walked to the fire, and held out my hands to it mechanically, for though the night was May, I was cold to the bone. There were some folks standing round the fire and lights flickering. Then an old woman came forward with the northern instinct of hospitality.

'Thou'rt tired,' she said, 'and mazed-like. Have a sup o' tea.'

I burst out laughing. I had travelled two hundred miles to see *her*. And she was dead, and they offered me tea. They drew back from me as if I had been a wild beast, but I could not stop laughing. Then a hand was laid on my shoulder and someone led me into a dark room, lighted a lamp, set me in a chair, and sat down opposite me. It was a bare parlour, coldly furnished with rush chairs and much-polished tables and presses. I caught my breath, and grew suddenly grave, and looked at the woman who sat opposite me.

'I was Miss Ida's nurse,' said she, 'and she told me to send for you. Who are you?'

'Her husband —'

The woman looked at me with hard eyes, where intense surprise struggled with resentment.

'Then may God forgive you!' she said. 'What you've done I don't know, but it'll be 'ard work forgivin' *you* — even for *Him!*'

'Tell me,' I said, 'my wife —'

'Tell you?' The bitter contempt in the woman's tone did not hurt me. What was it to the self-contempt that had gnawed my heart all these months? 'Tell you! Yes, I'll tell you. Your wife was that ashamed of you, she never so much as told me she was married. She let me think anything I pleased sooner than that. She just come 'ere, an' she said, "Nurse, take care of me, for I am in mortal trouble. And don't let them know where I am," says she. An' me bein' well married to an honest man, and well-to-do here, I was able to do it, by the blessing.'

'Why didn't you send for me before?' It was a cry of anguish wrung from me.

'I'd *never* 'a sent for you. It was *her* doin.' Oh, to think as God A'mighty's made men able to measure out such-like pecks o' trouble for us womenfolk! Young man, I don't know what you did to 'er to make 'er leave you; but it muster bin something cruel, for she loved the ground you walked on. She useter sit day after day a-lookin' at your picture an' talkin' to it, an' kissin' of it, when she thought I wasn't takin' no notice, and cryin' till she made me cry too. She useter cry all night 'most. An' one day, when I tells 'er to pray to God to 'elp 'er through 'er trouble, she outs with *your* putty face on a card, she does, an,' says she, with her poor little smile, "That's my god, Nursey," she says.'

'Don't!' I said feebly, putting out my hands to keep off the torture; 'not any more. Not now.'

'*Don't?*' she repeated. She had risen and was walking up and down the room with clasped hands. 'Don't, indeed! No, I won't; but I shan't forget you! I tell you, I've had you in my prayers time and again, when I thought you'd made a light-o'-love of my darling. I shan't drop you outer them now, when I know she was your own wedded wife as you chucked away when you tired of 'er, and left 'er to eat 'er 'art out with longin' for you. Oh! I pray to God above us to pay you scot and lot for all you done to 'er. You killed my pretty. The price will be required of you, young man, even to the uttermost farthing. O God in Heaven, make him suffer! Make him feel it!'

She stamped her foot as she passed me. I stood quite still. I bit my lip till I tasted the blood hot and salt on my tongue.

'She was nothing to you,' cried the woman, walking faster up and down between the rush chairs and the table; 'any fool can see that with half an eye. You didn't love her, so you don't feel nothin' now; but some day you'll care for someone, and then you shall know what she felt — if there's any justice in Heaven.'

I, too, rose, walked across the room, and leaned against the wall. I heard her words without understanding them.

'Can't you feel *nothin'*? Are you mader stone? Come an' look at 'er lyin' there so quiet. She don't fret arter the likes o' you no more now. She won't sit no more a-lookin' outer winder an' sayin' nothin' — only droppin' 'er tears one by one, slow, slow on her lap. Come an' see 'er; come an' see what you done to my pretty — an' then you can go. Nobody wants you 'ere. *She* don't want you now. But p'raps you'd like to see 'er safe underground afore you go? I'll be bound you'll put a big stone slab on 'er — to make sure she don't rise again.'

I turned on her. Her thin face was white with grief and rage. Her claw-like hands were clenched.

'Woman,' I said, 'have mercy.'

She paused and looked at me.

'Eh?' she said.

'Have mercy!' I said again.

'Mercy! You should 'a thought o' that before. You 'adn't no mercy on 'er. She loved you — she died lovin' you. An' if I wasn't a Christian woman, I'd kill you for it — like the rat you are! That I would, though I 'ad to swing for it arterwards.'

I caught the woman's hands and held them fast, though she writhed and resisted.

'Don't you understand?' I said savagely. 'We loved each other. She died loving me. I have to live loving her. And it's *her* you pity. I tell you it was all a mistake — a stupid, stupid mistake. Take me to her, and for pity's sake let me be left alone with her.'

She hesitated; then said in a voice only a shade less hard: 'Well, come along, then.'

We moved towards the door. As she opened it a faint, weak cry fell on my ear. My heart stood still.

'What's that?' I asked, stopping on the threshold.

'Your child,' she said shortly.

That too! Oh, my love! oh, my poor love! All these long months!

'She allus said she'd send for you when she'd got over her trouble,' the woman said as we climbed the stairs. "I'd like him to see his little baby, nurse," she says; "our little baby. It'll be all right when the baby's born," she says. "I know he'll come to me then. You'll see." And I never said nothin,' not thinkin' you'd come if she was your leavins,' and not dreamin' as you could be 'er husband an' could stay away from 'er a hour — 'er bein' as she was. Hush!'

She drew a key from her pocket and fitted it to the lock. She opened the door and I followed her in. It was a large, dark room, full of old-fashioned furniture and a smell of lavender, camphor, and narcissus.

The big four-post bed was covered with white.

'My lamb — my poor, pretty lamb!' said the woman, beginning to cry for the first time as she drew back the sheet. 'Don't she look beautiful?'

I stood by the bedstead. I looked down on my wife's face. Just so I had seen it lie on the pillow beside me in the early morning, when the wind and the dawn came up from beyond the sea. She did not look like one dead. Her lips were still red, and it seemed to me that a tinge of colour lay on her cheek. It seemed to me, too, that if I kissed her she would awaken, and put her slight hand on my neck, and lay her cheek against mine — and that we should tell each other everything, and weep together, and understand, and be comforted.

So I stooped and laid my lips to hers as the old nurse stole from the room.

But the red lips were like marble, and she did not waken. She will not waken now ever anymore.

I tell you again there are some things that cannot be written.

III

I lay that night in a big room filled with heavy, dark furniture, in a great four-poster hung with heavy, dark curtains — a bed the counterpart of that other bed from whose side they had dragged me at last.

They fed me, I believe, and the old nurse was kind to me. I think she saw now that it is not the dead who are to be pitied most.

I lay at last in the big, roomy bed, and heard the household noises grow fewer and die out, the little wail of my child sounding latest. They had brought the child to me, and I had held it in my arms, and bowed my head over its tiny face and frail fingers. I did not love it then. I told myself it had cost me her life. But my heart told me that it was I who had done that. The tall clock at the stairhead sounded the hours — eleven, twelve, one, and still I could not sleep. The room was dark and very still.

I had not yet been able to look at my life quietly. I had been full of the intoxication of grief — a real drunkenness, more merciful than the sober calm that comes afterwards.

Now I lay still as the dead woman in the next room, and looked at what was left of my life. I lay still, and thought, and thought, and thought. And in those hours I tasted the bitterness of death. It must have been about three when I first became aware of a slight sound that was not the ticking of the clock. I say I first became aware, and yet I knew perfectly that I had heard that sound more than once before, and had yet determined not to hear it, *because it came from the next room* — the room where the corpse lay.

And I did not wish to hear that sound, because I knew it meant that I was nervous — miserably nervous — a coward and a brute. It meant that I, having killed my wife as surely as though I had put a knife in her breast, had now sunk so low as to be afraid of her dead body — the dead body that lay in the room next to mine. The heads of the beds were placed against the same wall; and from that wall I had fancied I heard slight, slight, almost inaudible sounds. So that when I say I became aware of them, I mean that I, at last, heard a sound so distinct as to leave no room for doubt or question. It brought me to a sitting position in the bed, and the drops of sweat gathered heavily on my forehead and fell on my cold hands as I held my breath and listened.

I don't know how long I sat there — there was no further sound — and at last my tense muscles relaxed, and I fell back on the pillow.

'You fool!' I said to myself; 'dead or alive, is she not your darling, your heart's heart? Would you not go near to die of joy if she came back to you? Pray God to let her spirit come back and tell you she forgives you!'

'I wish she would come,' myself answered in words, while every fibre of my body and mind shrank and quivered in denial.

I struck a match, lighted a candle, and breathed more freely as I looked at the polished furniture — the commonplace details of an ordinary room. Then I thought of her, lying alone so near me, so quiet under the white sheet. She was dead; she would not wake or move. But suppose she did move? Suppose she turned back the sheet and got up and walked across the floor and turned the door-handle?

As I thought it, I heard — plainly, unmistakably heard — the door of the chamber of death open slowly. I heard slow steps in the passage, slow, heavy steps. I heard the touch of hands on my door outside, uncertain hands that felt for the latch.

Sick with terror, I lay clenching the sheet in my hands.

I knew well enough what would come in when that door opened — that door on which my eyes were fixed. I dreaded to look, yet dared not turn away my eyes. The door opened slowly, slowly, slowly, and the figure of my dead wife came in. It came straight towards the bed, and stood at the bed-foot in its white grave-clothes, with the white bandage under its chin. There was a scent of lavender and camphor and white narcissus. Its eyes were wide open, and looked at me with love unspeakable.

I could have shrieked aloud.

My wife spoke. It was the same dear voice that I had loved so to hear, but it was very weak and faint now; and now I trembled as I listened.

'You aren't afraid of me, darling, are you, though I am dead? I heard all you said to me when you came, but I couldn't answer. But now I've come back from the dead to tell you. I wasn't really so bad as you thought me. Elvira had told me she loved Oscar. I only wrote the letter to make it easier for you. I was too proud to tell you when you were so angry, but I am not proud anymore now. You'll love me again now, won't you, now I am dead? One always forgives dead people.'

The poor ghost's voice was hollow and faint. Abject terror paralysed me. I could answer nothing.

'Say you forgive me,' the thin, monotonous voice went on; 'say you love me again.'

I had to speak. Coward as I was, I did manage to stammer: 'Yes; I love you. I have always loved you, God help me.'

The sound of my own voice reassured me, and I ended more firmly than I began. The figure by the bed swayed a little, unsteadily.

'I suppose,' she said wearily, 'you would be afraid, now I am dead, if I came round to you and kissed you?'

She made a movement as though she would have come to me.

Then I did shriek aloud, again and again, and covered my face with the sheet and wound it round my head and body, and held it with all my force. There was a moment's silence. Then I heard my door close, and then a sound of feet and of voices, and I heard something heavy fall. I disentangled my head from the sheet. My room was empty. Then reason came back to me. I leaped from the bed.

'Ida, my darling, come back! I am not afraid! I love you. Come back! Come back!'

I sprang to my door and flung it open. Someone was bringing a light along the passage. On the floor, outside the door of the death chamber, was a huddled heap — the corpse, in its graveclothes. Dead, dead, dead.

✕

She is buried in Mellor churchyard, and there is no stone over her.

Now, whether it was catalepsy, as the doctor said, or whether my love came back, even from the dead, to me who loved her, I shall never know; but this I know, that if I had held out my arms to her as she stood at my bed-foot — if I had said, 'Yes, even from the grave, my darling — from hell itself, come back, come back to me!' — if I had had room in my coward's heart for anything but the unreasoning terror that killed love in that hour, I should not now be here alone. I shrank from her — I feared her — I would not take her to my heart. And now she will not come to me anymore.

Why do I go on living?

You see, there is the child. It is four years old now, and it has never spoken and never smiled.

6 Hurst of Hurstcote

We were at Eton together, and afterwards at Christchurch, and I always got on very well with him; but somehow he was a man about whom none of the other men cared very much. There was always something strange and secret about him; even at Eton he liked grubbing among books and trying chemical experiments, better than cricket or the boats. That sort of thing would make any boy unpopular. At Oxford it wasn't merely his studious ways and his love of science that went against him; it was a certain habit he had of gazing at us through narrowing lids, as though he were looking at us more from the outside than any one human being has a right to look at any other, and a bored air of belonging to another and higher race, whenever we talked the ordinary chatter about athletics and the Schools.

A wild paper on 'Black Magic', which he read to the Essay Society, filled to overflowing the cup of his college's contempt for him. I suppose no man was ever, for so little cause, so much disliked.

When we went down I noticed — for I knew his people at home — that the sentiment of dislike which he excited in most men was curiously in contrast to the emotions which he inspired in women. They all liked him, listened to him with rapt attention, talked of him with undisguised enthusiasm. I watched their strange infatuation with calmness for several years, but the day came when he met Kate Danvers, and then I was not calm anymore. She behaved like all the rest of the women, and to her, quite suddenly, Hurst threw the handkerchief. He was not Hurst of Hurstcote then, but his family was good, and his means not despicable, so he and she were conditionally engaged. People said it was a poor match for the beauty of the county; and her people, I know, hoped she would think better of it. As for me — well, this is not the story of my life, but of his. I need only say that I thought him a lucky man.

I went to town to complete the studies that were to make me MD; Hurst went abroad to Paris, or Leipzig, or somewhere, to study hypnotism and to prepare notes for his book on 'Black Magic'. This came out in the autumn, and had a strange and brilliant success. Hurst became famous, famous as men do become nowadays. His writings were asked for by all the big periodicals. His future seemed assured. In the spring they were married; I was not present at the wedding. The practice my father had bought for me in London claimed all my time, I said.

It was more than a year after their marriage that I had a letter from Hurst.

> Congratulate me, old man! Crowds of unknown uncles and cousins have died, and I am Hurst of Hurstcote, which, God wot, I never thought to be. The place is all to pieces, but we can't live anywhere else. If you can get away in September, come down and see us. We shall be installed. I have everything now that I ever longed for — cradle of our race and all that, the only woman in the world for my wife, and — But that's enough for any man, surely. — JOHN HURST OF HURSTCOTE.

Of course I knew Hurstcote. Who does not? Hurstcote, which, seventy years ago, was one of the most perfect, as well as the finest, brick Tudor mansions in England. The Hurst who lived there seventy years ago noticed one day that his chimneys smoked, and called in a Hastings architect. 'Your chimneys,' said the local man, 'are beyond me, but with the timbers and lead of your castle, and some nice new yellow bricks and stucco, I can build you a snug little house in the corner of your park, much more suitable for a residence than this old red brick building.' So they gutted Hurstcote, and built the new house and faced it with stucco. All of which things you will find written in the Guide to Sussex. Hurstcote, when I had seen it, had been the merest shell. How would Hurst make it habitable? Even if he had inherited much money with the castle and intended to restore the building, that would be a work of years, not months. What would he do?

In September I went to see.

Hurst met me at Pevensey Station.

'Let's walk up,' he said; 'there's a cart to bring your traps. Eh, but it's good to see you again, Bernard.'

It was good to see him again. And to see him so changed. And so changed for good, too. He was much stouter, and no longer wore the untidy, ill-fitting clothes of the old days. He was rather smartly dressed in grey stockings and knee-breeches, and wore a velvet shooting-coat. But the most noteworthy change was in his face; it bore no more the eager, inquiring, half-scornful, half-tolerant look that had won him such ill-will at Oxford. His face now was the face of a man completely at peace with himself and the world.

'How well you look!' I said, as we walked along the level, winding road through the still marshes.

'How much better, you mean!' he laughed. 'I know it. Bernard, you'll hardly believe it, but I'm on the way to be a popular man!'

He had not lost his old knack of reading one's thoughts.

'Don't trouble yourself to find the polite answer to that,' he hastened to add. 'No one knows as well as I how unpopular I was; and no one knows so well why,' he added in a very low voice. 'However,' he went on gaily, 'unpopularity is a thing of the past. The folk hereabout call on us, and condole with us on our hutch. A thing of the past, as I said — but what a past it was, eh? You're the only man who ever liked me. You don't know what that's been to me many a dark day and night. When the others were — you know — it was like a hand holding mine, to think of you. I've always thought I was sure of one soul in the world to stand by me.'

'Yes,' I said — 'Yes.'

He flung his arm over my shoulder with a frank, boyish gesture of affection, quite foreign to his nature as I had known it. Foreign as the bright frankness of his speech to his old scowling reticence.

'And I know why you didn't come to our wedding,' he went on, 'but that's all right now, isn't it?'

'Yes,' I said again, for indeed it was. There are brown eyes in the world, after all, as well as blue.

'That's well,' Hurst answered, and we walked on in satisfied silence, till we passed across the furze-crowned ridge, and went down the hill to Hurstcote. It lies in the hollow, ringed round by its moat, its dark red walls showing the sky behind them. There was no welcoming sparkle of early litten candle, only the pale amber of the September evening shining through the gaunt unglazed windows.

Three planks and a rough handrail had replaced the old drawbridge. We passed across the moat, and Hurst pulled a knotted rope that hung beside the great iron-bound door. A bell clanged loudly inside. In the moment we spent there waiting, Hurst pushed back a briar that was trailing across the arch, and let it fall outside the handrail.

'Nature is too much with us here,' he said, laughing. 'The clematis spends its time tripping one up or clawing at one's hair, and we are always expecting the ivy to force itself through the window and make an uninvited third at our dinner-table.'

Then the great door of Hurstcote Castle swung back, and there stood Kate, a thousand times sweeter and more beautiful than ever. I looked at her with momentary terror and dazzlement. She was indeed much more beautiful than any woman with brown eyes could be. My heart almost stopped beating.

'With life or death in the balance: Right!'

To be beautiful is not the same thing as to be dear, thank God. I went forward and took her hand with a free heart.

It was a pleasant fortnight I spent with them. They had had one tower completely repaired, and in its queer, eight-sided rooms we lived, when we were not out among the marshes or by the blue sea at Pevensey.

Mrs Hurst had made the rooms pleasant with stuffs from Liberty's, and odds and ends of old oak and beechwood. The grassy space within the castle walls, with its underground passages, its crumbling heaps of masonry, overgrown with lush creepers, was better than any garden. There we met the fresh morning; there we lounged through lazy noons; there the grey evenings found us.

I have never seen any two married people so utterly, so undisguisedly in love as these were. I, the third, had no embarrassment in so being — for their love had in it a completeness, a childish abandonment, to which the presence of a third — a friend — was no burden. A happiness, reflected from theirs, shone on me. The days went by, dreamlike, and brought the eve of my return to London and to the commonplaces of life.

We were sitting in the courtyard; Hurst had gone to the village to post some letters. A big moon was just showing over the battlements when Mrs Hurst shivered.

'It's late,' she said, 'and cold; the summer is gone. Let us go in.' So we went in to the little warm room, where a wood fire flickered on a brick hearth, and a shaded lamp was already glowing softly. Here we sat on the cushioned seat in the open window, and looked out through the lozenge panes at the gold moon and at the light of her making ghosts in the white mist that rose thick and heavy from the moat.

'I am so sorry that you are going,' she said, presently, 'but you will come and skate on the moat with us at Christmas, won't you? We mean to have a mediæval Christmas. You don't know what that is? Neither do I; but John does. He is very, very wise.'

'Yes,' I answered, 'he used to know many things that most men don't even dream of as possible to know.'

She was silent a minute and then shivered again. I picked up the shawl she had thrown down when we came in, and put it round her.

'Thank you! I think — don't you? — that there are some things that one is not meant to know, and some that one is meant *not* to know. You see the distinction?'

'I suppose so — yes.'

'Did it never frighten you in the old days,' she went on, 'to see that John would never — was always —'

'But he has given all that up now.'

'Oh yes, ever since our honeymoon. Do you know, he used to mesmerise me. It was horrible. And that book of his —'

'I didn't know you believed in Black Magic.'

'Oh, I don't — not the least bit. I never was at all superstitious, you know. But those things always frighten me just as much as if I believed in them. And besides — I think they are wicked; but John — Ah! there he is! Let's go and meet him.'

His dark figure was outlined against the sky behind the hill. She wrapped the soft shawl more closely around her, and we went out into the moonlight to meet her husband.

The next morning when I entered the parlour, I found that it lacked its chief ornament. The sparkling, white and silver breakfast accessories were there, but for my beautiful hostess I looked in vain. At ten minutes past nine Hurst came in looking horribly worried, and more like his old self than I had ever expected to see him.

'I say, old man,' he said hurriedly, 'are you really set on going back to town today? — because Kate's ill — really ill I'm afraid. I can't think what's wrong. I want you to see her after breakfast.'

I reflected a minute. 'I can stay if I send a wire,' I said.

'I wish you would then,' Hurst said, wringing my hand and turning away; 'she's been off her head most of the night, talking the most astounding nonsense. You must see her after breakfast. Will you pour out the coffee?'

'I'll see her first, please,' I said, and he led me up the winding stair to the room at the top of the tower.

I found her quite sensible, but very feverish. I wrote a prescription, and rode Hurst's mare over to Eastbourne to get it made up. When I got back she was worse. It seemed to be a sort of aggravated marsh fever. I reproached myself with having let her sit by the open window the night before. But I remembered with some satisfaction that I had told Hurst that the place was not quite healthy. I only wished I had insisted on it more strongly.

For the first day or two, I thought it was merely a touch of marsh fever that would pass off with no worse consequence than a little weakness; but on the third day, I perceived that she would die.

Hurst met me as I came from her bedside, stood back on the narrow landing for me to pass, and followed me down into the little sitting-room, which, deprived for three days of her presence, already bore the air of a room long deserted. He came in after me and shut the door.

'You're wrong,' he said abruptly, reading my thoughts as usual; 'she won't die — she can't die.'

'She will,' I bluntly answered, for I am no believer in that worst refinement of torture known as 'breaking bad news gently.' 'Send for any other man you choose. I'll consult with the whole College of Physicians if you like. But nothing short of a miracle can save her.'

'And you don't believe in miracles,' he answered quietly. 'I do, you see.'

'My dear old fellow, don't buoy yourself up with false hopes. I know my trade; I wish I could believe I didn't! Go back to her now; you have not very long to be together.'

I wrung his hand; he returned the pressure, but said almost cheerfully:

'You know your trade, old man, but there are some things you don't know. Mine, for instance — I mean my wife's constitution. Now, I know that thoroughly. And you mark my words — she won't die. You might as well say *I* was not long for this world.'

'*You*,' I said, with a touch of annoyance, 'you're good for another thirty or forty years.'

'Exactly so,' he rejoined quickly, 'and so is she. Her life's as good as mine; you'll see — she won't die.'

At dusk on the next day she died. He was with her; he had not left her since he had told me that she would not die. He was sitting by her, holding her hand. She had been unconscious for some time, when suddenly she dragged her hand from his, raised herself in bed, and cried out in a tone of acutest anguish:

'John! John! Let me go! For Heaven's sake, let me go!'

Then she fell back dead.

He would not understand — would not believe; he still sat by her, holding her hand, and calling on her by every name that love could teach him. I began to fear for his brain. He would not leave her, so by-and-by I brought him a cup of coffee in which I had mixed an opiate. In about an hour I went back and found him fast asleep, with his face on the pillow close by the face of his dead wife. The gardener and I carried him down to my bedroom, and I sent for a woman from the village. He slept for twelve hours. When he awoke his first words were:

'She is not dead! I must go to her!'

I hoped that the sight of her — pale and beautiful and still — with the white asters about her, and her cold hands crossed on her breast, would convince him; but no. He looked at her and said:

'Bernard, you're no fool; you know as well as I do that this is not death. Why treat it so? It is some form of catalepsy. If she should awake and find herself like this, the shock might destroy her reason.'

And to the horror of the woman from the village, he flung the asters on to the floor, covered the body with blankets, and sent for hot-water bottles.

I was now quite convinced that his brain was affected, and I saw plainly enough that he would never consent to take the necessary steps for the funeral.

I began to wonder whether I had not better send for another doctor, for I felt that I did not care to try the opiate again on my own responsibility, and something must be done about the funeral.

I spent a day in considering the matter — a day passed by John Hurst beside his wife's body. Then I made up my mind to try all my powers to bring him to reason, and to this end I went once more into the chamber of death. I found Hurst talking wildly in low whispers. He seemed to be talking to someone who was not there. He did not know me, and suffered himself to be led away. He was in a high fever. He had broken down completely, the kind of breakdown which in old novels used to be called brain fever. I actually blessed his illness, because it opened a way out of the dilemma in which I found myself. I wired for a trained nurse from town, and for the local undertaker. In a week she was buried, and John Hurst still lay unconscious and unheeding; but I did not look forward to his first renewal of consciousness.

Yet his first conscious words were not the inquiry I dreaded.

He only asked whether he had been ill long, and what had been the matter. When I had told him, he just nodded and went off to sleep again.

A few evenings later, I found him excited and feverish, but quite himself mentally. I said as much to him in answer to a question which he put to me:

'There's no brain disturbance now? I'm not mad or anything?'

'No, no, my dear fellow. Everything as it should be.'

'Then,' he answered slowly, 'I must get up and go to her.'

My worst fears were realised.

In moments of intense mental strain the truth sometimes overpowers all one's better resolves. It sounds brutal, horrible. I don't know what I meant to say; what I said was:

'You can't; she's buried.'

He sprang up in bed, and I caught him by the shoulders.

'Then it's true!' he cried, 'and I'm not mad. Oh, great God in Heaven, let me go to her; let me go! It's true! It's true!'

I held him fast, and spoke.

'I am strong — you know that. You are weak and ill; you are quite in my power — we're old friends, and there's nothing I wouldn't do to serve you. Tell me what you mean; I will do anything you wish.' This I said to soothe him.

'Let me go to her,' he said again.

'Tell me all about it,' I repeated. 'You are too ill to go to her. I will go, if you can collect yourself and tell me why. You could not walk five yards.'

He looked at me doubtfully.

'You'll help me? You won't say I'm mad, and have me shut up? You'll help me?'

'Yes, yes — I swear it.' All the time I was wondering what I should do to keep him where he was.

He lay back on his pillows, white and ghastly; his thin features and sunken eyes showed hawklike above the rough growth of his four weeks' beard. I took his hand. His pulse was rapid, and his lean fingers clenched themselves round mine.

'Look here,' he said, 'I don't know — There aren't any words to tell you how true it is. I am not mad, I am not wandering. I am as sane as you are. Now listen, and if you have a human heart in you, you'll help me. When I married her, I gave up hypnotism and all the old studies; she hated the whole business. But before I gave it up, I hypnotised her, and when she was completely under my control I forbade her soul to leave her body till my time came to die.'

I breathed more freely. Now I understood why he had said: 'She *cannot* die.'

'My dear old man,' I said gently, 'dismiss these fancies, and face your grief bravely. You can't control the great facts of life and death by hypnotism. She is dead; she is dead, and the body lies in its place. But her soul is with God who gave it.'

'No!' he cried, with such strength as the fever had left in him. 'No! no! Ever since I have been ill I have seen her, every day, every night, and always wringing her hands and moaning, "Let me go, John — let me go".'

'Those were her last words indeed,' I said; 'it is natural that they should haunt you. See, you bade her soul not leave her body. It has left it, for she is dead.'

His answer came almost in a whisper, borne on the wings of a long, breathless pause.

'*She is dead, but her soul has not left her body.*'

I held his hand more closely, still debating what I should do.

'She comes to me,' he went on; 'she comes to me continually. She does not reproach, but she implores: "Let me go, John — let me go." And I have no more power now; I cannot let her go, I cannot reach her; I can do nothing, nothing. Ah!' he cried, with a sudden sharp change of voice that thrilled through me to the ends of my fingers and feet. 'Ah, Kate, my life, I will come to you! No, no, you shan't be left alone among the dead. I am coming, dear.'

He reached his arms out towards the door with a look of longing and love, so really, so patently addressed to a sentient presence, that I turned sharply to see if, in truth, perhaps — Nothing, of course, nothing.

'She is dead,' I repeated stupidly. 'I was obliged to bury her.'

A shudder ran through him.

'I must go and see for myself,' he said.

Then I knew — all in a minute — what to do.

'I will go,' I said. 'I will open her coffin, and if she is not — is not as other dead folk, I will bring her body back to this house.'

'Will you go now?' he asked, with set lips.

It was nigh on midnight. I looked into his eyes.

'Yes, now,' I said, 'but you must swear to lie still till I return.'

'I swear it.' I saw that I could trust him, and I went to wake the nurse. He called weakly after me, 'There's a lanthorn in the tool-shed — and, Bernard —'

'Yes, my poor old chap?'

'There's a screwdriver in the sideboard drawer.'

I think until he said that, I really meant to go. I am not accustomed to lie, even to mad people, and I think I meant it till then.

He leaned on his elbow, and looked at me with wide open eyes.

'Think,' he said, 'what she must feel. Out of the body, and yet tied to it, all alone among the dead. Oh, make haste, make haste, for if I am not mad, and I have really fettered her soul, there is but one way.'

'And that is?'

'I must die too. Her soul can leave her body when I die.'

I called the nurse and left him. I went out, and across the wold to the church, but I did not go in. I carried the screwdriver and the lanthorn, lest he should send the nurse to see if I had taken them. I leaned on the churchyard wall and thought of her. I had loved the woman, and I remembered it in that hour.

As soon as I dared, I went back to him — remember I believed him mad — and told the lie that I thought would give him most ease.

'Well?' he said eagerly, as I entered.

I signed to the nurse to leave us.

'There is no hope,' I said. 'You will not see your wife again till you meet her in heaven.'

I laid down the screwdriver and the lanthorn and sat down by him.

'You have seen her?'

'Yes.'

'And there's no doubt?'

'There is no doubt.'

'Then I *am* mad; but you're a good fellow, Bernard, and I'll never forget it, in this world or the next.'

He seemed calmer, and fell asleep with my hand in his. His last word was a 'thank you' that cut me like a knife.

When I went into his room next morning, he was gone. But on his pillow a letter lay, painfully scrawled in pencil, and addressed to me.

'You lied. Perhaps you meant kindly. You didn't understand. She is not dead. She has been with me again. Though her soul may not leave her body, thank God it can still speak to mine. That vault — it is worse than a mere churchyard grave. Goodbye!'

I ran all the way to the church and entered by the open door. The air was chill and dank after the crisp October sunlight.

The stone that closed the vault of the Hursts of Hurstcote had been raised and was lying beside the dark, gaping hole in the chancel floor. The nurse, who had followed me, came in before I could shake off the horror that held me moveless. We both went down into the vault. Weak, exhausted by illness and sorrow, John Hurst had yet found strength to follow his love to the grave. I tell you he had crossed that wold alone, in the grey of the cold dawn; alone he had raised the stone and gone down to her. He had opened his wife's coffin, and he lay on the floor of the vault with his wife's body in his arms.

He had been dead some hours.

✖

When I told my wife this story, her brown eyes filled with tears.

'You were quite right, he was mad,' she said. 'Poor things — poor lovers!'

But sometimes when I wake in the grey morning, and, between waking and sleeping, think of all those things that I must shut out from my sleeping and waking thoughts, I wonder was I right, or was he? Was he mad, or was I idiotically incredulous? For — and it is this thing that haunts me — when I found them dead together in the vault, she had been buried five weeks. But the body that lay in John Hurst's arms, among the mouldering coffins of the Hursts of Hurstcote, was perfect and beautiful as it had been when first he clasped her in his arms, a bride.

7 The White Lady

We were a great houseful of people. They always had a houseful for Christmas at the Court. I have spent many a merry Christmas there since, but never one so merry as that.

I suppose it was because we were all young, and at that time of life when you only see the lights and none of the shadows. Besides Julian loved me. I had been certain of that ever since we met at Scarborough in the summer; and since I had been staying in his father's house, he had found a thousand little ways of making me more than sure that this dear old house was to be my home, and I the happiest mistress that ever owned it, because Julian loved me.

It was the night before Christmas Eve, and all we young folks were dancing in the big hall; and it was between two waltzes, as I sat resting in one of the deep window seats, sheltered by the heavy curtain, that Julian lifted the curtain, and passed in, and sat beside me. The window seat was in the shadow of the great stair, and the rest of the company were gathered round the piano, and were laughing and talking so gaily, that his words were no more heard by them than the soft sighing of the pine trees outside.

No one heard what he said but I, and no one ever shall hear; for you need not suppose that I am going to write down here what he said to me. But it was one of those happy moments that come so very seldom and that light one's life, when they do come, for a long, long way back and forward. And he told me he should speak to his father the next day.

Now I come of good family, and had a handsome property of my own. I was a nice-looking girl in those days, and considered agreeable and accomplished, as girls went. So next day when I met Julian in the hall for a moment after breakfast, I never expected the answer to be anything but 'yes' when I said:

'Is your father pleased with your choice?'

To my surprise Julian hesitated, then he answered: 'I think he is pleased with my choice, but he begs us to consider nothing as settled until after Christmas Eve.'

'Why?' I asked, naturally enough.

'I can't tell you now. It's a long tale, and those Danvers girls will be here in a minute. I promised, like the fool I am, to go skating with them. But this afternoon when we come in to tea, if you should happen to be in the library instead of the hall, one might perhaps get a word with one's sweetheart.'

The Danvers girls came in while he was speaking, but he finished his speech in my ear with great calmness, and I went off to nurse my new happiness, and wonder at and delight in it until the time was come when I should see him again.

I softly slipped into the library and closed the heavy door after me. The dusk was falling, the fire light shone pleasantly on the glass of the bookcases and the gilt backs of the books, and I stood by the window and watched the skating-party come up from the lake. I hadn't had a word with Julian all day. I couldn't skate, for I had promised my dear mother years before that I would never go on the ice, because my father had been killed by an ice accident.

I saw them come up, jingling their skates and talking merrily, and two minutes later Julian was with me.

'How nice and warm it is in here, my dear little love,' he began. 'I have been in purgatory all day — such a cold purgatory too.'

And indeed his face was as cold as ice. When he had thawed his hands a little by the fire, we sat down together on one of the leather-covered settees, and he said:

'Now, heart of mine, we have only a few, few minutes for all our stories and explanations, for I must get back to the other people before the tea comes in. The real fact is — there's a ghost in our family.'

I turned my foot this way and that, to watch the play of the firelight on my patent leather shoe. 'I don't think,' I remarked, still looking down, 'that a ghost would be an insuperable objection.'

'It's not quite that,' he said, hesitatingly.

'What is it?' I asked. 'The story is sure to be interesting; tell it to me.'

'Well, the story runs that a certain ancestress of mine ran away and got married without her parents' consent. The marriage didn't turn out well or something. At any rate, she was plagued with remorse in her later years, and very inconsistently undertook to appear and give her blessing whenever the heir of this house becomes engaged to a suitable young person; and if she doesn't appear the engagement doesn't come off. That's all.'

'But do you mean to tell me,' I exclaimed, for I could not help thinking he was laughing at me, 'that you would give me up just because a stupid old ghost didn't put in its appearance at a certain hour and place?'

'No, I wouldn't,' he replied, 'but my father would never consent, and I am sure you would never marry me without his consent.'

'I'm not so sure of that,' I said to myself in a low voice.

'I don't want to have any secrets from you, little woman; so I won't pretend that I shan't feel a good deal happier if the ghost does appear on Christmas Eve, as I have no doubt she will do.'

'But am I to understand then, that ever since your ancestors took this ridiculous resolution, her ghost has appeared to sanction the engagement of each heir of the house in succession?'

'Of course you will laugh at it,' he went on in rather an

injured way, 'but that really is the story. My father will tell
you that he saw it, and his father before him; and I haven't the
slightest doubt I shall see it on Christmas Eve. My father and
I will sit up for the purpose.'

'A pack of old wives' stories!' I rejoined indignantly, 'Look
here, Julian, I'm not going to wait for the ghost to refuse me
and I'm not going to marry into a family that believes in such
nonsense.'

'Oh! aren't you?' said Julian, quite calmly, 'we shall see
about that, my dear. You know perfectly well that I love
you so much that nothing on earth would ever induce me
to give you up. But you see how much pleasanter it would
be for everybody if the ghost gave us her blessing and in the
orthodox manner.'

I really even then thought he was playing some sort of joke
on me, but no, he was quite serious, and I had actually to be
in that ridiculous position of being engaged and not engaged
for more than three days. And Julian was very careless and
people were always coming in and finding us at different
corners of the room as if we had just jumped there; and once
I am certain one of those Danvers girls saw him kiss my ear
as we went upstairs before dinner.

The night before Christmas Eve I really felt almost worried
out of my life, and when I went up to bed I sent away my
maid, put on my dressing gown, let down my hair and settled
down in front of the fire to have a good cry. I had hardly
begun, however, when there was a soft tap at my door and
Lady Cary herself came in.

She was a dear little old lady. At least, she couldn't have
been more than forty-five, but that seems old when you are
only eighteen.

'May I come in?' she asked, in her soft pretty voice, and
came in at once, shut the door and sat down opposite me in
the other chair.

'Dear, dear, dear!' she said. 'Now whatever is the matter?'

'I'm tired,' I replied, 'and I've got a cold in my head.'

Lady Cary turned her eyes to the fire and fixed them there.

'Such a model of frankness and candor!' she said, slowly; 'that's what Julian said when he told me he was engaged to you. It came, it's true, at the end of a list of your more important qualities, beauty and sweetness and angelic charm.'

She suddenly raised her eyes to me, and I crept humiliated to the low stool at her feet.

'I'm very sorry,' I murmured; 'I didn't know that Julian had told you anything, and it seems so strange to be engaged and nobody to wish you happiness, or good luck, or anything, and to be depending on a stupid ghost; and I think I was wishing, when you came in, that there was someone, that — that my mother hadn't died when I was quite a little thing.'

Lady Cary stroked my hair. 'There, poor child,' she said; 'there is someone. Tell me all about it.'

And I told her all about it as well as I could, and when I had finished she broke out with a funny little laugh.

'My dear, I felt just as you do about it when I was your age, and Lord Cary's mother came to my assistance exactly as I am coming to yours, and as I believe the lady of the house has always come to her son's assistance ever since the White Lady promised to "walk". It depends on you, my dear, whether Julian and his father receive a satisfactory ghostly blessing on the engagement or not.'

'I wasn't crying a bit about the ghost,' I said, hardly hearing what she said, 'if you will only say that you would like me to be —'

'Of course I would, that's why I'm here. It's my belief that the Lady Cary has always had a good bit of a voice in her son's choice. My dear, the White Lady walked before I was engaged, and I had to undergo just such a tiresome probation as you are writhing under tonight, and my future mother-in-law showed me how to end it as you will end it tomorrow.'

'I?'

'Yes; I have no doubt Julian told you that on Christmas Eve the intending bridegroom and his father, if the father be alive, are bound to watch in the chapel from eleven till one, and across the gallery at the end the White Lady glides as the clock strikes twelve. You will have to practise gliding, my dear; it's a difficult art.'

'Then you mean that I — that you —'

'I mean that you must, in the character of the White Lady, pronounce your own blessing on your own engagement, as I did on mine, and as I believe all the ladies of Cary have done on theirs. It's the secret of the ladies of his house, and I should never have told it to you if I hadn't believed that you are the best wife in the world for my Julian.'

'Then you mean to tell me, Lady Cary,' I said, when I had recovered from my delight at this little speech, 'that you yourself played the part of the ghost in this house.'

'I did indeed, my dear,' she replied, 'and it was the best night's work I ever did.'

And her voice trembled, and her face lighted up with the recollection of old happiness.

'I have got the dress still, the white satin and the pearls, and the veil that my mother-in-law gave me, they were miles too big for me, and you shall wear them. The men are bound not to move from the chapel for an hour after midnight, which is a merciful provision to give one time to get comfortably out of the way before they can find any traces of one. The way to the gallery is rather peculiar; there are two secret doors to pass, but I will show you the trick of these tomorrow, and I will be there to receive you when you find your way back to the modern side of the Court. You mustn't be nervous about it.'

'Nervous!' I exclaimed, 'there is nothing to be nervous about; only one can't help —'

'No, don't say you can't help despising Julian for it. It runs in their blood, my dear, like their fair hair and their blue eyes, and you must take people as you find them, and make the best of them.'

She gave me another good kiss, and walked off with her bedroom candle.

The next night at eleven she came again to my room. She dressed me in the white satin and pearls, and powdered my face thickly to give me the pallid look necessary for my ghostly character.

It was always the custom at the Court to go to bed early on Christmas Eve, so that by a quarter to twelve the house was perfectly quiet. I took up the heavy, old-fashioned silver candlestick I was to carry, and crept out of the room, my white satin and pearls covered by a dark cloak. I found the spring Lady Cary had shown me under a carved wreath on an oak panel, pressed it, the panel turned on a pivot, I passed in and it closed behind me. Then I stood quite still, holding my breath, and listening lest anyone should have heard me pass from my room to this. But there was no sound — only I could hear my own heart beating.

I walked along the passage in which I found myself. The dust lay thickly under foot, so that my steps made no noise as I walked. It was a narrow passage made of rough stonework, and a door at the other end, which stood ajar and was easily opened, led me into a part of the house that I had never been in before. It was the suite of apartments that had been occupied by the White Lady, and since her time no one else had lived in them.

Everything was just as she had left it. Her garments and personal possessions were littered on the tables and chairs.

There was a lute, all its strings broken but one; and one stiff dress on a chair looked to me so like a human being that I paused for at least a minute before I had courage to go up to it and see that it was only heavy gold brocade. The dull, dark tapestries on the wall swayed a little now and then — with the wind, I suppose — but it seemed to me that something, anything, might be hidden behind them. My hand trembled so that I could hardly hold the candlestick, and the wax of the candle ran in a warm stream over my fingers. Lady Cary had said I should be nervous, and I certainly was. Then quite suddenly a thought came to me that sent all the blood rushing to my heart and nearly choked me. Suppose Lady Cary was wrong; suppose there was a ghost after all, and here was I alone in the rooms sacred to its use and memory. It wouldn't bear thinking of. I grasped the silver candlestick and hurried on through the long suite of rooms. At the end of the last ante-chamber I came to another panel like the one in the corridor, pressed a similar spring, and found myself on a little flight of stairs which Lady Cary had warned me led directly to the gallery. At the foot of this I was to wait till I heard the church clock begin to strike, then to walk forward boldly across the gallery, and descend a flight of steps at the other side, which would lead me into a passage communicating with the suite of rooms I had just left.

I didn't like the idea of that long sequence of mouldering emptiness behind me. I tried to get the panel to shut, but it wouldn't act; its hinges were stiff, and I was afraid of making them creak.

There I waited; and if it was a wrong thing to do to deceive my future husband in that way, I can only say I was well punished for it. What I suffered in those five minutes no one can believe who simply sees it written down here.

What I should have liked to do was to bolt back to my room like a rabbit and marry Julian in spite of all his father's opposition. But I have a habit of carrying a thing through when once I have begun it. Besides, I didn't want Lady Cary to think me a fool.

So I stayed there with my heart beating to that degree that I felt as if they could hear it in the chapel.

At last came the long, dull, slow stroke of the clock. I gathered up my satin draperies, held the candle high, and walked up the steps. It was a short flight, and in another moment I was in the gallery. My knees were knocking together with the double fear of being found out, and of diving again out of the comparative light and safety of the chapel into the unknown depths of that little dark stair beyond. The white moon shone through the windows of the clerestory, and there was air here as well as light, and movement, and human companionship; for, as I stepped into the gallery, I saw in the chancel below the two figures of my lover and his father. They had two tapers beside them and watched as one watches the dead.

I drew my veil over my face, held my candle high and walked forward. I felt rather than heard the hushed 'Ah!' from the chancel which told that they had seen me.

Holding my candle high above me I walked — for in that hour of terror my gliding lessons vanished from my memory, leaving no trace — to the other side of the gallery, and passed under the low wooden doorway and down the flight of stairs. The way was easy to find and, somehow, I felt that the worst was over now.

True, there were those deadly deserted rooms to traverse, but at the end of them, warmth, light, fire, my own room and Lady Cary, who was there waiting for me. So I followed the passage I found at the foot of the stairs till it brought me to the sliding panel I had been unable to shut, which let me into the ante-room of the White Lady's bedroom.

It was with a sigh of relief that I pushed it open and passed through it.

I hastened through the dark rooms and was beginning to feel something approaching a return of what I always like to consider my natural fearlessness, when I saw that I wasn't alone. There was another light in the great dark room and it was advancing towards me. My first thought was — Lady Cary — and I hurried to meet her.

The next moment I saw the fear I had thrust from me in this room ten minutes before had been no idle terror. It was not Lady Cary, who was coming towards me with candle in hand, up-raised in a silver candlestick. It was not Lady Cary who wore satin and pearls and a death-white face. It was the White Lady — the ghost herself — in whose character and in whose rooms I was madly masquerading.

In the frantic struggle not to shriek, not to scream, not to betray my presence here to Julian and his father, my candle slipped from my hand. At the same instant the ghost's light, too, was extinguished, and I was alone in the dark — in the rooms of a dead woman, with that dead woman's face and form not three yards from me — in the dark.

✕

'Ah!' I drew a long breath. There was a smell of vinegar and smelling salts. Somebody was rubbing my hands. It was very cold.

'Oh! thank God, you are better.' It was Lady Cary who was speaking. I opened my eyes, and looked at her. I was in my own room, pleasant and bright with fire and lamp-light. Lady Cary was bending over me with a very anxious face indeed.

'It's all right, my dear. You fainted in those dreadful dark rooms. It must have been a great trial. I knew it would be. But you are quite safe now.'

I sat up; the wet vinegar cloth flopped from my forehead as I did so, and fell on my hands.

'Lady Cary,' I said, 'I have seen the ghost, the real ghost, and it came close to me in that dreadful room.'

'Your nerves are over-wrought,' answered Lady Cary, calmly. 'I don't wonder. You must have fancied some bit of drapery or shadow to be a ghost.'

'It was as real as I am,' I said; 'I thought it was you at first. Oh, it is horrible, most horrible!'

Lady Cary would not let me talk about it anymore. She stayed with me that night, and in the morning gave out that I was too unwell to come to breakfast, which I certainly was, and about noon she came up to my room.

'Now,' she said, 'everyone is out skating. Have you the courage to come with me to the White Lady's rooms, and find out what optical illusion it was that so frightened you last night?'

'I have a thousand things to ask you,' I said. 'How did I get back to my room?'

'I got uneasy about you at last, and came to look for you,' she answered.

'And did you carry me back?'

Lady Cary laughed. 'My dear, if we are to go we must go at once, or we shall have the maids upon us.'

She threw a shawl round me, and we crossed the corridor. The oak panel swung on its pivot, we passed through and it closed behind us. In another minute we were in the White Lady's rooms.

Seen by the dim daylight that filtered through the cobwebbed panes, the rooms were more desolate than ever, and almost as eerie. But with Lady Cary's arm round me I could have faced it even in the dark, I thought.

We passed through one room after another, but nowhere was there anything that could by the wildest imagination be made to resemble white satin and pearls, and a raised arm holding a lighted candle. We walked to the further end and then retraced our steps. Lady Cary was just saying, 'It must have been pure imagination,' when I caught a glimpse of something moving at the end of the room — something white — and stopping short, rigid with terror, I pointed towards it.

'Look!' I said. 'Look there — there it is again.'

Lady Cary put up her double eye-glass and looked.

'You poor, dear, blessed little innocent,' she said. 'Don't you see that it's a looking-glass, and reflects nothing worse than your pretty self in your white dressing gown?'

Even then I was hardly to be convinced. Not till she led me up to the glass panel and I saw my own furred gown and scared face reflected in its depths did I understand the height of my own folly the night before. But then I was convinced, and Lady Cary led me back to my own room to pet and coax and laugh at me till I should be in a fit frame of mind to meet my lover.

When I went down to luncheon Lord Cary rose up before all the company and kissed my forehead, and welcomed me as his daughter and his son's wife; and such before the next Christmas Eve I became.

It was on the evening of our wedding day that I felt I could keep my secret no longer.

'Julian,' I said, 'I hope you will forgive me. I have something horrible to tell you.'

'Proceed,' he answered, with a twinkle in his eyes.

'But it really is horrible, and I don't know whether you will forgive me. But I couldn't bear to tell you before, for fear it should interfere somehow with our marriage.'

'You rack me with suspense,' he replied, cheerfully. 'What is this horror that might have parted us at the altar steps?'

Then I told him how I had played the ghost on Christmas Eve; and when my tale was ended, I hung my head, waiting his reproaches.

'My dear little woman,' he said, putting his arm round me, 'this is ancient history. Who, do you suppose, carried you out of the ghost's room that night?'

'Did you? Did Lady Cary —?'

'Of course she did. You didn't suppose that a dear little shrimp of a woman, such as my mother is, could carry my big, blonde beauty?'

'And you are not angry?'

'Do I look it?' he asked.

'And you think I was right, and your mother was right?'

'Yes, sweetheart, and all the other fair ladies who have played the ghost on Christmas Eve to win a superstitious Cary for a husband. I only wish we were better worth the trouble.'

As to that I have my own opinion.

8 The Haunted Inheritance

The most extraordinary thing that ever happened to me was my going back to town on that day. I am a reasonable being; I do not do such things. I was on a bicycling tour with another man. We were far from the mean cares of an unremunerative profession; we were men not fettered by any given address, any pledged date, any preconcerted route. I went to bed weary and cheerful, fell asleep a mere animal — a tired dog after a day's hunting — and awoke at four in the morning that creature of nerves and fancies which is my other self, and which has driven me to all the follies I have ever kept company with. But even that second self of mine, whining beast and traitor as it is, has never played me such a trick as it played then. Indeed, something in the result of that day's rash act sets me wondering whether after all it could have been I, or even my other self, who moved in the adventure; whether it was not rather some power outside both of us … but this is a speculation as idle in me as uninteresting to you, and so enough of it.

From four to seven I lay awake, the prey of a growing detestation of bicycling tours, friends, scenery, physical exertion, holidays. By seven o'clock I felt that I would rather perish than spend another day in the society of the other man — an excellent fellow, by the way, and the best of company.

At half-past seven the post came. I saw the postman through my window as I shaved. I went down to get my letters — there were none, naturally.

At breakfast I said: 'Edmundson, my dear fellow, I am extremely sorry; but my letters this morning compel me to return to town at once.'

'But I thought,' said Edmundson — then he stopped, and I saw that he had perceived in time that this was no moment for reminding me that, having left no address, I could have had no letters.

He looked sympathetic, and gave me what there was left of the bacon. I suppose he thought that it was a love affair or some such folly. I let him think so; after all, no love affair but would have seemed wise compared with the blank idiocy of this sudden determination to cut short a delightful holiday and go back to those dusty, stuffy rooms in Gray's Inn.

After that first and almost pardonable lapse, Edmundson behaved beautifully. I caught the 9.17 train, and by half-past eleven I was climbing my dirty staircase.

I let myself in and waded through a heap of envelopes and wrappered circulars that had drifted in through the letter-box, as dead leaves drift into the areas of houses in squares. All the windows were shut. Dust lay thick on everything. My laundress had evidently chosen this as a good time for her holiday. I wondered idly where she spent it. And now the close, musty smell of the rooms caught at my senses, and I remembered with a positive pang the sweet scent of the earth and the dead leaves in that wood through which, at this very moment, the sensible and fortunate Edmundson would be riding.

The thought of dead leaves reminded me of the heap of correspondence. I glanced through it. Only one of all those letters interested me in the least. It was from my mother:

Elliot's Bay, Norfolk,
17th August.

DEAR LAWRENCE, — I have wonderful news for you. Your great-uncle Sefton has died, and left you half his immense property. The other half is left to your second cousin Selwyn. You must come home at once. There are heaps of letters here for you, but I dare not send them on, as goodness only knows where you may be. I do wish you would remember to leave an address. I send this to your rooms, in case you have had the forethought to instruct your charwoman to send your letters on to you. It is a most handsome fortune, and I am too happy about your accession to it to scold you as you deserve, but I hope this will be a lesson to you to leave an address when next you go away. Come home at once. — Your loving Mother,

MARGARET SEFTON

P.S. — It is the maddest will; everything divided evenly between you two except the house and estate. The will says you and your cousin Selwyn are to meet there on the 1st September following his death, in presence of the family, and decide which of you is to have the house. If you can't agree, it's to be presented to the county for a lunatic asylum. I should think so! He was always so eccentric. The one who doesn't have the house, etc, gets £20,000 extra. Of course you will choose *that*.

P.P.S. — Be sure to bring your under-shirts with you — the air here is very keen of an evening.

I opened both the windows and lit a pipe. Sefton Manor, that gorgeous old place — I knew its picture in Hasted, cradle of our race, and so on — and a big fortune. I hoped my cousin Selwyn would want the £20,000 more than he wanted the house. If he didn't — well, perhaps my fortune might be large enough to increase that £20,000 to a sum that he *would* want.

And then, suddenly, I became aware that this was the 31st of August, and that tomorrow was the day on which I was to meet my cousin Selwyn and 'the family', and come to a decision about the house. I had never, to my knowledge, heard of my cousin Selwyn. We were a family rich in collateral branches. I hoped he would be a reasonable young man. Also, I had never seen Sefton Manor House, except in a print. It occurred to me that I would rather see the house before I saw the cousin.

I caught the next train to Sefton.

'It's but a mile by the field way,' said the railway porter. 'You take the stile — the first on the left — and follow the path till you come to the wood. Then skirt along the left of it, cater across the meadow at the end, and you'll see the place right below you in the vale.'

'It's a fine old place, I hear,' said I.

'All to pieces, though,' said he. 'I shouldn't wonder if it cost a couple o' hundred to put it to rights. Water coming through the roof and all.'

'But surely the owner —'

'Oh, he never lived there; not since his son was taken. He lived in the lodge; it's on the brow of the hill looking down on the Manor House.'

'Is the house empty?'

'As empty as a rotten nutshell, except for the old sticks o' furniture. Anyone who likes,' added the porter, 'can lie there o' nights. But it wouldn't be me!'

'Do you mean there's a ghost?' I hope I kept any note of undue elation out of my voice.

'I don't hold with ghosts,' said the porter firmly, 'but my aunt was in service at the lodge, and there's no doubt but *something* walks there.'

'Come,' I said, 'this is very interesting. Can't you leave the station, and come across to where beer is?'

'I don't mind if I do,' said he. 'That is so far as your standing a drop goes. But I can't leave the station, so if you pour my beer you must pour it dry, sir, as the saying is.'

So I gave the man a shilling, and he told me about the ghost at Sefton Manor House. Indeed, about the ghosts, for

THE HOUSE OF SILENCE

there were, it seemed, two; a lady in white, and a gentleman in a slouch hat and black riding cloak.

'They do say,' said my porter, 'as how one of the young ladies once on a time was wishful to elope, and started so to do — not getting further than the hall door; her father, thinking it to be burglars, fired out of the window, and the happy pair fell on the doorstep, corpses.'

'Is it true, do you think?'

The porter did not know. At any rate there was a tablet in the church to Maria Sefton and George Ballard — 'and something about in their death them not being divided.'

I took the stile, I skirted the wood, I 'catered' across the meadow — and so I came out on a chalky ridge held in a net of pine roots, where dog violets grew. Below stretched the green park, dotted with trees. The lodge, stuccoed but solid, lay below me. Smoke came from its chimneys. Lower still lay the Manor House — red brick with grey lichened mullions, a house in a thousand, Elizabethan — and from its twisted beautiful chimneys no smoke arose. I hurried across the short turf towards the Manor House.

I had no difficulty in getting into the great garden. The bricks of the wall were everywhere displaced or crumbling. The ivy had forced the coping stones away; each red buttress offered a dozen spots for foothold. I climbed the wall and found myself in a garden — oh! but such a garden. There are not half a dozen such in England — ancient box hedges, rosaries, fountains, yew tree avenues, bowers of clematis (now feathery in its seeding time), great trees, grey-grown marble balustrades and steps, terraces, green lawns, one green lawn, in especial, girt round with a sweet briar hedge, and in the middle of this lawn a sundial. All this was mine, or, to be more exact, might be mine, should my cousin Selwyn prove to be a person of sense. How I prayed that he might not be a person of taste! That he might be a person who liked yachts

90

or racehorses or diamonds, or motor-cars, or anything that money can buy, not a person who liked beautiful Elizabethan houses, and gardens old beyond belief.

The sundial stood on a mass of masonry, too low and wide to be called a pillar. I mounted the two brick steps and leaned over to read the date and the motto:

Tempus fugit manet amor.

The date was 1617, the initials S S surmounted it. The face of the dial was unusually ornate — a wreath of stiffly drawn roses was traced outside the circle of the numbers. As I leaned there a sudden movement on the other side of the pedestal compelled my attention. I leaned over a little further to see what had rustled — a rat — a rabbit? A flash of pink struck at my eyes. A lady in a pink dress was sitting on the step at the other side of the sundial.

I suppose some exclamation escaped me — the lady looked up. Her hair was dark, and her eyes; her face was pink and white, with a few little gold-coloured freckles on nose and on cheek bones. Her dress was of pink cotton stuff, thin and soft. She looked like a beautiful pink rose.

Our eyes met.

'I beg your pardon,' said I, 'I had no idea —' There I stopped and tried to crawl back to firm ground. Graceful explanations are not best given by one sprawling on his stomach across a sundial.

By the time I was once more on my feet she too was standing.

'It is a beautiful old place,' she said gently, and, as it seemed, with a kindly wish to relieve my embarrassment. She made a movement as if to turn away.

'Quite a show place,' said I stupidly enough, but I was still a little embarrassed, and I wanted to say something — anything — to arrest her departure. You have no idea how pretty she was. She had a straw hat in her hand, dangling by soft black ribbons. Her hair was all fluffy-soft — like a child's. 'I suppose you have seen the house?' I asked.

She paused, one foot still on the lower step of the sundial, and her face seemed to brighten at the touch of some idea as sudden as welcome.

'Well — no,' she said. 'The fact is — I wanted frightfully to see the house; in fact, I've come miles and miles on purpose, but there's no one to let me in.'

'The people at the lodge?' I suggested.

'Oh no,' she said. 'I — the fact is I — I don't want to be shown round. I want to explore!'

She looked at me critically. Her eyes dwelt on my right hand, which lay on the sundial. I have always taken reasonable care of my hands, and I wore a good ring, a sapphire, cut with the Sefton arms: an heirloom, by the way. Her glance at my hand preluded a longer glance at my face. Then she shrugged her pretty shoulders.

'Oh well,' she said, and it was as if she had said plainly, 'I see that you are a gentleman and a decent fellow. Why should I not look over the house in your company? Introductions? Bah!'

All this her shrug said without ambiguity as without words.

'Perhaps,' I hazarded, 'I could get the keys.'

'Do you really care very much for old houses?'

'I do,' said I, 'and you?'

'I care so much that I nearly broke into this one. I should have done it quite if the windows had been an inch or two lower.'

'I am an inch or two higher,' said I, standing squarely so as to make the most of my six feet beside her five-feet-five or thereabouts.

'Oh — if you only would!' said she.

'Why not?' said I.

She led the way past the marble basin of the fountain,

and along the historic yew avenue, planted, like all old yew avenues, by that industrious gardener our Eighth Henry. Then across a lawn, through a winding, grassy, shrubbery path, that ended at a green door in the garden wall.

'You can lift this latch with a hairpin,' said she, and therewith lifted it.

We walked into a courtyard. Young grass grew green between the grey flags on which our steps echoed.

'This is the window,' said she. 'You see there's a pane broken. If you could get on to the window-sill, you could get your hand in and undo the hasp, and —'

'And you?'

'Oh, you'll let me in by the kitchen door.'

I did it. My conscience called me a burglar — in vain. Was it not my own, or as good as my own house?

I let her in at the back door. We walked through the big dark kitchen where the old three-legged pot towered large on the hearth, and the old spits and firedogs still kept their ancient place. Then through another kitchen where red rust was making its full meal of a comparatively modern range.

Then into the great hall, where the old armour and the buff-coats and round-caps hang on the walls, and where the carved stone staircases run at each side up to the gallery above.

The long tables in the middle of the hall were scored by the knives of the many who had eaten meat there — initials and dates were cut into them. The roof was groined, the windows low-arched.

'Oh, but what a place!' said she; 'this must be much older than the rest of it —'

'Evidently. About 1300, I should say.'

'Oh, let us explore the rest,' she cried; 'it is really a comfort not to have a guide, but only a person like you who just guesses comfortably at dates. I should hate to be told *exactly* when this hall was built.'

We explored ball-room and picture gallery, white parlour and library. Most of the rooms were furnished — all heavily, some magnificently — but everything was dusty and faded.

It was in the white parlour, a spacious panelled room on the first floor, that she told me the ghost story, substantially the same as my porter's tale, only in one respect different.

'And so, just as she was leaving this very room — yes, I'm sure it's this room, because the woman at the inn pointed out this double window and told me so — just as the poor lovers were creeping out of the door, the cruel father came quickly out of some dark place and killed them both. So now they haunt it.'

'It is a terrible thought,' said I gravely. 'How would you like to live in a haunted house?'

'I couldn't,' she said quickly.

'Nor I; it would be too —' my speech would have ended flippantly, but for the grave set of her features.

'I wonder who *will* live here?' she said. 'The owner is just dead. They say it is an awful house, full of ghosts. Of course one is not afraid now' — the sunlight lay golden and soft on the dusty parquet of the floor — 'but at night, when the wind wails, and the doors creak, and the things rustle, oh, it must be awful!'

'I hear the house has been left to two people, or rather one is to have the house, and the other a sum of money,' said I. 'It's a beautiful house, full of beautiful things, but I should think at least one of the heirs would rather have the money.'

'Oh yes, I should think so. I wonder whether the heirs know about the ghost? The lights can be seen from the inn, you know, at twelve o'clock, and they see the ghost in white at the window.'

'Never the black one?'

'Oh yes, I suppose so.'

'The ghosts don't appear together?'

'No.'

'I suppose,' said I, 'whoever it is that manages such things knows that the poor ghosts would like to be together, so it won't let them.'

She shivered.

'Come,' she said, 'we have seen all over the house; let us get back into the sunshine. Now I will go out, and you shall bolt the door after me, and then you can come out by the window. Thank you so much for all the trouble you have taken. It has really been quite an adventure ...'

I rather liked that expression, and she hastened to spoil it.

'... Quite an adventure going all over this glorious old place, and looking at everything one wanted to see, and not just at what the housekeeper didn't mind one's looking at.'

She passed through the door, but when I had closed it and prepared to lock it, I found that the key was no longer in the lock. I looked on the floor — I felt in my pockets, and at last, wandering back into the kitchen, discovered it on the table, where I swear I never put it.

When I had fitted that key into the lock and turned it, and got out of the window and made that fast, I dropped into the yard. No one shared its solitude with me. I searched garden and pleasure grounds, but never a glimpse of pink rewarded my anxious eyes. I found the sundial again, and stretched myself along the warm brick of the wide step where she had sat: and called myself a fool.

I had let her go. I did not know her name; I did not know where she lived; she had been at the inn, but probably only for lunch. I should never see her again, and certainly in that event I should never see again such dark, soft eyes, such hair, such a contour of cheek and chin, such a frank smile — in a word, a girl with whom it would be so delightfully natural for me to fall in love. For all the time she had been talking to me of architecture and archaeology, of dates and periods, of carvings and mouldings, I had been recklessly falling in love with the idea of falling in love with her. I had cherished and adored this delightful possibility, and now my chance was over. Even I could not definitely fall in love after one interview with a girl I was never to see again! And falling in love is so pleasant! I cursed my lost chance, and went back to the inn. I talked to the waiter.

'Yes, a lady in pink had lunched there with a party. Had gone on to the Castle. A party from Tonbridge it was.'

Barnhurst Castle is close to Sefton Manor. The inn lays itself out to entertain persons who come in brakes and carve their names on the walls of the Castle keep. The inn has a visitors' book. I examined it. Some twenty feminine names. Any one might be hers. The waiter looked over my shoulder. I turned the pages.

'Only parties staying in the house in this part of the book,' said the waiter.

My eye caught one name. 'Selwyn Sefton', in a clear, round, black handwriting.

'Staying here?' I pointed to the name.

'Yes, sir; came today, sir.'

'Can I have a private sitting-room?'

I had one. I ordered my dinner to be served in it, and I sat down and considered my course of action. Should I invite my cousin Selwyn to dinner, ply him with wine, and exact promises? Honour forbade. Should I seek him out and try to establish friendly relations? To what end?

Then I saw from my window a young man in a light-checked suit, with a face at once pallid and coarse. He strolled along the gravel path, and a woman's voice in the garden called 'Selwyn'.

He disappeared in the direction of the voice. I don't think I ever disliked a man so much at first sight.

'Brute,' said I, 'why should he have the house? He'd stucco

it all over as likely as not; perhaps let it! He'd never stand the ghosts, either —'

Then the inexcusable, daring idea of my life came to me, striking me rigid — a blow from my other self. It must have been a minute or two before my muscles relaxed and my arms fell at my sides.

'I'll do it,' I said.

I dined. I told the people of the house not to sit up for me. I was going to see friends in the neighbourhood, and might stay the night with them. I took my Inverness cape with me on my arm and my soft felt hat in my pocket. I wore a light suit and a straw hat.

Before I started I leaned cautiously from my window. The lamp at the bow window next to mine showed me the pallid young man, smoking a fat, reeking cigar. I hoped he would continue to sit there smoking. His window looked the right way; and if he didn't see what I wanted him to see someone else in the inn would. The landlady had assured me that I should disturb no one if I came in at half-past twelve.

'We hardly keep country hours here, sir,' she said, 'on account of so much excursionist business.'

I bought candles in the village, and, as I went down across the park in the soft darkness, I turned again and again to be sure that the light and the pallid young man were still at that window. It was now past eleven.

I got into the house and lighted a candle, and crept through the dark kitchens, whose windows, I knew, did not look towards the inn. When I came to the hall I blew out my candle. I dared not show light prematurely, and in the unhaunted part of the house.

I gave myself a nasty knock against one of the long tables, but it helped me to get my bearings, and presently I laid my hand on the stone balustrade of the great staircase. You would hardly believe me if I were to tell you truly of my sensations as I began to go up these stairs. I am not a coward — at least, I had never thought so till then — but the absolute darkness unnerved me. I had to go slowly, or I should have lost my head and blundered up the stairs three at a time, so strong was the feeling of something — something uncanny — just behind me.

I set my teeth. I reached the top of the stairs, felt along the walls, and after a false start, which landed me in the great picture gallery, I found the white parlour, entered it, closed the door, and felt my way to a little room without a window, which we had decided must have been a powdering-room.

Here I ventured to re-light my candle.

The white parlour, I remembered, was fully furnished. Returning to it I struck one match, and by its flash determined the way to the mantelpiece.

Then I closed the powdering-room door behind me. I felt my way to the mantelpiece and took down the two brass twenty-lighted candelabra. I placed these on a table a yard or two from the window, and in them set up my candles. It is astonishingly difficult in the dark to do anything, even a thing so simple as the setting up of a candle.

Then I went back into my little room, put on the Inverness cape and the slouch hat, and looked at my watch. Eleven-thirty. I must wait. I sat down and waited. I thought how rich I was — the thought fell flat; I wanted this house. I thought of my beautiful pink lady; but I put that thought aside; I had an inward consciousness that my conduct, more heroic than enough in one sense, would seem mean and crafty in her eyes. Only ten minutes had passed. I could not wait till twelve. The chill of the night and of the damp, unused house, and, perhaps, some less material influence, made me shiver.

I opened the door, crept on hands and knees to the table, and, carefully keeping myself below the level of the window,

I reached up a trembling arm, and lighted, one by one, my forty candles. The room was a blaze of light. My courage came back to me with the retreat of the darkness. I was far too excited to know what a fool I was making of myself. I rose boldly, and struck an attitude over against the window, where the candlelight shone upon as well as behind me. My Inverness was flung jauntily over my shoulder, my soft, black felt twisted and slouched over my eyes.

There I stood for the world, and particularly for my cousin Selwyn, to see, the very image of the ghost that haunted that chamber. And from my window I could see the light in that other window, and indistinctly the lounging figure there. Oh, my cousin Selwyn, I wished many things to your address in that moment! For it was only a moment that I had to feel brave and daring in. Then I heard, deep down in the house, a sound, very slight, very faint. Then came silence. I drew a deep breath. The silence endured. And I stood by my lighted window.

After a very long time, as it seemed, I heard a board crack, and then a soft rustling sound that drew near and seemed to pause outside the very door of my parlour.

Again I held my breath, and now I thought of the most horrible story Poe ever wrote — 'The Fall of the House of Usher' — and I fancied I saw the handle of that door move. I fixed my eyes on it. The fancy passed: and returned.

Then again there was silence. And then the door opened with a soft, silent suddenness, and I saw in the doorway a figure in trailing white. Its eyes blazed in a death-white face. It made two ghostly, gliding steps forward, and my heart stood still. I had not thought it possible for a man to experience so sharp a pang of sheer terror. I had masqueraded as one of the ghosts in this accursed house. Well, the other ghost — the real one — had come to meet me. I do not like to dwell on that moment. The only thing which it pleases me to remember is that I did not scream or go mad. I think I stood on the verge of both.

The ghost, I say, took two steps forward; then it threw up its arms, the lighted taper it carried fell on the floor, and it reeled back against the door with its arms across its face.

The fall of the candle woke me as from a nightmare. It fell solidly, and rolled away under the table.

I perceived that my ghost was human. I cried incoherently: 'Don't, for Heaven's sake — it's all right.'

The ghost dropped its hands and turned agonised eyes on me. I tore off my cloak and hat.

'I — didn't — scream,' she said, and with that I sprang forward and caught her in my arms — my poor, pink lady — white now as a white rose.

I carried her into the powdering-room, and left one candle with her, extinguishing the others hastily, for now I saw what in my extravagant folly had escaped me before, that my ghost exhibition might bring the whole village down on the house. I tore down the long corridor and double locked the doors leading from it to the staircase, then back to the powdering-room and the prone white rose. How, in the madness of that night's folly, I had thought to bring a brandy-flask passes my understanding. But I had done it. Now I rubbed her hands with the spirit. I rubbed her temples, I tried to force it between her lips, and at last she sighed and opened her eyes.

'Oh — thank God — thank God!' I cried, for indeed I had almost feared that my mad trick had killed her. 'Are you better? oh, poor little lady, are you better?'

She moved her head a little on my arm.

Again she sighed, and her eyes closed. I gave her more brandy. She took it, choked, raised herself against my shoulder.

'I'm all right now,' she said faintly. 'It served me right.

How silly it all is!' Then she began to laugh, and then she began to cry.

It was at this moment that we heard voices on the terrace below. She clutched at my arm in a frenzy of terror, the bright tears glistening on her cheeks.

'Oh! not any more, not any more,' she cried. 'I can't bear it.'

'Hush,' I said, taking her hands strongly in mine. 'I've played the fool; so have you. We must play the man now. The people in the village have seen the lights — that's all. They think we're burglars. They can't get in. Keep quiet, and they'll go away.'

But when they did go away they left the local constable on guard. He kept guard like a man till daylight began to creep over the hill, and then he crawled into the hayloft and fell asleep, small blame to him.

But through those long hours I sat beside her and held her hand. At first she clung to me as a frightened child clings, and her tears were the prettiest, saddest things to see. As we grew calmer we talked.

'I did it to frighten my cousin,' I owned. 'I meant to have told you today, I mean yesterday, only you went away. I am Lawrence Sefton, and the place is to go either to me or to my cousin Selwyn. And I wanted to frighten him off it. But you, why did you —?'

Even then I couldn't see. She looked at me.

'I don't know how I ever could have thought I was brave enough to do it, but I did want the house so, and I wanted to frighten you —'

'To frighten *me*. Why?'

'Because I am your cousin Selwyn,' she said, hiding her face in her hands.

'And you knew me?' I asked.

'By your ring,' she said. 'I saw your father wear it when I was a little girl. Can't we get back to the inn now?'

'Not unless you want everyone to know how silly we have been.'

'I wish you'd forgive me,' she said when we had talked awhile, and she had even laughed at the description of the pallid young man on whom I had bestowed, in my mind, her name.

'The wrong is mutual,' I said; 'we will exchange forgivenesses.'

'Oh, but it isn't,' she said eagerly. 'Because I knew it was you, and you didn't know it was me: you wouldn't have tried to frighten *me*.'

'You know I wouldn't.' My voice was tenderer than I meant it to be.

She was silent.

'And who is to have the house?' she said.

'Why you, of course.'

'I never will.'

'Why?'

'Oh, because!'

'Can't we put off the decision?' I asked.

'Impossible. We must decide tomorrow — today I mean.'

'Well, when we meet tomorrow — I mean today — with lawyers and chaperones and mothers and relations, give me one word alone with you.'

'Yes,' she answered, with docility.

✕

'Do you know,' she said presently, 'I can never respect myself again? To undertake a thing like that, and then be so horribly frightened. Oh! I thought you really *were* the other ghost.'

'I will tell you a secret,' said I. 'I thought *you* were, and I was much more frightened than you.'

'Oh well,' she said, leaning against my shoulder as a tired

child might have done, 'if you were frightened too, Cousin Lawrence, I don't mind so very, very much.'

It was soon afterwards that, cautiously looking out of the parlour window for the twentieth time, I had the happiness of seeing the local policeman disappear into the stable rubbing his eyes.

We got out of the window on the other side of the house and went back to the inn across the dewy park. The French window of the sitting-room which had let her out let us both in. No one was stirring, so no one save she and I were any the wiser as to that night's work.

✖

It was like a garden party next day, when lawyers and executors and aunts and relations met on the terrace in front of Sefton Manor House.

Her eyes were downcast. She followed her aunt demurely over the house and the grounds.

'Your decision,' said my great-uncle's solicitor, 'has to be given within the hour.'

'My cousin and I will announce it within that time,' I said, and I at once gave her my arm.

Arrived at the sundial we stopped.

'This is my proposal,' I said: 'we will say that we decide that the house is yours — we will spend the £20,000 in restoring it and the grounds. By the time that's done we can decide who is to have it.'

'But how?'

'Oh, we'll draw lots, or toss a halfpenny, or anything you like.'

'I'd rather decide now,' she said; '*you* take it.'

'No, *you* shall.'

'I'd rather you had it. I — I don't feel so greedy as I did yesterday,' she said.

'Neither do I. Or at any rate not in the same way.'

'Do — do take the house,' she said very earnestly.

Then I said: 'My cousin Selwyn, unless you take the house, I shall make you an offer of marriage.'

'*Oh!*' she breathed.

'And when you have declined it, on the very proper ground of our too slight acquaintance, I will take my turn at declining. I will decline the house. Then, if you are obdurate, it will become an asylum. Don't be obdurate. Pretend to take the house and —'

She looked at me rather piteously.

'Very well,' she said, 'I will pretend to take the house, and when it is restored —'

'We'll spin the penny.'

So before the waiting relations the house was adjudged to my cousin Selwyn. When the restoration was complete I met Selwyn at the sundial. We had met there often in the course of the restoration, in which business we both took an extravagant interest.

'Now,' I said, 'we'll spin the penny. Heads you take the house, tails it comes to me.'

I spun the coin — it fell on the brick steps of the sundial, and stuck upright there, wedged between two bricks. She laughed; I laughed.

'It's not *my* house,' I said.

'It's not *my* house,' said she.

'Dear,' said I, and we were neither of us laughing then, 'can't it be *our* house?'

And, thank God, our house it is.

9 The Power of Darkness

It was an enthusiastic send-off. Half the students from her Atelier were there, and twice as many more from other studios. She had been the belle of the Artists' Quarter in Montparnasse for three golden months. Now she was off to the Riviera to meet her people, and everyone she knew was at the Gare de Lyons to catch the pretty last glimpse of her. And, as had been more than once said late of an evening, 'to see her was to love her'. She was one of those agitating blondes, with the naturally rippled hair, the rounded rose-leaf cheeks, the large violet-blue eyes that look all things and mean Heaven alone knows how little. She held her court like a queen, leaning out of the carriage window and receiving bouquets, books, journals, long last words, and last longing looks. All eyes were on her, and her eyes were for all — and her smile. For all but one, that is. Not a single glance went Edward's way, and Edward, tall, lean, gaunt, with big eyes, straight nose, and mouth somewhat too small, too beautiful, seemed to grow thinner and paler before one's eyes. One pair of eyes at least saw the miracle worked, the paling of what had seemed absolute pallor, the revelation of the bones of a face that seemed already covered but by the thinnest possible veil of flesh.

And the man whose eyes saw this rejoiced, for he loved her, like the rest, or not like the rest; and he had had Edward's face before him for the last month, in that secret shrine where we set the loved and the hated, the shrine that is lighted by a million lamps kindled at the soul's flame, the shrine that leaps into dazzling glow when the candles are out and one lies alone on hot pillows to outface the night and the light as best one may.

'Oh, goodbye, goodbye, all of you,' said Rose. 'I shall miss you — oh, you don't know how I shall miss you all!'

She gathered the glances of her friends and her worshippers on her own glance, as one gathers jewels on a silken string. The eyes of Edward alone seemed to escape her.

'En voiture, messieurs et dames.'

Folk drew back from the train. There was a whistle. And then at the very last little moment of all, as the train pulled itself together for the start, her eyes met Edward's eyes. And the other man saw the meeting, and he knew — which was more than Edward did.

So, when the light of life having been borne away in the retreating train, the broken-hearted group dispersed, the other man, whose name by the way was Vincent, linked his arm in Edward's and asked cheerily: 'Whither away, sweet nymph?'

'I'm off home,' said Edward. 'The 7.20 to Calais.'

'Sick of Paris?'

'One has to see one's people sometimes, don't you know, hang it all!' was Edward's way of expressing the longing that tore him for the old house among the brown woods of Kent.

'No attraction here now, eh?'

'The chief attraction has gone, certainly,' Edward made himself say.

'But there are as good fish in the sea —?'

'Fishing isn't my trade,' said Edward.

'The beautiful Rose! —' said Vincent.

Edward raised hurriedly the only shield he could find. It happened to be the truth as he saw it.

'Oh,' he said, 'of course, we're all in love with her — and all hopelessly.'

Vincent perceived that this was truth, as Edward saw it.

'What are you going to do till your train goes?' he asked.

'I don't know. Café, I suppose, and a vilely early dinner.'

'Let's look in at the Musée Grévin,' said Vincent.

The two were friends. They had been school-fellows, and this is a link that survives many a strain too strong to be resisted by more intimate and vital bonds. And they were fellow-students, though that counts for little or much — as you take it. Besides, Vincent knew something about Edward that no one else of their age and standing even guessed. He knew that Edward was afraid of the dark, and why. He had found it out that Christmas that the two had spent at an English country house. The house was full: there was a dance. There were to be theatricals. Early in the new year the hostess meant to 'move house' to an old convent, built in Tudor times, a beautiful place with terraces and clipped yew trees, castellated battlements, a moat, swans, and a ghost story.

'You boys,' she said, 'must put up with a shake-down in the new house. I hope the ghost won't worry you. She's a nun with a bunch of keys and no eyes. Comes and breathes softly on the back of your neck when you're shaving. Then you see her in the glass, and, as often as not, you cut your throat.' She laughed. So did Edward and Vincent, and the other young men; there were seven or eight of them.

But that night, when sparse candles had lighted 'the boys' to their rooms, when the last pipe had been smoked, the last goodnight said, there came a fumbling with the handle of Vincent's door. Edward entered an unwieldy figure clasping pillows, trailing blankets.

'What the deuce?' queried Vincent in natural amazement.

'I'll turn in here on the floor, if you don't mind,' said Edward. 'I know it's beastly rot, but I can't stand it. The room they've put me into, it's an attic as big as a barn — and there's a great door at the end, eight feet high — raw oak it is — and it leads into a sort of horror-hole — bare beams and rafters, and black as Hell. I know I'm an abject duffer, but there it is — I can't face it.'

Vincent was sympathetic, though he had never known a night-terror that could not be exorcised by pipe, book, and candle.

'I know, old chap. There's no reasoning about these things,' said he, and so on.

'You can't despise me more than I despise myself,' Edward said. 'I feel a crawling hound. But it is so. I had a scare when I was a kid, and it seems to have left a sort of brand on me. I'm branded 'coward', old man, and the feel of it's not nice.'

Again Vincent was sympathetic, and the poor little tale came out. How Edward, eight years old, and greedy as became his little years, had sneaked down, night-clad, to pick among the outcomings of a dinner party, and how, in the hall, dark with the light of an 'artistic' coloured glass lantern, a white figure had suddenly faced him — leaned towards him it seemed, pointed lead-white hands at his heart. That next day, finding him weak from his fainting fit, had shown the horror to be but a statue, a new purchase of his father's, had mattered not one whit.

Edward had shared Vincent's room, and Vincent, alone of all men, shared Edward's secret.

And now, in Paris, Rose speeding away towards Cannes, Vincent said: 'Let's look in at the Musée Grévin.'

The Musée Grévin is a wax-work show. Your mind, at the word, flies instantly to the excellent exhibition founded by the worthy Madame Tussaud, and you think you know what wax-works mean. But you are wrong. The exhibition of Madame Tussaud — in these days, at any rate — is the work of *bourgeois* for a *bourgeois* class. The Musée Grévin contains the work of artists for a nation of artists. Wax, modelled and retouched till it seems as near life as death is: this is what one sees at the Musée Grévin.

'Let's look in at the Musée Grévin,' said Vincent. He remembered the pleasant thrill the Musée had given him, and wondered what sort of a thrill it would give his friend.

'I hate museums,' said Edward.

'This isn't a museum,' Vincent said, and truly; 'it's just wax-works.'

'All right,' said Edward indifferently. And they went. They reached the doors of the Musée in the grey-brown dusk of a February evening.

One walks along a bare, narrow corridor, much like the entrance to the stalls of the Standard Theatre, and such daylight as there may be fades away behind one, and one finds oneself in a square hall, heavily decorated, and displaying with its electric lights Loie Fuller in her accordion-pleated skirts, and one or two other figures not designed to quicken the pulse.

'It's very like Madame Tussaud's,' said Edward.

'Yes,' Vincent said, 'isn't it?'

Then they passed through an arch, and behold, a long room with waxen groups life-like behind glass — the *coulisses* of the Opéra, Kitchener at Fashoda — this last with a desert background lit by something convincingly like desert sunlight.

'By Jove!' said Edward, 'that's jolly good.'

'Yes,' said Vincent again, 'isn't it?'

Edward's interest grew. The things were so convincing, so very nearly alive. Given the right angle, their glass eyes met one's own, and seemed to exchange with one meaning glances.

Vincent led the way to an arched door labelled: 'Gallerie de la Revolution.'

There one saw, almost in the living, suffering body, poor Marie Antoinette in prison in the Temple, her little son on his couch of rags, the rats eating from his platter, the brutal Simon calling to him from the grated window; one almost heard the words, 'Ho la, little Capet — are you asleep?'

One saw Marat bleeding in his bath — the brave Charlotte eyeing him — the very tiles of the bath-room, the glass of the windows with, outside, the very sunlight, as it seemed, of 1793 on that 'yellow July evening, the thirteenth of the month'.

The spectators did not move in a public place among wax-work figures. They peeped through open doors into rooms where history seemed to be re-lived. The rooms were lighted each by its own sun, or lamp, or candle. The spectators walked among shadows that might have oppressed a nervous person.

'Fine, eh?' said Vincent.

'Yes,' said Edward, 'it's wonderful.'

A turn of a corner brought them to a room. Marie Antoinette fainting, supported by her ladies; poor fat Louis by the window looking literally sick.

'What's the matter with them all?' said Edward.

'Look at the window,' said Vincent.

There was a window to the room. Outside was sunshine — the sunshine of 1792 — and, gleaming in it, blonde hair flowing, red mouth half open, what seemed the just-severed head of a beautiful woman. It was raised on a pike, so that it seemed to be looking in at the window.

'I say!' said Edward, and the head on the pike seemed to sway before his eyes.

'Madame de Lamballe. Good thing, isn't it?' said Vincent.

'It's altogether too much of a good thing,' said Edward. 'Look here — I've had enough of this.'

'Oh, you must just see the Catacombs,' said Vincent; 'nothing bloody, you know. Only Early Christians being married and baptized, and all that.'

He led the way, down some clumsy steps to the cellars which the genius of a great artist has transformed into the exact semblance of the old Catacombs at Rome. The same rough hewing of rock, the same sacred tokens engraved strongly and simply; and among the arches of these subterranean burrowings the life of the Early Christians, their sacraments, their joys, their sorrows — all expressed in groups of wax-work as like life as Death is.

'But this is very fine, you know,' said Edward, getting his breath again after Madame de Lamballe, and his imagination loved the thought of the noble sufferings and refrainings of these first lovers of the Crucified Christ.

'Yes,' said Vincent for the third time, 'isn't it?'

They passed the baptism and the burying and the marriage. The tableaux were sufficiently lighted, but little light strayed to the narrow passage where the two men walked, and the darkness seemed to press, tangible as a bodily presence, against Edward's shoulder. He glanced backward.

'Come,' he said, 'I've had enough.'

'Come on, then,' said Vincent.

They turned the corner — and a blaze of Italian sunlight struck at their eyes with positive dazzlement. There lay the Coliseum — tier on tier of eager faces under the blue sky of Italy. They were level with the arena. In the arena were crosses; from them drooped bleeding figures. On the sand beasts prowled, bodies lay. They saw it all through bars. They seemed to be in the place where the chosen victims waited their turn, waited for the lions and the crosses, the palm and the crown. Close by Edward was a group — an old man, a woman — children. He could have touched them with his hand. The woman and the man stared in an agony of terror straight in the eyes of a snarling tiger, ten feet long, that stood up on its hind feet and clawed through the bars at them. The youngest child, only, unconscious of the horror, laughed in the very face of it. Roman soldiers, unmoved in military vigilance, guarded the group of martyrs. In a low cage to the left more wild beasts cringed and seemed to growl, unfed. Within the grating on the wide circle of yellow sand lions and tigers drank the blood of Christians. Close against the bars a great lion sucked the chest of a corpse on whose blood-stained face the horror of the death-agony was printed plain.

'Good God!' said Edward. Vincent took his arm suddenly, and he started with what was almost a shriek.

'What a nervous chap you are!' said Vincent complacently, as they regained the street where the lights were, and the sound of voices and the movement of live human beings — all that warms and awakens nerves almost paralysed by the life in death of waxen immobility.

'I don't know,' said Edward. 'Let's have a vermouth, shall we? There's something uncanny about those wax things. They're like life — but they're much more like death. Suppose they moved? I don't feel at all sure that they don't move, when the lights are all out, and there's no one there.' He laughed. 'I suppose you were never frightened, Vincent?'

'Yes, I was once,' said Vincent, sipping his absinthe. 'Three other men and I were taking turns by twos to watch a dead man. It was a fancy of his mother's. Our time was up, and the other watch hadn't come. So my chap — the one who was watching with me, I mean — went to fetch them. I didn't think I should mind. But it was just like you say.'

'How?'

'Why, I kept thinking: suppose it should move — it was so like life. And if it did move, of course it would have been because it *was* alive, and I ought to have been glad, because the man was my friend. But all the same, if it had moved I should have gone mad.'

'Yes,' said Edward, 'that's just exactly it.'

Vincent called for a second absinthe.

'But a dead body's different to wax-works,' he said. 'I can't understand anyone being frightened of *them*.'

'Oh, can't you?' The contempt in the other's tone stung him. 'I bet you wouldn't spend a night alone in that place.'

'I bet you five pounds I do!'

'Done!' said Edward briskly. 'At least, I would if you'd got five pounds.'

'But I have. I'm simply rolling. I've sold my Deianira, didn't you know? I shall win your money, though, anyway. But *you* couldn't do it, old man. I suppose you'll never outgrow that childish scare.'

'You might shut up about that,' said Edward shortly.

'Oh, it's nothing to be ashamed of; some women are afraid of mice or spiders. I say, does Rose know you're a coward?'

'Vincent!'

'No offence, old boy. One may as well call a spade a spade. Of course, you've got tons of moral courage, and all that. But you *are* afraid of the dark — and wax-works!'

'Are you trying to quarrel with me?'

'Heaven in its mercy forbid; but I bet *you* wouldn't spend a night in the Musée Grévin and keep your senses.'

'What's the stake?'

'Anything you like.'

'Make it, that if I do, you'll never speak to Rose again — and what's more, that you'll never speak to me,' said Edward, white-hot, knocking down a chair as he rose.

'Done!' said Vincent; 'but you'll never do it. Keep your hair on. Besides, you're off home.'

'I shall be back in ten days. I'll do it then,' said Edward, and was off before the other could answer.

Then Vincent, left alone, sat still, and over his third absinthe remembered how, before she had known Edward, Rose had smiled on him; more than on the others, he had thought. He thought of her wide, lovely eyes, her wild-rose cheeks, the scented curves of her hair, and then and there the devil entered into him.

In ten days Edward would undoubtedly try to win his wager. He would try to spend the night in the Musée Grévin. Perhaps something could be arranged before that. If one knew the place thoroughly! A little scare would serve Edward right for being the man to whom that last glance of Rose's had been given.

Vincent dined lightly, but with conscientious care — and as he dined, he thought. Something might be done by tying a string to one of the figures, and making it move, when Edward was going through that impossible night among the effigies that are so like life — so like death. Something that was not the devil said: 'You may frighten him out of his wits.' And the devil answered: 'Nonsense! do him good. He oughtn't to be such a schoolgirl.'

Anyway, the five pounds might as well be won tonight as any other night. He would take a great coat, sleep sound in the place of horrors, and the people who opened it in the morning to sweep and dust would bear witness that he had passed the night there. He thought he might trust to the French love of a sporting wager to keep him from any bother with the authorities.

So he went in among the crowd, and looked about among the wax-works for a place to hide in. He was not in the least afraid of these lifeless images. He had always been able to control his nervous tremors. He was not even afraid of being frightened, which, by the way, is the worst fear of all. As one looks at the room of the poor little Dauphin, one sees a door to the left. It opens out of the room on to blackness. There were few people in the gallery. Vincent watched, and in a moment when he was alone he stepped over the barrier and through this door. A narrow passage ran round behind the wall of the room. Here he hid, and when the gallery was deserted he looked out across the body of little Capet to the gaolers at the window. There was a soldier at the window, too. Vincent amused himself with the fancy that this soldier might walk round the passage at the back of the room and tap him on the shoulder in the darkness. Only the head and shoulders of the soldier and the gaoler showed, so, of course, they could not walk, even if they were something that was not wax-work.

Presently he himself went along the passage and round to the window where they were. He found that they had legs. They were full-sized figures dressed completely in the costume of the period.

'Thorough the beggars are, even the parts that don't show — artists, upon my word,' said Vincent, and went back to his doorway, thinking of the hidden carving behind the capitols of Gothic cathedrals.

But the idea of the soldier who might come behind him in the dark stuck in his mind. Though still a few visitors strolled through the gallery, the closing hour was near. He supposed it would be quite dark then. And now he had allowed himself to be amused by the thought of something that should creep up behind him in the dark, he might possibly be nervous in that passage round which, if wax-works could move, the soldier might have come.

'By Jove!' he said, 'one might easily frighten oneself by just fancying things. Suppose there were a back way from Marat's bath-room, and instead of the soldier Marat came out of his bath, with his wet towels stained with blood, and dabbed them against your neck.'

When next the gallery was empty he crept out. Not because he was nervous, he told himself, but because one might be, and because the passage was draughty, and he meant to sleep.

He went down the steps into the Catacombs, and here he spoke the truth to himself.

'Hang it all!' he said, 'I *was* nervous. That fool Edward must have infected me. Mesmeric influences, or something.'

'Chuck it and go home,' said Commonsense.

'I'm damned if I do!' said Vincent.

There were a good many people in the Catacombs at the

moment — live people. He sucked confidence from their nearness, and went up and down looking for a hiding-place.

Through rock-hewn arches he saw a burial scene — a corpse on a bier surrounded by mourners; a great pillar cut off half the still, lying figure. It was all still and unemotional as a Sunday School oleograph. He waited till no one was near, then slipped quickly through the mourning group and hid behind the pillar. Surprising — heartening too — to find a plain rushed chair there, doubtless set for the resting of tired officials. He sat down in it, comforted his hand with the commonplace lines of its rungs and back. A shrouded waxen figure just behind him to the left of his pillar worried him a little, but the corpse left him unmoved as itself. A far better place this than that draughty passage where the soldier with legs kept intruding on the darkness that is always behind one.

Custodians went along the passages issuing orders. A stillness fell. Then suddenly all the lights went out.

'That's all right,' said Vincent, and composed himself to sleep.

But he seemed to have forgotten what sleep was like. He firmly fixed his thoughts on pleasant things — the sale of his picture, dances with Rose, merry evenings with Edward and the others. But the thoughts rushed by him like motes in sunbeams — he could not hold a single one of them, and presently it seemed that he had thought of every pleasant thing that had ever happened to him, and that now, if he thought at all, he must think of the things one wants most to forget. And there would be time in this long night to think much of many things. But now he found that he could no longer think.

The draped effigy just behind him worried him again. He had been trying, at the back of his mind, behind the other thoughts, to strangle the thought of it. But it was there — very close to him. Suppose it put out its hand, its wax hand,

and touched him. But it was of wax: it could not move. No, of course not. But suppose it *did*?

He laughed aloud, a short, dry laugh that echoed through the vaults. The cheering effect of laughter has been over-estimated, perhaps. Anyhow, he did not laugh again.

The silence was intense, but it was a silence thick with rustlings and breathings, and movements that his ear, strained to the uttermost, could just not hear. Suppose, as Edward had said, when all the lights were out, these things did move. A corpse was a thing that had moved — given a certain condition — Life. What if there were a condition, given which these things could move? What if such conditions were present now? What if all of them — Napoleon, yellow-white from his death sleep — the beasts from the Amphitheatre, gore dribbling from their jaws — that soldier with the legs — all were drawing near to him in this full silence? Those death masks of Robespierre and Mirabeau, they might float down through the darkness till they touched his face. That head of Madame de Lamballe on the pike might be thrust at him from behind the pillar. The silence throbbed with sounds that could not quite be heard.

'You fool,' he said to himself, 'your dinner has disagreed with you, with a vengeance. Don't be an ass. The whole lot are only a set of big dolls.'

He felt for his matches, and lighted a cigarette. The gleam of the match fell on the face of the corpse in front of him. The light was brief, and it seemed, somehow, impossible to look, by that light, in every corner where one would have wished to look. The match burnt his fingers as it went out; and there were only three more matches in the box.

It was dark again, and the image left on the darkness was that of the corpse in front of him. He thought of his dead friend. When the cigarette was smoked out, he thought of him more and more, till it seemed that what lay on the bier was not wax. His hand reached forward, and drew back more than once. But at last he made it touch the bier, and through the blackness travel up along a lean, rigid arm to the wax face that lay there so still. The touch was not reassuring. Just so, and not otherwise, had his dead friend's face felt, to the last touch of his lips: cold, firm, waxen. People always said the dead were 'waxen.' How true that was! He had never thought of it before. He thought of it now.

He sat still, so still that every muscle ached, because if you wish to hear the sounds that infest silence, you must be very still indeed. He thought of Edward, and of the string he had meant to tie to one of the figures.

'That wouldn't be needed,' he told himself. And his ears ached with listening — listening for the sound that, it seemed, *must* break at last from that crowded silence.

He never knew how long he sat there. To move, to go up, to batter at the door and clamour to be let out — that one could have done if one had had a lantern, or even a full matchbox. But in the dark, not knowing the turnings, to feel one's way among these things that were so like life and yet were not alive — to touch, perhaps, these faces that were not dead, and yet felt like death. His heart beat heavily in his throat at the thought.

No, he must sit still till morning. He had been hypnotised into this state, he told himself, by Edward, no doubt; it was not natural to him.

Then suddenly the silence was shattered. In the dark something moved. And, after those sounds that the silence teemed with, the noise seemed to him thunder-loud. Yet it was only a very, very little sound, just the rustling of drapery, as though something had turned in its sleep. And there was a sigh — not far off.

Vincent's muscles and tendons tightened like fine-drawn wire. He listened. There was nothing more: only the silence, the thick silence.

The sound had seemed to come from a part of the vault where, long ago, when there was light, he had seen a grave being dug for the body of a young girl martyr.

'I will get up and go out,' said Vincent. 'I have three matches. I am off my head. I shall really be nervous presently if I don't look out.'

He got up and struck a match, refused his eyes the sight of the corpse whose waxen face he had felt in the blackness, and made his way through the crowd of figures. By the match's flicker they seemed to make way for him, to turn their heads to look after him. The match lasted till he got to a turn of the rock-hewn passage. His next match showed him the burial scene: the little, thin body of the martyr, palm in hand, lying on the rock floor in patient waiting, the grave-digger, the mourners. Some standing, some kneeling, one crouched on the ground.

This was where that sound had come from, that rustle, that sigh. He had thought he was going away from it: instead, he had come straight to the spot where, if anywhere, his nerves might be expected to play him false.

'Bah!' he said, and he said it aloud, 'the silly things are only wax. Who's afraid?' His voice sounded loud in the silence that lives with the wax people. 'They're only wax,' he said again, and touched with his foot, contemptuously, the crouching figure in the mantle.

And, as he touched it, it raised its head and looked vacantly at him, and its eyes were mobile and alive. He staggered back against another figure, and dropped the match. In the new darkness he heard the crouching figure move towards him. Then the darkness fitted in round him very closely.

✕

'What was it exactly that sent poor Vincent mad: you've never told me?' Rose asked the question. She and Edward were looking out over the pines and tamarisks, across the blue Mediterranean. They were very happy, because it was their honeymoon.

He told her about the Musée Grévin and the wager, but he did not state the terms of it.

'But why did he think you would be afraid?'

He told her why.

'And then what happened?'

'Why, I suppose he thought there was no time like the present — for his five pounds, you know — and he hid among the wax-works. And I missed my train, and *I* thought there was no time like the present. In fact, dear, I thought if I waited I should have time to make certain of funking it, so I hid there, too. And I put on my big black capuchon, and sat down right in one of the wax-work groups — they couldn't see me from the passage where you walk. And after they put the lights out I simply went to sleep; and I woke up — and there was a light, and I heard someone say: 'They're only wax,' and it was Vincent. He thought I was one of the wax people, till I looked at him; and I expect he thought I was one of them even then, poor chap. And his match went out, and while I was trying to find my railway reading-lamp that I'd got near me, he began to scream, and the night watchman came running. And now he thinks everyone in the asylum is made of wax, and he screams if they come near him. They have to put his food beside him while he's asleep. It's horrible. I can't help feeling as if it were my fault, somehow.'

'Of course it's not,' said Rose. 'Poor Vincent! Do you know I never *really* liked him.' There was a pause. Then she said: 'But how was it *you* weren't frightened?'

'I was,' he said, 'horribly frightened. I — I — it sounds idiotic, but I thought I should go mad at first — I did really:

and yet I *had* to go through with it. And then I got among the figures of the people in the Catacombs, the people who died for — for things, don't you know, died in such horrible ways. And there they were, so calm — and believing it was all all right. And I thought about what they'd gone through. It sounds awful rot I know, dear — but I expect I was sleepy. Those wax people, they sort of seemed as if they were alive, and were telling me there wasn't anything to be frightened about. I felt as if I were one of them, and they were all my friends, and they'd wake me if anything went wrong, so I just went to sleep.'

'I think I understand,' she said. But she didn't.

'And the odd thing is,' he went on, 'I've never been afraid of the dark since. Perhaps his calling me a coward had something to do with it.'

'I don't think so,' said she. And she was right. But she would never have understood how, nor why.

10 The Shadow

This is not an artistically rounded off ghost story, and nothing is explained in it, and there seems to be no reason why any of it should have happened. But that is no reason why it should not be told. You must have noticed that all the real ghost stories you have ever come close to, are like this in these respects — no explanation, no logical coherence. Here is the story.

⁂

There were three of us and another, but she had fainted suddenly at the second extra of the Christmas Dance, and had been put to bed in the dressing-room next to the room which we three shared. It had been one of those jolly, old-fashioned dances where nearly everybody stays the night, and the big country house is stretched to its utmost containing — guests harbouring on sofas, couches, settles, and even mattresses on floors. Some of the young men actually, I believe, slept on the great dining-table. We had talked of our partners, as girls will, and then the stillness of the manor house, broken only by the whisper of the wind in the cedar branches, and the scraping of their harsh fingers against our window panes, had pricked us to such a luxurious confidence in our surroundings of bright chintz and candle-flame and fire-light, that we had dared to talk of ghosts — in which, said we all, we did not believe one bit. We had told the story of the phantom coach, and the horribly strange bed, and the lady in the sacque, and the house in Berkeley Square.

We none of us believed in ghosts, but my heart, at least, seemed to leap to my throat and choke me there, when a tap came to our door — a tap faint, not to be mistaken.

'Who's there?' said the youngest of us, craning a lean neck towards the door. It opened slowly, and I give you my word the instant of suspense that followed is still reckoned among my life's least confident moments. Almost at once the door opened fully, and Miss Eastwich, my aunt's housekeeper, companion and general stand-by, looked in on us.

We all said 'Come in,' but she stood there. She was, at all normal hours, the most silent woman I have ever known. She stood and looked at us, and shivered a little. So did we — for in those days corridors were not warmed by hot-water pipes, and the air from the door was keen.

'I saw your light,' she said at last, 'and I thought it was late for you to be up — after all this gaiety. I thought perhaps —' her glance turned towards the door of the dressing-room.

'No,' I said, 'she's fast asleep.' I should have added a good-night, but the youngest of us forestalled my speech. She did not know Miss Eastwich as we others did; did not know how her persistent silence had built a wall round her — a wall that no one dared to break down with the commonplaces of talk, or the littlenesses of mere human relationship. Miss Eastwich's silence had taught us to treat her as a machine; and as other than a machine we never dreamed of treating her. But the youngest of us had seen Miss Eastwich for the first time that day. She was young, crude, ill-balanced, subject to blind, calf-like impulses. She was also the heiress of a rich tallow-chandler, but that has nothing to do with this part of the story. She jumped up from the hearth-rug, her unsuitably rich silk lace-trimmed dressing-gown falling back from her thin collar-bones, and ran to the door and put an arm round Miss Eastwich's prim, lisse-encircled neck. I gasped. I should as soon have dared to embrace Cleopatra's Needle. 'Come in,' said the youngest of us — 'come in and get warm. There's lots of cocoa left.' She drew Miss Eastwich in and shut the door.

The vivid light of pleasure in the housekeeper's pale eyes went through my heart like a knife. It would have been so easy to put an arm round her neck, if one had only thought she wanted an arm there. But it was not I who had thought that — and indeed, my arm might not have brought the light envoked by the thin arm of the youngest of us.

'Now,' the youngest went on eagerly, 'you shall have the very biggest, nicest chair, and the cocoa-pot's here on the hob as hot as hot — and we've all been telling ghost stories, only we don't believe in them a bit; and when you get warm you ought to tell one too.'

Miss Eastwich — that model of decorum and decently done duties, tell a ghost story!

'You're sure I'm not in your way,' Miss Eastwich said, stretching her hands to the blaze. I wondered whether housekeepers have fires in their rooms even at Christmas time. 'Not a bit' — I said it, and I hope I said it as warmly as I felt it. 'I — Miss Eastwich — I'd have asked you to come in other times — only I didn't think you'd care for girls' chatter.'

The third girl, who was really of no account, and that's why I have not said anything about her before, poured cocoa for our guest. I put my fleecy Madeira shawl round her shoulders. I could not think of anything else to do for her, and I found myself wishing desperately to do something. The smiles she gave us were quite pretty. People can smile prettily at forty or fifty, or even later, though girls don't realise this. It occurred to me, and this was another knife-thrust, that I had never seen Miss Eastwich smile — a real smile, before. The pale smiles of dutiful acquiescence were not of the same blood as this dimpling, happy, transfiguring look.

'This is very pleasant,' she said, and it seemed to me that I had never before heard her real voice. It did not please me to think that at the cost of cocoa, a fire, and my arm round her neck, I might have heard this new voice any time these six years.

'We've been telling ghost stories,' I said. 'The worst of it is, we don't believe in ghosts. No one one knows has ever seen one.'

'It's always what somebody told somebody who told somebody you know,' said the youngest of us, 'and you can't believe that, can you?'

'What the soldier said, is not evidence,' said Miss Eastwich. Will it be believed that the little Dickens quotation pierced one more keenly than the new smile or the new voice?

'And all the ghost stories are so beautifully rounded off — a murder committed on the spot — or a hidden treasure, or a warning ... I think that makes them harder to believe. The most horrid ghost-story I ever heard was one that was quite silly.'

'Tell it.'

'I can't — it doesn't sound anything to tell. Miss Eastwich ought to tell one.'

'Oh do,' said the youngest of us, and her salt cellars loomed dark, as she stretched her neck eagerly and laid an entreating arm on our guest's knee.

'The only thing that I ever knew of was — was hearsay,' she said slowly, 'till just the end.'

I knew she would tell her story, and I knew she had never before told it, and I knew she was only telling it now because she was proud, and this seemed the only way to pay for the fire and the cocoa, and the laying of that arm round her neck.

'Don't tell it,' I said suddenly, 'I know you'd rather not.'

'I daresay it would bore you,' she said meekly, and the youngest of us, who, after all, did not understand everything, glared resentfully at me.

'We should just *love* it,' she said. '*Do* tell us. Never mind if it isn't a real, proper, fixed up story. I'm certain anything *you* think ghostly would be quite too beautifully horrid for anything.'

Miss Eastwich finished her cocoa and reached up to set the cup on the mantelpiece.

'It can't do any harm,' she said to herself, 'they don't believe in ghosts, and it wasn't exactly a ghost either. And they're all over twenty — they're not babies.'

There was a breathing time of hush and expectancy. The fire crackled and the gas suddenly glared higher because the billiard lights had been put out. We heard the steps and voices of the men going along the corridors.

'It is really hardly worth telling,' Miss Eastwich said doubtfully, shading her faded face from the fire with her thin hand.

We all said, 'Go on — oh, go on — do!'

'Well,' she said, 'twenty years ago — and more than that, I had two friends, and I loved them more than anything in the world. And they married each other —'

She paused, and I knew just in what way she had loved each of them. The youngest of us said —

'How awfully nice for you. Do go on.'

She patted the youngest's shoulder, and I was glad that I had understood, and that the youngest of all hadn't. She went on.

'Well, after they were married, I didn't see much of them for a year or two; and then he wrote and asked me to come and stay, because his wife was ill, and I should cheer her up, and cheer him up as well; for it was a gloomy house, and he himself was growing gloomy too.'

I knew, as she spoke, that she had every line of that letter by heart.

'Well, I went. The address was in Lee, near London; in those days there were streets and streets of new villa-houses growing up round old brick mansions standing in their own grounds, with red walls round, you know, and a sort of flavour of coaching days, and post chaises, and Blackheath highwaymen about them. He had said the house was gloomy, and it was called 'The Firs', and I imagined my cab going through a dark, winding shrubbery, and drawing up in front of one of these sedate, old, square houses. Instead, we drew up in front of a large, smart villa, with iron railings, gay encaustic tiles leading from the iron gate to the stained-glass-panelled door, and for shrubbery only a few stunted cypresses and aucubas in the tiny front garden. But inside it was all warm and welcoming. He met me at the door.'

She was gazing into the fire, and I knew she had forgotten us. But the youngest girl of all still thought it was to us she was telling her story.

'He met me at the door,' she said again, 'and thanked me for coming, and asked me to forgive the past.'

'What past?' said that high priestess of the *inapropos*, the youngest of all.

'Oh — I suppose he meant because they hadn't invited me before, or something,' said Miss Eastwich worriedly, 'but it's a very dull story, I find, after all, and —'

'Do go on,' I said — then I kicked the youngest of us, and got up to rearrange Miss Eastwich's shawl, and said in blatant dumb show, over the shawled shoulder: 'Shut up, you little idiot —'

After another silence, the housekeeper's new voice went on.

'They were very glad to see me, and I was very glad to be there. You girls, now, have such troops of friends, but these two were all I had, all I had ever had. Mabel wasn't exactly ill, only weak and excitable. I thought he seemed more ill than she did. She went to bed early and before she went, she asked me to keep him company through his last pipe, so we went into the dining-room and sat in the two arm chairs on each side of the fireplace. They were covered with green leather I remember. There were bronze groups of horses and a black marble clock on the mantelpiece — all wedding-presents. He poured out some whisky for himself, but he hardly touched it. He sat looking into the fire. At last I said:

"What's wrong? Mabel looks as well as you could expect."

'He said, "Yes — but I don't know from one day to another that she won't begin to notice something wrong. That's why I wanted you to come. You were always so sensible and strong-minded, and Mabel's like a little bird on a flower."

'I said yes, of course, and waited for him to go on. I thought he must be in debt, or in trouble of some sort. So I just waited. Presently he said:

"Margaret, this is a very peculiar house —" he always called me Margaret. You see we'd been such old friends. I told him I thought the house was very pretty, and fresh, and homelike — only a little too new — but that fault would mend with time. He said:

"It *is* new: that's just it. We're the first people who've ever lived in it. If it were an old house, Margaret, I should think it was haunted."

'I asked if he had seen anything. "No," he said, "not yet."

'Heard then?' said I.

"No — not heard either," he said "but there's a sort of feeling: I can't describe it — I've seen nothing and I've heard nothing, but I've been so near to seeing and hearing, just near, that's all. And something follows me about — only when I turn round, there's never anything, only my shadow. And I always feel that I *shall* see the thing next minute — but I never do — not quite — it's always just not visible."

'I thought he'd been working rather hard — and tried to cheer him up by making light of all this. It was just nerves, I said. Then he said he had thought I could help him, and did I think anyone he had wronged could have laid a curse on him, and did I believe in curses. I said I didn't — and the only person anyone could have said he had wronged forgave him freely, I knew, if there was anything to forgive. So I told him this too.'

It was I, not the youngest of us, who knew the name of that person, wronged and forgiving.

'So then I said he ought to take Mabel away from the house and have a complete change. But he said No; Mabel had got everything in order, and he could never manage to get her away just now without explaining everything — "and, above all," he said, "she mustn't guess there's anything wrong. I daresay I shan't feel quite such a lunatic now you're here."

'So we said goodnight.'

'Is that all the story!' said the third girl, striving to convey that even as it stood it was a good story.

'That's only the beginning,' said Miss Eastwich. 'Whenever I was alone with him he used to tell me the same thing over and over again, and at first when I began to notice things, I tried to think that it was his talk that had upset my nerves. The odd thing was that it wasn't only at night — but in broad daylight — and particularly on the stairs and passages. On the staircase the feeling used to be so awful that I have had to bite my lips till they bled to keep myself from running upstairs at full speed. Only I knew if I did I should go mad at the top. There was always something behind me — exactly as he had said — something that one could just not see. And a sound that one could just not hear. There was a long corridor at the top of the house. I have sometimes almost seen something — you know how one sees things without looking — but if I turned round, it seemed as if the thing drooped and melted into my shadow. There was a little window at the end of the corridor.

'Downstairs there was another corridor, something like it, with a cupboard at one end and the kitchen at the other. One night I went down into the kitchen to heat some milk for Mabel. The servants had gone to bed. As I stood by the fire, waiting for the milk to boil, I glanced through the open door and along the passage. I never could keep my eyes on what I was doing in that house. The cupboard door was partly open; they used to keep empty boxes and things in it. And, as I looked, I knew that now it was not going to be 'almost' anymore. Yet I said, 'Mabel?' not because I thought it could be Mabel who was crouching down there, half in and half out of the cupboard. The thing was grey at first, and then it was black. And when I whispered, 'Mabel,' it seemed to sink down till it lay like a pool of ink on the floor, and then its edges drew in, and it seemed to flow, like ink when you tilt up the paper you have spilt it on; and it flowed into the cupboard till it was all gathered into the shadow there. I saw it go quite plainly. The gas was full on in the kitchen. I screamed aloud, but even then, I'm thankful to say, I had enough sense to upset the boiling milk, so that when he came downstairs three steps at a time, I had the excuse for my scream of a scalded hand. The explanation satisfied Mabel, but next night he said:

"Why didn't you tell me? It was that cupboard. All the horror of the house comes out of that. Tell me — have you seen anything yet? Or is it only the nearly seeing and nearly hearing still?"

'I said, "You must tell me first what you've seen." He told me, and his eyes wandered, as he spoke, to the shadows by the curtains, and I turned up all three gas lights, and lit the candles on the mantelpiece. Then we looked at each other and said we were both mad, and thanked God that Mabel at least was sane. For what he had seen was what I had seen.

'After that I hated to be alone with a shadow, because at any moment I might see something that would crouch, and sink, and lie like a black pool, and then slowly draw itself into the shadow that was nearest. Often that shadow was my own.

The thing came first at night, but afterwards there was no hour safe from it. I saw it at dawn and at noon, in the dusk and in the firelight, and always it crouched and sank, and was a pool that flowed into some shadow and became part of it. And always I saw it with a straining of the eyes — a pricking and aching. It seemed as though I could only just see it, as if my sight, to see it, had to be strained to the uttermost. And still the sound was in the house — the sound that I could just not hear. At last, one morning early, I did hear it. It was close behind me, and it was only a sigh. It was worse than the thing that crept into the shadows.

'I don't know how I bore it. I couldn't have borne it, if I hadn't been so fond of them both. But I knew in my heart that, if he had no one to whom he could speak openly, he would go mad, or tell Mabel. His was not a very strong character; very sweet, and kind, and gentle, but not strong. He was always easily led. So I stayed on and bore up, and we were very cheerful, and made little jokes, and tried to be amusing when Mabel was with us. But when we were alone, we did not try to be amusing. And sometimes a day or two would go by without our seeing or hearing anything, and we should perhaps have fancied that we had fancied what we had seen and heard — only there was always the feeling of there being something about the house, that one could just not hear and not see. Sometimes we used to try not to talk about it, but generally we talked of nothing else at all. And the weeks went by, and Mabel's baby was born. The nurse and the doctor said that both mother and child were doing well. He and I sat late in the dining-room that night. We had neither of us seen or heard anything for three days; our anxiety about Mabel was lessened. We talked of the future — it seemed then so much brighter than the past. We arranged that, the moment she was fit to be moved, he should take her away to the sea, and I should superintend the moving of their furniture into the new house he had already chosen. He was gayer than I had seen him since his marriage — almost like his old self. When I said goodnight to him, he said a lot of things about my having been a comfort to them both. I hadn't done anything much, of course, but still I am glad he said them.

'Then I went upstairs, almost for the first time without that feeling of something following me. I listened at Mabel's door. Everything was quiet. I went on towards my own room, and in an instant I felt that there *was* something behind me. I turned. It was crouching there; it sank, and the black fluidness of it seemed to be sucked under the door of Mabel's room.

'I went back. I opened the door a listening inch. All was still. And then I heard a sigh close behind me. I opened the door and went in. The nurse and the baby were asleep. Mabel was asleep too — she looked so pretty — like a tired child — the baby was cuddled up into one of her arms with its tiny head against her side. I prayed then that Mabel might never know the terrors that he and I had known. That those little ears might never hear any but pretty sounds, those clear eyes never see any but pretty sights. I did not dare to pray for a long time after that. Because my prayer was answered. She never saw, never heard anything more in this world. And now I could do nothing more for him or for her.

'When they had put her in her coffin, I lighted wax candles round her, and laid the horrible white flowers that people will send near her, and then I saw he had followed me. I took his hand to lead him away.

'At the door we both turned. It seemed to us that we heard a sigh. He would have sprung to her side, in I don't know what mad, glad hope. But at that instant we both saw it. Between us and the coffin, first grey, then black, it crouched an instant, then sank and liquified — and was gathered together and drawn till it ran into the nearest shadow. And the nearest shadow was the shadow of Mabel's coffin. I left the next day. His mother came. She had never liked me.'

Miss Eastwich paused. I think she had quite forgotten us.

'Didn't you see him again?' asked the youngest of us all.

'Only once,' Miss Eastwich answered, 'and something black crouched then between him and me. But it was only his second wife, crying beside his coffin. It's not a cheerful story is it? And it doesn't lead anywhere. I've never told anyone else. I think it was seeing his daughter that brought it all back.'

She looked towards the dressing-room door.

'Mabel's baby?'

'Yes — and exactly like Mabel, only with his eyes.'

The youngest of all had Miss Eastwich's hands, and was petting them.

Suddenly the woman wrenched her hands away, and stood at her gaunt height, her hands clenched, eyes straining. She was looking at something that we could not see, and I know what the man in the Bible meant when he said: 'The hair of my flesh stood up.'

What she saw seemed not quite to reach the height of the dressing-room door handle. Her eyes followed it down, down — widening and widening. Mine followed them — all the nerves of them seemed strained to the uttermost — and I almost saw — or did I quite see? I can't be certain. But we all heard the long-drawn, quivering sigh. And to each of us it seemed to be breathed just behind us.

It was I who caught up the candle — it dripped wax all over my trembling hand — and was dragged by Miss Eastwich to the girl who had fainted during the second extra. But it was the youngest of all whose lean arms were round the housekeeper when we turned away, and that have been round her many a time since, in the new home where she keeps house for the youngest of us.

The doctor who came in the morning said that Mabel's daughter had died of heart disease — which she had inherited from her mother. It was that that made her faint during the second extra. But I have sometimes wondered whether she may not have inherited something from her father. I have never been able to forget the look on her dead face.

11 The House of Silence

The thief stood close under the high wall, and looked to right and left. To the right the road wound white and sinuous, lying like a twisted ribbon over the broad grey shoulder of the hill; to the left the road turned sharply down towards the river; beyond the ford the road went away slowly in a curve, prolonged for miles through the green marshes.

No least black fly of a figure stirred on it. There were no travellers at such an hour on such a road.

The thief looked across the valley, at the top of the mountain flushed with sunset, and at the grey-green of the olives about its base. The terraces of olives were already dusk with twilight, but his keen eyes could not have missed the smallest variance or shifting of their lights and shadows. Nothing stirred there. He was alone.

Then, turning, he looked again at the wall behind him. The face of it was grey and sombre, but all along the top of it, in the crannies of the coping stones, orange wallflowers and sulphur-coloured snapdragons shone among the haze of feathery-flowered grasses. He looked again at the place where some of the stones had fallen from the coping — had fallen within the wall, for none lay in the road without. The bough of a mighty tree covered the gap with its green mantle from the eyes of any chance wayfarer; but the thief was no chance wayfarer, and he had surprised the only infidelity of the great wall to its trust.

To the chance wayfarer, too, the wall's denial had seemed absolute, unanswerable. Its solid stone, close knit by mortar hardly less solid, showed not only a defence, it offered a defiance — a menace. But the thief had learnt his trade; he saw that the mortar might be loosened a little here, broken a little there, and now the crumbs of it fell rustling on to the dry, dusty grass of the roadside. He drew back, took two quick steps forward, and, with a spring, sudden and agile as a cat's, grasped the wall where the gap showed, and drew himself up. Then he rubbed his hands on his knees, because his hands were bloody from the sudden grasping of the rough stones, and sat astride on the wall.

He parted the leafy boughs and looked down; below him lay the stones that had fallen from the wall — already grass was growing upon the mound they made. As he ventured his head beyond the green leafage, the level light of the sinking sun struck him in the eyes. It was like a blow. He dropped softly from the wall and stood in the shadow of the tree — looking, listening.

Before him stretched the park — wide and still; dotted here and there with trees, and overlaid with gold poured from the west. He held his breath and listened. There was no wind to stir the leaves to those rustlings which may deceive and disconcert the keenest and the boldest; only the sleepy twitter of birds, and the little sudden soft movements of them in the dusky privacy of the thick-leaved branches. There was in all the broad park no sign of any other living thing.

The thief trod softly along under the wall where the trees were thickest, and at every step he paused to look and listen.

It was quite suddenly that he came upon the little lodge near the great gates of wrought iron with the marble gate-posts bearing upon them the two gaunt griffins, the cognisance of the noble house whose lands these were. The thief drew back into the shadow and stood still, only his heart beat thickly. He stood still as the tree trunk beside him, looking, listening. He told himself that he heard nothing — saw nothing — yet he became aware of things. That the door of the lodge was not closed, that some of its windows were broken, and that into its little garden straw and litter had drifted from the open door: and that between the stone step and the threshold grass was growing inches high. When he was aware of this he stepped forward and entered the lodge. All the sordid sadness of a little deserted home met him here — broken crocks and bent pans, straw, old rags, and a brooding, dusty stillness.

'There has been no one here since the old keeper died. They told the truth,' said the thief; and he made haste to leave the lodge, for there was nothing in it now that any man need covet — only desolation and the memory of death.

So he went slowly among the trees, and by devious ways drew a little nearer to the great house that stood in its walled garden in the middle of the park. From very far off, above the green wave of trees that broke round it, he could see the towers of it rising black against the sunset; and between the trees came glimpses of its marble white where the faint grey light touched it from the east.

Moving slowly — vigilant, alert, with eyes turning always to right and to left, with ears which felt the intense silence more acutely than they could have felt any tumult — the thief reached the low wall of the garden, at the western side. The last redness of the sunset's reflection had lighted all the many windows, and the vast place blazed at him for an instant before the light dipped behind the black bar of the trees, and left him face to face with a pale house, whose windows now were black and hollow, and seemed like eyes that watched him. Every window was closed; the lower ones were guarded by jalousies; through the glass of the ones above he could see the set painted faces of the shutters.

From far off he had heard, and known, the plash-plash of fountains, and now he saw their white changing columns rise and fall against the background of the terrace. The garden was full of rose bushes trailing and unpruned; and the heavy, happy scent of the roses, still warm from the sun, breathed through the place, exaggerating the sadness of its tangled desolation. Strange figures gleamed in the deepening dusk, but they were too white to be feared. He crept into a corner where Psyche drooped in marble, and, behind her pedestal, crouched. He took food from his pockets and ate and drank. And between the mouthfuls he listened and watched.

The moon rose, and struck a pale fire from the face of the house and from the marble limbs of the statues, and the gleaming water of the fountains drew the moonbeams into the unchanging change of its rise and fall.

Something rustled and stirred among the roses. The thief grew rigid: his heart seemed suddenly hollow; he held his breath. Through the deepening shadows something gleamed white; and not marble, for it moved, it came towards him. Then the silence of the night was shattered by a scream, as the white shape glided into the moonlight. The thief resumed his munching, and another shape glimmered after the first. 'Curse the beasts!' he said, and took another draught from his bottle, as the white peacocks were blotted out by the shadows of the trees, and the stillness of the night grew more intense.

In the moonlight the thief went round and about the house, pushing through the trailing briers that clung to him — and now grown bolder he looked closely at doors and windows. But all were fast barred as the doors of a tomb. And the silence deepened as the moonlight waxed.

There was one little window, high up, that showed no shutter. He looked at it; measured its distance from the ground and from the nearest of the great chestnut trees. Then he walked along under the avenue of chestnuts with head thrown back and eyes fixed on the mystery of their interlacing branches.

At the fifth tree he stopped; leaped to the lowest bough, missed it; leaped again, caught it, and drew up his body. Then climbing, creeping, swinging, while the leaves, agitated by his progress, rustled to the bending of the boughs, he passed to that tree, to the next — swift, assured, unhesitating. And so from tree to tree, till he was at the last tree — and on the bough that stretched to touch the little window with its leaves.

He swung from this. The bough bent and cracked, and would have broken, but that at the only possible instant the thief swung forward, felt the edge of the window with his feet, loosed the bough, sprang, and stood, flattened against the mouldings, clutching the carved drip-stone with his hands. He thrust his knee through the window, waiting for the tinkle of the falling glass to settle into quietness, opened the window, and crept in. He found himself in a corridor: he could see the long line of its white windows, and the bars of moonlight falling across the inlaid wood of its floor.

He took out his thief's lantern — high and slender like a tall cup — lighted it, and crept softly along the corridor, listening between his steps till the silence grew to be like a humming in his ears.

And slowly, stealthily, he opened door after door; the rooms were spacious and empty — his lantern's yellow light flashing into their corners told him this. Some poor, plain furniture he discerned, a curtain or a bench here and there, but not what he sought. So large was the house, that presently it seemed to the thief that for many hours he had been wandering along its galleries, creeping down its wide stairs, opening the grudging doors of the dark, empty rooms, whose silence spoke ever more insistently in his ears.

'But it is as he told me,' he said inwardly; 'no living soul in all the place. The old man — a servant of this great house — he told me; he knew, and I have found all even as he said.'

Then the thief turned away from the arched emptiness of the grand staircase, and in a far corner of the hall he found himself speaking in a whisper because now it seemed to him that nothing would serve but that this clamorous silence should be stilled by a human voice.

'The old man said it would be thus — all emptiness, and not profit to a man; and he died, and I tended him. Dear Jesus! how our good deeds come home to us! And he told me how the last of the great family had gone away none knew whither. And the tales I heard in the town — how the great man had not gone, but lived here in hiding — It is not possible. There is the silence of death in this house.'

He moistened his lips with his tongue. The stillness of the place seemed to press upon him like a solid thing. 'It is like a dead man on one's shoulders,' thought the thief, and he straightened himself up and whispered again: 'The old man said, "The door with the carved griffin, and the roses enwreathed, and the seventh rose holds the secret in its heart."'

With that the thief set forth again, creeping softly across the bars of moonlight down the corridor.

And after much seeking he found at last, under the angle of the great stone staircase behind a mouldering tapestry wrought with peacocks and pines, a door, and on it carved a griffin, wreathed about with roses. He pressed his finger into the deep heart of each carven rose, and when he pressed the rose that was seventh in number from the griffin, he felt the inmost part of it move beneath his finger as though it sought to escape. So he pressed more strongly, leaning against the door till it swung open, and he passed through it, looking behind him to see that nothing followed. The door he closed as he entered.

And now he was, as it seemed, in some other house. The chambers were large and lofty as those whose hushed emptiness he had explored — but these rooms seemed warm with life, yet held no threat, no terror. To the dim yellow flicker from the lantern came out of the darkness hints of a crowded magnificence, a lavish profusion of beautiful objects such as he had never in his life dreamed of, though all that life had been one dream of the lovely treasures which rich men hoard, and which, by the thief's skill and craft, may come to be his.

He passed through the rooms, turning the light of his lantern this way and that, and ever the darkness withheld more than the light revealed. He knew that thick tapestries hung from the walls, velvet curtains masked the windows; his hand, exploring eagerly, felt the rich carving of chairs and presses; the great beds were hung with silken cloth wrought in gold thread with glimmering strange starry devices. Broad sideboards flashed back to his lantern's questionings the faint white laugh of silver; the tall cabinets could not, with all their reserve, suppress the confession of wrought gold, and, from the caskets into whose depths he flashed the light, came the trembling avowal of rich jewels. And now, at last, that carved door closed between him and the poignant silence of the deserted corridors, the thief felt a sudden gaiety of heart, a sense of escape, of security. He was alone, yet warmed and companioned. The silence here was no longer a horror, but a consoler, a friend.

And, indeed, now he was not alone. The ample splendours about him, the spoils which long centuries had yielded to the grasp of a noble family — these were companions after his own heart.

He flung open the shade of his lantern and held it high above his head. The room still kept half its secrets. The discretion of the darkness should be broken down. He must see more of this splendour — not in unsatisfying dim detail, but in the lit gorgeous mass of it. The narrow bar of the lantern's light chafed him. He sprang on to the dining-table, and began to light the half-burnt chandelier. There were a hundred candles, and he lighted all, so that the chandelier swung like a vast living jewel in the centre of the hall. Then, as he turned, all the colour in the room leapt out at him. The purple of the couches, the green gleam of the delicate glass, the blue of the tapestries, and the vivid scarlet of the velvet hangings, and with the colour sprang the gleams of white from the silver, of yellow from the gold, of many-coloured fire from strange inlaid work and jewelled caskets, till the thief stood aghast with rapture in the strange, sudden revelation of this concentrated splendour.

He went along the walls with a lighted candle in his hand — the wax dripped warm over his fingers as he went — lighting one after another, the tapers in the sconces of the silver-framed glasses. In the state bedchamber he drew back suddenly, face to face with a death-white countenance in which black eyes blazed at him with triumph and delight. Then he laughed aloud. He had not known his own face in the strange depths of this mirror. It had no sconces like the others, or he would have known it for what it was. It was framed in Venice glass — wonderful, gleaming, iridescent.

The thief dropped the candle and threw his arms wide with a gesture of supreme longing.

'If I could carry it all away! All, all! Every beautiful thing! To sell some — the less beautiful, and to live with the others all my days!'

And now a madness came over the thief. So little a part of all these things could he bear away with him; yet all were his — his for the taking — even the huge carved presses and the enormous vases of solid silver, too heavy for him to lift — even these were his: had he not found them — he, by his own skill and cunning? He went about in the rooms, touching one after the other the beautiful, rare things. He caressed the gold and the jewels. He threw his arms round the great silver vases; he wound round himself the heavy red velvet of the curtain where the griffins gleamed in embossed gold, and shivered with pleasure at the soft clinging of its embrace. He found, in a tall cupboard, curiously-shaped flasks of wine, such wine as he had never tasted, and he drank of it slowly — in little sips — from a silver goblet and from a green Venice glass, and from a cup of rare pink china, knowing that any one of his drinking vessels was worth enough to keep him in idleness for a long year. For the thief had learnt his trade, and it is a part of a thief's trade to know the value of things.

He threw himself on the rich couches, sat in the stately carved chairs, leaned his elbows on the ebony tables. He buried his hot face in the chill, smooth linen of the great bed, and wondered to find it still scented delicately as though some sweet woman had lain there but last night. He went hither and thither laughing with pure pleasure, and making to himself an unbridled carnival of the joys of possession.

In this wise the night wore on, and with the night his madness wore away. So presently he went about among the treasures — no more with the eyes of a lover, but with the eyes of a connoisseur — and he chose those precious stones which he knew for the most precious, and put them in the bag he had brought, and with them some fine-wrought goldsmith's work and the goblet out of which he had drunk the wine. Though it was but of silver, he would not leave it. The green Venice glass he broke and the cup, for he said: 'No man less fortunate than I, tonight, shall ever again drink from them.' But he harmed nothing else of all the beautiful things, because he loved them.

Then, leaving the low, uneven ends of the candles still alight, he turned to the door by which he had come in. There were two doors, side by side, carved with straight lilies, and between them a panel wrought with the griffin and the seven roses enwreathed. He pressed his finger in the heart of the seventh rose, hardly hoping that the panel would move, and indeed it did not; and he was about to seek for a secret spring among the lilies, when he perceived that one of the doors wrought with these had opened itself a little. So he passed through it and closed it after him.

'I must guard my treasures,' he said. But when he had passed through the door and closed it, and put out his hand to raise the tattered tapestry that covered it from without, his hand met the empty air, and he knew that he had not come out by the door through which he had entered.

When the lantern was lighted, it showed him a vaulted passage, whose floor and whose walls were stone, and there was a damp air and a mouldering scent in it, as of a cellar long unopened. He was cold now, and the room with the wine and the treasures seemed long ago and far away, though but a door and a moment divided him from it, and though some of the wine was in his body, and some of the treasure in his hands. He set about to find the way to the quiet night outside, for this seemed to him a haven and a safeguard since, with the closing of that door, he had shut away warmth, and light, and companionship. He was enclosed in walls once more, and once more menaced by the invading silence that was almost a presence. Once more it seemed to him that he must creep softly, must hold his breath before he ventured to turn a corner — for always he felt that he was not alone, that near him was something, and that its breath, too, was held.

So he went by many passages and stairways, and could find no way out; and after a long time of searching he crept by another way back to come unawares on the door which shut him off from the room where the many lights were, and the wine and the treasure. Then terror leaped out upon him from the dark hush of the place, and he beat on the door with his hands and cried aloud, till the echo of his cry in the groined roof cowed him back into silence.

Again he crept stealthily by strange passages, and again

could find no way except, after much wandering, back to the door where he had begun.

And now the fear of death beat in his brain with blows like a hammer. To die here like a rat in a trap, never to see the sun alight again, never to climb in at a window, or see brave jewels shine under his lantern, but to wander, and wander, and wander between these inexorable walls till he died, and the rats, admitting him to their brotherhood, swarmed round the dead body of him.

'I had better have been born a fool,' said the thief.

Then once more he went through the damp and the blackness of the vaulted passages, tremulously searching for some outlet, but in vain.

Only at last, in a corner behind a pillar, he found a very little door and a stair that led down. So he followed it, to wander among other corridors and cellars, with the silence heavy about him, and despair growing thick and cold like a fungus about his heart, and in his brain the fear of death beating like a hammer.

It was quite suddenly in his wanderings, which had grown into an aimless frenzy, having now less of search in it than of flight from the insistent silence, that he saw at last a light — and it was the light of day coming through an open door. He stood at the door and breathed the air of the morning. The sun had risen and touched the tops of the towers of the house with white radiance; the birds were singing loudly. It was morning, then, and he was a free man.

He looked about him for a way to come at the park, and thence to the broken wall and the white road, which he had come by a very long time before. For this door opened on an inner enclosed courtyard, still in damp shadow, though the sun above struck level across it — a courtyard where tall weeds grew thick and dank. The dew of the night was heavy on them.

As he stood and looked, he was aware of a low, buzzing sound that came from the other side of the courtyard. He pushed through the weeds towards it; and the sense of a presence in the silence came upon him more than ever it had done in the darkened house, though now it was day, and the birds sang all gaily, and the good sun shone so bravely overhead.

As he thrust aside the weeds which grew waist-high, he trod on something that seemed to writhe under his feet like a snake. He started back and looked down. It was the long, firm, heavy plait of a woman's hair. And just beyond lay the green gown of a woman, and a woman's hands, and her golden head, and her eyes; all about the place where she lay was the thick buzzing of flies, and the black swarming of them.

The thief saw, and he turned and he fled back to his doorway, and down the steps and through the maze of vaulted passages — fled in the dark, and empty-handed, because when he had come into the presence that informed that house with silence, he had dropped lantern and treasure, and fled wildly, the horror in his soul driving him before it. Now fear is more wise than cunning, so, whereas he had sought for hours with his lantern and with all his thief's craft to find the way out, and had sought in vain, he now, in the dark and blindly, without thought or will, without pause or let, found the one way that led to a door, shot back the bolts, and fled through the awakened rose garden and across the dewy park.

He dropped from the wall into the road, and stood there looking eagerly to right and left. To the right the road wound white and sinuous, like a twisted ribbon over the great, grey shoulder of the hill; to the left the road curved down towards the river. No least black fly of a figure stirred on it. There are no travellers on such a road at such an hour.

12 Number 17

I yawned. I could not help it. But the flat, inexorable voice went on.

'Speaking from the journalistic point of view — I may tell you, gentlemen, that I once occupied the position of advertisement editor to the *Bradford Woollen Goods Journal* — and speaking from that point of view, I hold the opinion that all the best ghost stories have been written over and over again; and if I were to leave the road and return to a literary career I should never be led away by ghosts. Realism's what's wanted nowadays, if you want to be up-to-date.'

The large commercial paused for breath.

'You never can tell with the public,' said the lean, elderly traveller; 'it's like in the fancy business. You never know how it's going to be. Whether it's a clockwork ostrich or Sometite silk or a particular shape of shaded glass novelty or a tobacco-box got up to look like a raw chop, you never know your luck.'

'That depends on who you are,' said the dapper man in the corner by the fire. 'If you've got the right push about you, you can make a thing go, whether it's a clockwork kitten or imitation meat, and with stories, I take it, it's just the same — realism or ghost stories. But the best ghost story would be the realest one, *I* think.'

The large commercial had got his breath.

'I don't believe in ghost stories, myself,' he was saying with earnest dullness; 'but there was rather a queer thing happened to a second cousin of an aunt of mine by marriage — a very sensible woman with no nonsense about her. And the soul of truth and honour. I shouldn't have believed it if she had been one of your flighty, fanciful sort.'

'Don't tell us the story,' said the melancholy man who travelled in hardware; 'you'll make us afraid to go to bed.'

The well-meant effort failed. The large commercial went on, as I had known he would; his words overflowed his mouth, as his person overflowed his chair. I turned my mind to my own affairs, coming back to the commercial room in time to hear the summing up.

'The doors were all locked, and she was quite certain she saw a tall, white figure glide past her and vanish. I wouldn't have believed it if —' And so on *da capo*, from 'if she hadn't been the second cousin' to the 'soul of truth and honour.'

I yawned again.

'Very good story,' said the smart little man by the fire. He was a traveller, as the rest of us were; his presence in the room told us that much. He had been rather silent during dinner, and afterwards, while the red curtains were being drawn and the red and black cloth laid between the glasses and the decanters and the mahogany, he had quietly taken the best chair in the warmest corner. We had got our letters written and the large traveller had been boring for some time before I even noticed that there was a best chair, and that this silent, bright-eyed, dapper, fair man had secured it.

'Very good story,' he said, 'but it's not what I call realism. You don't tell us half enough, sir. You don't say when it happened or where, or the time of year, or what colour your aunt's second cousin's hair was. Nor yet you don't tell us what it was she saw, nor what the room was like where she saw it, nor why she saw it, nor what happened afterwards. And I shouldn't like to breathe a word against anybody's aunt by marriage's cousin, first or second, but I must say I like a story about what a man's seen *himself*.'

'So do I,' the large commercial snorted, 'when I hear it.'

He blew his nose like a trumpet of defiance.

'But,' said the rabbit-faced man, 'we know nowadays, what with the advance of science and all that sort of thing, we know there aren't any such things as ghosts. They're hallucinations; that's what they are — hallucinations.'

'Don't seem to matter what you call them,' the dapper one urged. 'If you see a thing that looks as real as you do yourself, a thing that makes your blood run cold and turns you sick and silly with fear — well, call it ghost, or call it hallucination, or call it Tommy Dodd; it isn't the *name* that matters.'

The elderly commercial coughed and said, 'You might call it another name. You might call it —'

'No, you mightn't,' said the little man, briskly, 'not when the man it happened to had been a teetotal Bond of Joy for five years and is to this day.'

'Why don't you tell us the story?' I asked.

'I might be willing,' he said, 'if the rest of the company were agreeable. Only I warn you it's not that sort-of-a kind-of-a-somebody-fancied-they-saw-a-sort-of-a-kind-of-a-something-sort of a story. No, sir. Everything I'm going to tell you is plain and straightforward and as clear as a time-table — clearer than some. But I don't much like telling it, especially to people who don't believe in ghosts.'

Several of us said we did believe in ghosts. The heavy man snorted and looked at his watch. And the man in the best chair began.

'Turn the gas down a bit, will you? Thanks. Did any of you know Herbert Hatteras? He was on this road a good many years. No? Well, never mind. He was a good chap, I believe, with good teeth and a black whisker. But I didn't know him myself. He was before my time. Well, this that I'm going to tell you about happened at a certain commercial hotel. I'm not going to give it a name, because that sort of thing gets about, and in every other respects it's a good house and reasonable, and we all have our living to get. It was just a good ordinary old-fashioned commercial hotel, as it might be this. And I've often used it since, though they've never put me in that room again. Perhaps they shut it up after what happened.

'Well, the beginning of it was, I came across an old schoolfellow; in Boulter's Lock one Sunday it was, I remember. Jones was his name, Ted Jones. We both had canoes. We had tea at Marlow, and we got talking about this and that and old times and old mates; and do you remember Jim, and what's become of Tom, and so on. Oh, you know. And I happened to ask after his brother, Fred by name. And Ted turned pale and almost dropped his cup, and he said, "You don't mean to say you haven't heard?" "No," says I, mopping up the tea he'd slopped over with my handkerchief. "No, what?" I said.

"It was horrible," he said. "They wired for me, and I saw him afterwards. Whether he'd done it himself or not, nobody knows; but they'd found him lying on the floor with his throat cut." No cause could be assigned for the rash act, Ted told me. I asked him where it had happened, and he told me the name of this hotel — I'm not going to name it. And when I'd sympathized with him and drawn him out about old times and poor old Fred being such a good old sort and all that, I asked him what the room was like. I always like to know what the places look like where things happen.

'No, there wasn't anything specially rum about the room, only that it had a French bed with red curtains in a sort of alcove; and a large mahogany wardrobe as big as a hearse, with a glass door; and, instead of a swing-glass, a carved, black-framed glass screwed up against the wall between the windows, and a picture of 'Belshazzar's Feast' over the mantelpiece. I beg your pardon?' He stopped, for the heavy commercial had opened his mouth and shut it again.

'I thought you were going to say something,' the dapper man went on. 'Well, we talked about other things and parted, and I thought no more about it till business brought me to

— but I'd better not name the town either — and I found my firm had marked this very hotel — where poor Fred had met his death, you know — for me to put up at. And I had to put up there too, because of their addressing everything to me there. And, anyhow, I expect I should have gone there out of curiosity.

'No, I didn't believe in ghosts in those days. I was like you, sir.' He nodded amiably to the large commercial.

'The house was very full, and we were quite a large party in the room — very pleasant company, as it might be tonight; and we got talking of ghosts — just as it might be us. And there was a chap in glasses, sitting just over there, I remember — an old hand on the road, he was; and he said, just as it might be any of you, "I don't believe in ghosts but I wouldn't care to sleep in Number Seventeen, for all that"; and, of course, we asked him why. "Because," said he, very short, "that's why."

'But when we'd persuaded him a bit, he told us.

'"Because that's the room where chaps cut their throats," he said. "There was a chap called Bert Hatteras began it. They found him weltering in his gore. And since that every man that's slept there's been found with his throat cut."

'I asked him how many had slept there. "Well, only two beside the first," he said; "they shut it up then." "Oh, did they?" said I. "Well, they've opened it again. Number Seventeen's my room!"

'I tell you those chaps looked at me.

'"But you aren't going to sleep in it?" one of them said. And I explained that I didn't pay half a dollar for a bedroom to keep awake in.

'"I suppose it's press of business has made them open it up again," the chap in spectacles said. "It's a very mysterious affair. There's some secret horror about that room that we don't understand," he said, "and I'll tell you another queer thing. Every one of those poor chaps was a commercial gentleman. That's what I don't like about it. There was Bert Hatteras — he was the first, and a chap called Jones — Frederick Jones, and then Donald Overshaw — a Scotchman he was, and travelled in child's underclothing."

'Well, we sat there and talked a bit, and if I hadn't been a Bond of Joy, I don't know that I mightn't have exceeded, gentlemen — yes, positively exceeded; for the more I thought about it the less I liked the thought of Number Seventeen. I hadn't noticed the room particularly, except to see that the furniture had been changed since poor Fred's time. So I just slipped out, by and by, and I went out to the little glass case under the arch where the booking clerk sits — just like here, that hotel was — and I said:

"'Look here, miss, haven't you another room empty except seventeen?"

"'No,' she said, "I don't think so."

"'Then what's that?" I said, and pointed to a key hanging on the board, the only one left.

"'Oh,' she said, "that's sixteen."

"'Anyone in sixteen?" I said. "Is it a comfortable room?"

"'No,' said she. "Yes, quite comfortable. It's next door to yours — much the same class of room."

"'Then I'll have sixteen, if you've no objection," I said, and went back to the others feeling very clever.

'When I went up to bed I locked my door, and, though I didn't believe in ghosts, I wished seventeen wasn't next door to me, and I wished there wasn't a door between the two rooms, though the door was locked right enough and the key on my side. I'd only got the one candle besides the two on the dressing-table, which I hadn't lighted; and I got my collar and tie off before I noticed that the furniture in my new room was the furniture out of Number Seventeen; French bed with red curtains, mahogany wardrobe as big as a hearse, and the carved mirror over the dressing-table between the two windows, and 'Belshazzar's Feast' over the mantelpiece. So that, though I'd not got the room where the commercial gentlemen had cut their throats, I'd got the *furniture* out of it. And for a moment I thought that was worse than the other. When I thought of what that furniture could tell, if it could speak —

'It was a silly thing to do — but we're all friends here and I don't mind owning up — I looked under the bed and I looked inside the hearse-wardrobe and I looked in a sort of narrow cupboard there was, where a body could have stood upright —'

'A body?' I repeated.

'A man, I mean. You see, it seemed to me that either these poor chaps had been murdered by someone who hid himself in Number Seventeen to do it, or else there was something there that frightened them into cutting their throats; and upon my soul, I can't tell you which idea I liked least!'

He paused, and filled his pipe very deliberately. 'Go on,' someone said. And he went on.

'Now, you'll observe,' he said, 'that all I've told you up to the time of my going to bed that night's just hearsay. So I don't ask you to believe it — though the three coroners' inquests would be enough to stagger most chaps, I should say. Still, what I'm going to tell you now's *my* part of the story — what happened to me myself in that room.'

He paused again, holding the pipe in his hand, unlighted.

There was a silence, which I broke.

'Well, what *did* happen?' I asked.

'I had a bit of a struggle with myself,' he said. 'I reminded myself it was not *that* room, but the next one that it had happened in. I smoked a pipe or two and read the morning paper, advertisements and all. And at last I went to bed. I left the candle burning, though, I own that.'

'Did you sleep?' I asked.

'Yes. I slept. Sound as a top. I was awakened by a soft tapping on my door. I sat up. I don't think I've ever been so frightened in my life. But I made myself say, "Who's there?" in a whisper. Heaven knows I never expected anyone to answer. The candle had gone out and it was pitch-dark. There was a quiet murmur and a shuffling sound outside. And no one answered. I tell you I hadn't expected anyone to. But I cleared my throat and cried out, "Who's there?" in a real out-loud voice. And "Me, sir," said a voice. "Shaving-water, sir, six o'clock, sir."

'It was the chambermaid.'

A movement of relief ran round our circle.

'I don't think much of your story,' said the large commercial.

'You haven't heard it yet,' said the story-teller, dryly. 'It was six o'clock on a winter's morning, and pitch-dark. My train went at seven. I got up and began to dress. My one candle wasn't much use. I lighted the two on the dressing table to see to shave by. There wasn't any shaving-water outside my door, after all. And the passage was as black as a coal-hole. So I started to shave with cold water; one has to sometimes, you know. I'd gone over my face, and I was just going lightly round under my chin, when I saw something move in the looking-glass. I mean something that moved was reflected in the looking-glass. The big door of the wardrobe had swung open, and by a sort of double reflection I could see the French bed with the red curtains. On the edge of it sat a man in his shirt and trousers — a man with black hair and whiskers, with the most awful look of despair and fear on his face that I've ever seen or dreamt of. I stood paralyzed, watching him in the mirror. I could not have turned round to save my life. Suddenly he laughed. It was a horrid, silent laugh, and showed all his teeth. They were very white and even. And the next moment he had cut his throat from ear to ear, there before my eyes. Did you ever see a man cut his throat? The bed was all white before.'

The story-teller had laid down his pipe, and he passed his hand over his face before he went on.

'When I could look round I did. There was no one in the room. The bed was as white as ever. Well, that's all,' he said, abruptly, 'except that now, of course, I understood how these poor chaps had come by their deaths. They'd all seen this horror — the ghost of the first poor chap, I suppose — Bert Hatteras, you know; and with the shock their hands must have slipped and their throats got cut before they could stop themselves. Oh! by the way, when I looked at my watch it was two o'clock; there hadn't been any chambermaid at all. I must have dreamed that. But I didn't dream the other. Oh! and one thing more. It was the same room. They hadn't changed the room, they'd only changed the number. *It was the same room!*'

'Look here,' said the heavy man, 'the room you've been talking about. *My* room's sixteen. And it's got that same furniture in it as what you describe, and the same picture and all.'

'Oh, has it?' said the story-teller, a little uncomfortable, it seemed. 'I'm sorry. But the cat's out of the bag now, and it can't be helped. Yes, it *was* this house I was speaking of. I suppose they've opened the room again. But you don't believe in ghosts; *you'll* be all right.'

'Yes,' said the heavy man, and presently got up and left the room.

'He's gone to see if he can get his room changed. You see if he hasn't,' said the rabbit-faced man, 'and I don't wonder.'

The heavy man came back and settled into his chair.

'I could do with a drink,' he said, reaching to the bell.

'I'll stand some punch, gentlemen, if you'll allow me,' said our dapper story-teller. 'I rather pride myself on my punch. I'll step out to the bar and get what I need for it.'

'I thought he said he was a teetotaller,' said the heavy

traveller when he had gone. And then our voices buzzed like a hive of bees. When our story-teller came in again we turned on him — half-a-dozen of us at once — and spoke.

'One at a time,' he said, gently. 'I didn't quite catch what you said.'

'We want to know,' I said, 'how it was — if seeing that ghost made all those chaps cut their throats by startling them when they were shaving — how was it *you* didn't cut *your* throat when you saw it?'

'I should have,' he answered, gravely, 'without the slightest doubt — I should have cut my throat, only,' he glanced at our heavy friend, 'I always shave with a safety razor. I travel in them,' he added, slowly, and bisected a lemon.

'But — but,' said the large man, when he could speak through our uproar, 'I've gone and given up my room.'

'Yes,' said the dapper man, squeezing the lemon; 'I've just had my things moved into it. It's the best room in the house. I always think it worthwhile to take a little pains to secure it.'

13 In the Dark

It may have been a form of madness. Or it may be that he really was what is called haunted. Or it may — though I don't pretend to understand how — have been the development, through intense suffering, of a sixth sense in a very nervous, highly-strung nature. Something certainly led him where They were. And to him They were all one.

He told me the first part of the story, and the last part of it I saw with my own eyes.

I

Haldane and I were friends even in our school-days. What first brought us together was our common hatred of Visger, who came from our part of the country. His people knew our people at home, so he was put on to us when he came. He was the most intolerable person, boy and man, that I have ever known. He would not tell a lie. And that was all right. But he didn't stop at that. If he were asked whether any other chap had done anything — been out of bounds, or up to any sort of lark — he would always say, 'I don't know, sir, but I believe so.' He never did know — we took care of that. But what he believed was always right. I remember Haldane twisting his arm to say how he knew about that cherry-tree business, and he only said, 'I don't know — I just feel sure. And I was right, you see.' What can you do with a boy like that?

We grew up to be men. At least Haldane and I did. Visger grew up to be a prig. He was a vegetarian and a teetotaller, and an all-wooler and a Christian Scientist, and all the things that prigs are — but he wasn't a common prig. He knew all sorts of things that he oughtn't to have known, that he *couldn't* have known in any ordinary decent way. It wasn't that he found things out. He just knew them. Once, when I was very unhappy, he came into my rooms — we were all in our last year at Oxford — and talked about things I hardly knew myself. That was really why I went to India that winter. It was bad enough to be unhappy, without having that beast knowing all about it.

I was away over a year. Coming back, I thought a lot about how jolly it would be to see old Haldane again. If I thought about Visger at all, I wished he was dead. But I didn't think about him much.

I did want to see Haldane. He was always such a jolly chap — gay, and kindly, and simple, honourable, upright, and full of practical sympathies. I longed to see him, to see the smile in his jolly blue eyes, looking out from the net of wrinkles that laughing had made round them, to hear his jolly laugh, and feel the good grip of his big hand. I went straight from the docks to his chambers in Gray's Inn, and I found him cold, pale, anæmic, with dull eyes and a limp hand, and pale lips that smiled without mirth, and uttered a welcome without gladness.

He was surrounded by a litter of disordered furniture and personal effects half packed. Some big boxes stood corded, and there were cases of books, filled and waiting for the enclosing boards to be nailed on.

'Yes, I'm moving,' he said. 'I can't stand these rooms. There's something rum about them — something devilish rum. I clear out tomorrow.'

The autumn dusk was filling the corners with shadows. 'You got the furs,' I said, just for something to say, for I saw the big case that held them lying corded among the others.

'Furs?' he said. 'Oh yes. Thanks awfully. Yes. I forgot about the furs.' He laughed, out of politeness, I suppose, for there was no joke about the furs. They were many and fine — the best I could get for money, and I had seen them packed and sent off when my heart was very sore. He stood looking at me, and saying nothing.

'Come out and have a bit of dinner,' I said as cheerfully as I could.

'Too busy,' he answered, after the slightest possible pause, and a glance round the room —'Look here — I'm awfully glad to see you — If you'd just slip over and order in dinner — I'd go myself — only — Well, you see how it is.'

I went. And when I came back, he had cleared a space near the fire, and moved his big gate-table into it. We dined there by candlelight. I tried to be amusing. He, I am sure, tried to be amused. We did not succeed, either of us. And his haggard eyes watched me all the time, save in those fleeting moments when, without turning his head, he glanced back over his shoulder into the shadows that crowded round the little lighted place where we sat.

When we had dined and the man had come and taken away the dishes, I looked at Haldane very steadily, so that he stopped in a pointless anecdote, and looked interrogatively at me.

'Well?' I said.

'You're not listening,' he said petulantly. 'What's the matter?'

'That's what you'd better tell me,' I said.

He was silent, gave one of those furtive glances at the shadows, and stooped to stir the fire to — I knew it — a blaze that must light every corner of the room.

'You're all to pieces,' I said cheerfully. 'What have you been up to? Wine? Cards? Speculation? A woman? If you won't tell me, you'll have to tell your doctor. Why, my dear chap, you're a wreck.'

'You're a comfortable friend to have about the place,' he said, and smiled a mechanical smile not at all pleasant to see.

'I'm the friend you want, I think,' said I. 'Do you suppose

I'm blind? Something's gone wrong and you've taken to something. Morphia, perhaps? And you've brooded over the thing till you've lost all sense of proportion. Out with it, old chap. I bet you a dollar it's not so bad as you think it.'

'If I could tell you — or tell anyone,' he said slowly, 'it wouldn't be so bad as it is. If I could tell anyone, I'd tell you. And even as it is, I've told you more than I've told anyone else.'

I could get nothing more out of him. But he pressed me to stay — would have given me his bed and made himself a shake-down, he said. But I had engaged my room at the Victoria, and I was expecting letters. So I left him, quite late — and he stood on the stairs, holding a candle over the bannisters to light me down.

When I went back next morning, he was gone. Men were moving his furniture into a big van with somebody's Pantechnicon painted on it in big letters.

He had left no address with the porter, and had driven off in a hansom with two portmanteaux — to Waterloo, the porter thought.

Well, a man has a right to the monopoly of his own troubles, if he chooses to have it. And I had troubles of my own that kept me busy.

II

It was more than a year later that I saw Haldane again. I had got rooms in the Albany by this time, and he turned up there one morning, very early indeed — before breakfast in fact. And if he looked ghastly before, he now looked almost ghostly. His face looked as though it had worn thin, like an oyster shell that has for years been cast up twice a day by the sea on a shore all pebbly. His hands were thin as bird's claws, and they trembled like caught butterflies.

I welcomed him with enthusiastic cordiality and pressed breakfast on him. This time, I decided, I would ask no questions. For I saw that none were needed. He would tell me. He intended to tell me. He had come here to tell me, and for nothing else.

I lit the spirit lamp — I made coffee and small talk for him, and I ate and drank, and waited for him to begin. And it was like this that he began:

'I am going,' he said, 'to kill myself — oh, don't be alarmed,' — I suppose I had said or looked something — 'I sha'n't do it here, or now. I shall do it when I have to — when I can't bear it any longer. And I want someone to know why. I don't want to feel that I'm the only living creature who does know. And I can trust you, can't I?'

I murmured something reassuring.

'I should like you, if you don't mind, to give me your word, that you won't tell a soul what I'm going to tell you, as long as I'm alive. Afterwards ... you can tell whom you please.'

I gave him my word.

He sat silent looking at the fire. Then he shrugged his shoulders.

'It's extraordinary how difficult it is to say it,' he said, and smiled. 'The fact is — you know that beast, George Visger.'

'Yes,' I said. 'I haven't seen him since I came back. Some one told me he'd gone to some island or other to preach vegetarianism to the cannibals. Anyhow, he's out of the way, bad luck to him.'

'Yes,' said Haldane, 'he's out of the way. But he's not preaching anything. In point of fact, he's dead.'

'Dead?' was all I could think of to say.

'Yes,' said he, 'it's not generally known, but he is.'

'What did he die of?' I asked, not that I cared. The bare fact was good enough for me.

'You know what an interfering chap he always was. Always

knew everything. Heart to heart talks — and have everything open and above board. Well, he interfered between me and someone else — told her a pack of lies.'

'Lies?'

'Well, the *things* were true, but he made lies of them the way he told them — *you* know.' I did. I nodded. 'And she threw me over. And she died. And we weren't even friends. And I couldn't see her — before — I couldn't even … Oh, my God … But I went to the funeral. He was there. They'd asked *him*. And then I came back to my rooms. And I was sitting there, thinking. And he came up.'

'He would do. It's just what he would do. The beast! I hope you kicked him out.'

'No, I didn't. I listened to what he'd got to say. He came to say, no doubt it was all for the best. And he hadn't known the things he told her. He'd only guessed. He'd guessed right, damn him. What right had he to guess right? And he said it was all for the best, because, besides that, there was madness in my family. He'd found that out too —'

'And is there?'

'If there is, I didn't know it. And that was why it was all for the best. So then I said, "There wasn't any madness in my family before, but there is now," and I got hold of his throat. I am not sure whether I meant to kill him; I ought to have meant to kill him. Anyhow, I did kill him. What did you say?'

I had said nothing. It is not easy to think at once of the tactful and suitable thing to say, when your oldest friend tells you that he is a murderer.

'When I could get my hands out of his throat — it was as difficult as it is to drop the handles of a galvanic battery — he fell in a lump on the hearthrug. And I saw what I'd done. How is it that murderers ever get found out?'

'They're careless, I suppose,' I found myself saying, 'they

lose their nerve.'

'I didn't,' he said. 'I never was calmer. I sat down in the big chair and looked at him, and thought it all out. He was just off to that island — I knew that. He'd said good-bye to everyone. He'd told me that. There was no blood to get rid of — or only a touch at the corner of his slack mouth. He wasn't going to travel in his own name because of interviewers. Mr Somebody Something's luggage would be unclaimed and his cabin empty. No one would guess that Mr Somebody Something was Sir George Visger, FRS. It was all as plain as plain. There was nothing to get rid of, but the man. No weapon, no blood — and I got rid of him all right.'

'How?'

He smiled cunningly.

'No, no,' he said, 'that's where I draw the line. It's not that I doubt your word, but if you talked in your sleep, or had a fever or anything. No, no. As long as you don't know where the body is, don't you see, I'm all right. Even if you could prove that I've said all this — which you can't — it's only the wanderings of my poor unhinged brain. See?'

I saw. And I was sorry for him. And I did not believe that he had killed Visger. He was not the sort of man who kills people. So I said:

'Yes, old chap, I see. Now look here. Let's go away together, you and I — travel a bit and see the world, and forget all about that beastly chap.'

His eyes lighted up at that.

'Why,' he said, 'you understand. You don't hate me and shrink from me. I wish I'd told you before — you know — when you came and I was packing all my sticks. But it's too late now.'

'Too late? Not a bit of it,' I said. 'Come, we'll pack our traps and be off tonight — out into the unknown, don't you know.'

'That's where *I'm* going,' he said. 'You wait. When you've

heard what's been happening to me, you won't be so keen to go travelling about with me.'

'But you've told me what's been happening to you,' I said, and the more I thought about what he had told me, the less I believed it.

'No,' he said, slowly, 'no — I've told you what happened to *him*. What happened to me is quite different. Did I tell you what his last words were? Just when I was coming at him. Before I'd got his throat, you know. He said, "Look out. You'll never to able to get rid of the body — Besides, anger's sinful." You know that way he had, like a tract on its hind legs. So afterwards I got thinking of that. But I didn't think of it for a year. Because I did get rid of his body all right. And then I was sitting in that comfortable chair, and I thought, "Hullo, it must be about a year now, since that —" and I pulled out my pocket-book and went to the window to look at a little almanack I carry about — it was getting dusk — and sure enough it was a year, to the day. And then I remembered what he'd said. And I said to myself, "Not much trouble about getting rid of *your* body, you brute." And then I looked at the hearthrug and — Ah!' he screamed suddenly and very loud — 'I can't tell you — no, I can't.'

My man opened the door — he wore a smooth face over his wriggling curiosity. 'Did you call, sir?'

'Yes,' I lied. 'I want you to take a note to the bank, and wait for an answer.'

When he was got rid of, Haldane said, 'Where was I?'

'You were just telling me what happened after you looked at the almanack. What was it?'

'Nothing much,' he said, laughing softly, 'oh, nothing much — only that I glanced at the hearthrug — and there *he* was — the man I'd killed a year before. Don't try to explain, or I shall lose my temper. The door was shut. The windows were shut. He hadn't been there a minute before. And he was there then. That's all.'

Hallucination was one of the words I stumbled among.

'Exactly what I thought,' he said triumphantly, 'but — I touched it. It was quite real. Heavy, you know, and harder than live people are somehow, to the touch — more like a stone thing covered with kid the hands were, and the arms like a marble statue in a blue serge suit. Don't you hate men who wear blue serge suits?'

'There are hallucinations of touch too,' I found myself saying.

'Exactly what I thought,' said Haldane more triumphant than ever, 'but there are limits, you know — limits. So then I thought someone had got him out — the real him — and stuck him there to frighten me while my back was turned, and I went to the place where I'd hidden him, and he was there — ah! — just as I'd left him. Only ... it was a year ago. There are two of him there now.'

'My dear chap,' I said, 'this is simply comic.'

'Yes,' he said, 'it is amusing. I find it so myself. Especially in the night when I wake up and think of it. I hope I shan't die in the dark, Winston. That's one of the reasons why I think I shall have to kill myself. I could be sure then of not dying in the dark.'

'Is *that* all?' I asked, feeling sure that it must be.

'No,' said Haldane at once, 'that's *not* all. He's come back to me again. In a railway carriage it was. I'd been asleep. When I woke up, there he was lying on the seat opposite me. Looked just the same. I pitched him out on the line in Red Hill Tunnel. And if I see him again, I'm going out myself. I can't stand it. It's too much. I'd sooner go. Whatever the next world's like, there aren't things like that. We leave them here, in graves and boxes and ... You think I'm mad. But I'm not. You can't help me — no one can help me. He *knew*, you see. He said I shouldn't be able to get rid of the body. And I can't get rid of it. I can't. I can't. He knew. He always did know things that he *couldn't* know. But I'll cut his game short. After all, I've got the ace of trumps, and I play it on his next trick. I give you my word of honour, Winston, that I'm not mad.'

'My dear old man,' I said, 'I don't think you're mad. But I do think your nerves are very much upset. Mine are a bit, too. Do you know why I went to India? It was because of you and her. I couldn't stay and see it, though I wished for your happiness and all that; you know I did. And when I came back, she ... and you ... Let's see it out together,' I said. 'You won't keep fancying things if you've got me to talk to. And I always said you weren't half a bad old duffer.'

'She liked you,' he said.

'Oh, yes,' I said, 'she liked me.'

III

That was how we came to go abroad together. I was full of hope for him. He'd always been such a splendid chap — so sane and strong. I couldn't believe that he was gone mad, gone forever, I mean, so that he'd never come right again. Perhaps my own trouble made it easy for me to see things not quite straight. Anyway, I took him away to recover his mind's health, exactly as I should have taken him away to get strong after a fever. And the madness seemed to pass away, and in a month or two we were perfectly jolly, and I thought I had cured him. And I was very glad because of that old friendship of ours, and because she had loved him and liked me.

We never spoke of Visger. I thought he had forgotten all about him. I thought I understood how his mind, overstrained by sorrow and anger, had fixed on the man he hated, and woven a nightmare web of horror round that detestable personality. And I had got the whip hand of my own trouble. And we were as jolly as sandboys together all those months.

And we came to Bruges at last in our travels, and Bruges was very full, because of the Exhibition. We could only get one room and one bed. So we tossed for the bed, and the one who lost the toss was to make the best of the night in the arm-chair. And the bed-clothes we were to share equitably.

We spent the evening at a *café chantant* and finished at a beer hall, and it was late and sleepy when we got back to the Grande Vigne. I took our key from its nail in the concierge's room, and we went up. We talked awhile, I remember, of the town, and the belfry, and the Venetian aspect of the canals by moonlight, and then Haldane got into bed, and I made a chrysalis of myself with my share of the blankets and fitted the tight roll into the arm-chair. I was not at all comfortable, but I was compensatingly tired, and I was nearly asleep when Haldane roused me up to tell me about his will.

'I've left everything to you, old man,' he said. 'I know I can trust you to see to everything.'

'Quite so,' said I, 'and if you don't mind, we'll talk about it in the morning.'

He tried to go on about it, and about what a friend I'd been, and all that, but I shut him up and told him to go to sleep. But no. He wasn't comfortable, he said. And he'd got a thirst like a lime kiln. And he'd noticed that there was no water-bottle in the room. 'And the water in the jug's like pale soup,' he said.

'Oh, all right,' said I. 'Light your candle and go and get some water, then, in Heaven's name, and let me get to sleep.'

But he said, 'No — you light it. I don't want to get out of bed in the dark. I might — I might step on something, mightn't I — or walk into something that wasn't there when I got into bed.'

'Rot,' I said, 'walk into your grandmother.' But I lit the

candle all the same. He sat up in bed and looked at me — very pale — with his hair all tumbled from the pillow, and his eyes blinking and shining.

'That's better,' he said. And then, 'I say — look here. Oh — yes — I see. It's all right. Queer how they mark the sheets here. Blest if I didn't think it was blood, just for the minute.'

The sheet was marked, not at the corner, as sheets are marked at home, but right in the middle where it turns down, with big, red, cross-stitching.

'Yes, I see,' I said, 'it is a queer place to mark it.'

'It's queer letters to have on it,' he said. 'G.V.'

'Grande Vigne,' I said. 'What letters do you expect them to mark things with? Hurry up.'

'You come too,' he said. 'Yes, it does stand for Grande Vigne, of course. I wish you'd come down too, Winston.'

'I'll go down,' I said and turned with the candle in my hand.

He was out of bed and close to me in a flash. 'No,' said he, 'I don't want to stay alone in the dark.'

He said it just as a frightened child might have done.

'All right then, come along,' I said. And we went. I tried to make some joke, I remember, about the length of his hair, and the cut of his pyjamas — but I was sick with disappointment. For it was almost quite plain to me, even then, that all my time and trouble had been thrown away, and that he wasn't cured after all. We went down as quietly as we could, and got a carafe of water from the long bare dining table in the *salle-à-manger*. He got hold of my arm at first, and then he got the candle away from me, and went very slowly, shading the light with his hand, and looking very carefully all about, as though he expected to see something that he wanted very desperately not to see. And of course, I knew what that something was. I didn't like the way he was going on. I can't at all express how deeply I didn't like it. And he looked over his shoulder every now and then, just as he did that first evening after I came back from India.

The thing got on my nerves so that I could hardly find the way back to our room. And when we got there, I give you my word, I more than half expected to see what *he* had expected to see — that, or something like that, on the hearthrug. But of course there was nothing.

I blew out the light and tightened my blankets round me — I'd been trailing them after me in our expedition. And I was settled in my chair when Haldane spoke.

'You've got all the blankets,' he said.

'No, I haven't,' said I, 'only what I've always had.'

'I can't find mine then,' he said, and I could hear his teeth chattering. 'And I'm cold. I'm ... For God's sake, light the candle. Light it. Light it. Something horrible ...'

And I couldn't find the matches.

'Light the candle, light the candle,' he said, and his voice broke, as a boy's does sometimes in chapel. 'If you don't he'll come to me. It is so easy to come at anyone in the dark. Oh Winston, light the candle, for the love of God! I can't die in the dark.'

'I am lighting it,' I said savagely, and I was feeling for the matches on the marble-topped chest of drawers, on the mantelpiece — everywhere but on the round centre table where I'd put them. 'You're not going to die. Don't be a fool,' I said. 'It's all right. I'll get a light in a second.'

He said, 'It's cold. It's cold. It's cold,' like that, three times. And then he screamed aloud, like a woman — like a child — like a hare when the dogs have got it. I had heard him scream like that once before.

'What is it?' I cried, hardly less loud. 'For God's sake, hold your noise. What is it?'

There was an empty silence. Then, very slowly:

'It's Visger,' he said. And he spoke thickly, as through some stifling veil.

'Nonsense. Where?' I asked, and my hand closed on the matches as he spoke.

'Here,' he screamed sharply, as though he had torn the veil away, 'here, beside me. In the bed.'

I got the candle alight. I got across to him.

He was crushed in a heap at the edge of the bed. Stretched on the bed beyond him was a dead man, white and very cold.

Haldane had died in the dark.

✕

It was all so simple.

We had come to the wrong room. The man the room belonged to was there, on the bed he had engaged and paid for before he died of heart disease, earlier in the day. A French *commis-voyageur* representing soap and perfumery: his name, Felix Leblanc.

Later, in England, I made cautious enquiries. The body of a man had been found in the Red Hill tunnel — a haberdasher named Simmons, who had drunk spirits of salts, owing to the depression of trade. The bottle was clutched in his dead hand.

For reasons that I had, I took care to have a police inspector with me when I opened the boxes that came to me by Haldane's will. One of them was the big box, metal-lined, in which I had sent him the skins from India — for a wedding present, God help us all!

It was closely soldered.

Inside were the skins of beasts? No. The bodies of two men. One was identified, after some trouble, as that of a hawker of pens in city offices — subject to fits. He had died in one, it seemed. The other body was Visger's, right enough.

Explain it as you like. I offered you, if you remember, a choice of explanations before I began the story. I have not yet found the explanation that can satisfy me.

14 The Violet Car

Do you know the downs — the wide windy spaces, the rounded shoulders of the hills leaned against the sky, the hollows where farms and homesteads nestle sheltered, with trees round them pressed close and tight as a carnation in a button-hole? On long summer days it is good to lie on the downs, between short turf and pale, clear sky, to smell the wild thyme, and hear the tiny tinkle of the sheep-bells and the song of the skylark. But on winter evenings when the wind is waking up to its work, spitting rain in your eyes, beating the poor, naked trees and shaking the dusk across the hills like a gray pall, then it is better to be by a warm fireside, in one of the farms that lie lonely where shelter is, and oppose their windows glowing with candlelight and firelight to the deepening darkness, as faith holds up its love-lamp in the night of sin and sorrow that is life.

✳

I am unaccustomed to literary effort — and I feel that I shall not say what I have to say, or that it will convince you, unless I say it very plainly. I thought I could adorn my story with pleasant words, prettily arranged. But as I pause to think of what really happened, I see that the plainest words will be the best. I do not know how to weave a plot, nor how to embroider it. It is best not to try. These things happened. I have no skill to add to what happened; nor is any adding of mine needed.

I am a nurse — and I was sent for to go to Charlestown — a mental case. It was November — and the fog was thick in London, so that my cab went at a foot's pace, so I missed the train by which I should have gone. I sent a telegram to Charlestown, and waited in the dismal waiting room at London Bridge. The time was passed for me by a little child. Its mother, a widow, seemed too crushed to be able to respond to its quick questionings. She answered briefly, and not, as it seemed, to the child's satisfaction. The child itself presently seemed to perceive that its mother was not, so to speak, available. It leaned back on the wide, dusty seat and yawned. I caught its eye, and smiled. It would not smile, but it looked. I took out of my bag a silk purse, bright with beads and steel tassels, and turned it over and over. Presently, the child slid along the seat and said, 'Let me' — After that all was easy. The mother sat with eyes closed. When I rose to go, she opened them and thanked me. The child, clinging, kissed me. Later, I saw them get into a first class carriage in my train. My ticket was a third class one.

I expected, of course, that there would be a conveyance of some sort to meet me at the station — but there was nothing. Nor was there a cab or a fly to be seen. It was by this time nearly dark, and the wind was driving the rain almost horizontally along the unfrequented road that lay beyond the door of the station. I looked out, forlorn and perplexed.

'Haven't you engaged a carriage?' It was the widow lady who spoke.

I explained.

'My motor will be here directly,' she said, 'you'll let me drive you? Where is it you are going?'

'Charlestown,' I said, and as I said it, I was aware of a very odd change in her face. A faint change, but quite unmistakable.

'Why do you look like that?' I asked her bluntly. And, of course, she said, 'Like what?'

'There's nothing wrong with the house?' I said, for that, I found, was what I had taken that faint change to signify; and I was very young, and one has heard tales. 'No reason why I shouldn't go there, I mean?'

'No — oh no —' she glanced out through the rain, and I knew as well as though she had told me that there was a reason why *she* should not wish to go there.

'Don't trouble,' I said, 'its very kind of you — but it's probably out of your way and...'

'Oh — but I'll take you — of *course* I'll take you,' she said, and the child said, 'Mother, here comes the car.'

And come it did, though neither of us heard it till the child had spoken. I know nothing of motor cars, and I don't know the names of any of the parts of them. This was like a brougham — only you got in at the back, as you do in a waggonette; the seats were in the corners, and when the door was shut there was a little seat that pulled up, and the child sat on it between us. And it moved like magic — or like a dream of a train.

We drove quickly through the dark — I could hear the wind screaming, and the wild dashing of the rain against the windows, even through the whirring of the machinery. One could see nothing of the country — only the black night, and the shafts of light from the lamps in front.

After, as it seemed, a very long time, the chauffeur got down and opened a gate. We went through it, and after that the road was very much rougher. We were quite silent in the car, and the child had fallen asleep.

We stopped, and the car stood pulsating, as though it were out of breath, while the chauffeur hauled down my box. It was so dark that I could not see the shape of the house, only the lights in the downstairs windows, and the low-walled front garden faintly revealed by their light and the light of the motor lamps. Yet I felt that it was a fair-sized house, that it was surrounded by bog trees, and that there was a pond or river close by. In daylight next day I found that all this was so. I have never been able to tell how I knew it that first night, in the dark, but I did know it. Perhaps there was something in the way the rain fell on the trees and on the water. I don't know.

The chauffeur took my box up a stone path, whereon I got out, and said goodbyes and thanks.

'Don't wait, please don't,' I said. 'I'm all right now. Thank you a thousand times!'

The car, however, stood pulsating till I had reached the doorstep, then it caught its breath, as it were, throbbed more loudly, turned, and went.

And still the door had not opened. I felt for the knocker, and rapped smartly. Inside the door I was sure I heard whispering. The car light was fast diminishing to a little distant star, and its panting sounded now hardly at all. When it ceased to sound at all, the place was quiet as death. The lights glowed redly from curtained windows, but there was no other sign of life. I wished I had not been in such a hurry to part from my escort, from human companionship, and from the great, solid, competent presence of the motor car.

I knocked again, and this time I followed the knock by a shout.

'Hullo!' I cried. 'Let me in. I'm the nurse!'

There was a pause, such a pause as would allow time for whisperers to exchange glances on the other side of a door.

Then a bolt ground back, a key turned, and the doorway framed no longer cold, wet wood, but light and a welcoming warmth — and faces.

'Come in, oh, come in,' said a voice, a woman's voice, and the voice of a man said: 'We didn't know there was anyone there.'

And I had shaken the very door with my knockings!

I went in, blinking at the light, and the man called a servant, and between them they carried my box upstairs.

The woman took my arm and led me into a low, square room, pleasant, homely, and comfortable, with solid mid-Victorian comfort — the kind that expressed itself in rep and mahogany. In the lamplight I turned to look at her. She was small and thin, her hair, her face, and her hands were of the same tint of greyish yellow.

'Mrs Eldridge?' I asked.

'Yes,' said she, very softly. 'Oh! I am so glad you've come. I hope you won't be dull here. I hope you'll stay. I hope I shall be able to make you comfortable.'

She had a gentle, urgent way of speaking that was very winning.

'I'm sure I shall be very comfortable,' I said; 'but it's I that am to take care of you. Have you been ill long?'

'It's not me that's ill, really,' she said, 'it's him —'

Now, it was Mr Robert Eldridge who had written to engage me to attend on his wife, who was, he said, slightly deranged.

'I see,' said I. One must never contradict them, it only aggravates their disorder.

'The reason ...' she was beginning, when his foot sounded on the stairs, and she fluttered off to get candles and hot water.

He came in and shut the door. A fair bearded, elderly man, quite ordinary.

'You'll take care of her,' he said. 'I don't want her to get talking to people. She fancies things.'

'What form do the illusions take?' I asked, prosaically.

'She thinks I'm mad,' he said, with a short laugh.

'It's a very usual form. Is that all?'

'It's about enough. And she can't hear things that I can hear, see things that I can see, and she can't smell things. By the way, you didn't see or hear anything of a motor as you came up, did you?'

'I came up *in* a motor car,' I said shortly. 'You never sent to meet me, and a lady gave me a lift.' I was going to explain about my missing the earlier train, when I found that he was not listening to me. He was watching the door. When his wife came in, with a steaming jug in one hand and a flat candlestick in the other, he went towards her, and whispered eagerly. The only words I caught were: 'She came in a real motor.'

Apparently, to these simple people a motor was as great a novelty as to me. My telegram, by the way, was delivered next morning.

They were very kind to me; they treated me as an honoured guest. When the rain stopped, as it did late the next day, and I was able to go out, I found that Charlestown was a farm, a large farm, but even to my inexperienced eyes it seemed neglected and unprosperous. There was absolutely nothing for me to do but to follow Mrs Eldridge, helping her where I could in her household duties, and to sit with her while she sewed in the homely parlour. When I had been in the house a few days, I began to put together the little things that I had noticed singly, and the life at the farm seemed suddenly to come into focus, as strange surroundings do after a while.

I found that I had noticed that Mr and Mrs Eldridge were very fond of each other, and that it was a fondness, and their way of shewing it was a way that told that they had known sorrow, and had borne it together. That she shewed no sign of mental derangement, save in the persistent belief of hers that *he* was deranged. That the morning found them fairly cheerful; that after the early dinner they seemed to grow more and more depressed; that after the 'early cup of tea' — that is just as dusk was falling — they always went for a walk together. That they never asked me to join them in this walk, and that it always took the same direction — across the downs towards the sea. That they always returned from this walk pale and dejected; that she sometimes cried afterwards alone in their bedroom, while he was shut up in the little room they called the office, where he did his accounts, and paid his men's wages, and where his hunting-crops and guns were kept. After supper, which was early, they always made an effort to be cheerful. I knew that this effort was for my sake, and I knew that each of them thought it was good for the other to make it.

Just as I had known before they shewed it to me that Charlestown was surrounded by big trees and had a great pond beside it, so I knew, and in as inexplicable a way, that with these two fear lived. It looked at me out of their eyes. And I knew, too, that this fear was not her fear. I had not been two days in the place before I found that I was beginning to be fond of them both. They were so kind, so gentle, so ordinary, so homely — the kind of people who ought not to have known the name of fear — the kind of people to whom all honest, simple joys should have come by right, and no sorrows but such as come to us all, the death of old friends, and the slow changes of advancing years.

They seemed to belong to the land — to the downs, and the copses, and the old pastures, and the lessening corn-fields. I found myself wishing that I, too, belonged to these, that I had been born a farmer's daughter. All the stress and struggle of cram and exam, of school, and college, and hospital, seemed so loud and futile, compared with these open secrets of the down life. And I felt this the more, as more and more I felt that I must leave it all — that there was, honestly, no work for me here such as for good or ill I had been trained to do.

'I ought not to stay,' I said to her one afternoon, as we stood at the open door. It was February now, and the snowdrops were thick in tufts beside the flagged path. 'You are quite well.'

'I am,' she said.

'You are quite well, both of you,' I said. 'I oughtn't to be taking your money and doing nothing for it.'

'You're doing everything,' she said; 'you don't know how much you're doing.'

'We had a daughter of our own once,' she added vaguely, and then, after a very long pause, she said very quietly and distinctly:

'He has never been the same since.'

'How not the same?' I asked, turning my face up to the thin February sunshine.

She tapped her wrinkled, yellow-grey forehead, as country people do.

'Not right here,' she said.

'How?' I asked. 'Dear Mrs Eldridge, tell me; perhaps I could help somehow.'

Her voice was so sane, so sweet. It had come to this with me, that I did not know which of those two was the one who needed my help.

'He sees things that no one else sees, and hears things no one else hears, and smells things that you can't smell if you're standing there beside him.'

I remembered with a sudden smile his words to me on the evening of my arrival:

'She can't see, or hear, or smell.'

And once more I wondered to which of the two I owed my service.

'Have you any idea why?' I asked. She caught at my arm.

'It was after our Bessie died,' she said — 'the very day she was buried. The motor that killed her — they said it was an accident — it was on the Brighton Road. It was a violet colour. They go into mourning for Queens with violet, don't they?' she added; 'and my Bessie, she was a Queen. So the motor was violet. That was all right, wasn't it?'

I told myself now that I saw that the woman was not normal, and I saw why. It was grief that had turned her brain. There must have been some change in my look, though I ought to have known better, for she said suddenly, 'No. I'll not tell you any more.'

And then he came out. He never left me alone with her for very long. Nor did she ever leave him for very long alone with me.

I did not intend to spy upon them, though I am not sure that my position as nurse to one mentally afflicted would not have justified such spying. But I did not spy. It was chance. I had been to the village to get some blue sewing silk for a blouse I was making, and there was a royal sunset which tempted me to prolong my walk. That was how I found myself on the high downs where they slope to the broken edge of England — the sheer, white cliffs against which the English Channel beats forever. The furze was in flower, and skylarks were singing, and my thoughts were with my own life, my own hopes and dreams. So I found that I had struck a road, without knowing when I had struck it. I followed it towards the sea, and quite soon it ceased to be a road, and merged in the pathless turf as a stream sometimes disappears in sand. There was nothing but turf and furze bushes, the song of the skylarks, and beyond the slope that ended at the cliff's edge, the booming of the sea. I turned back, following the road, which defined itself again a few yards back, and presently sank to a lane, deep-banked and bordered with brown hedge stuff. It was there that I came upon them in the dusk. And I heard their voices before I saw them, and before it was possible for them to see me. It was her voice that I heard first.

'No, no, no, no, no,' it said.

'I tell you yes,' that was his voice; 'there — can't you hear it, that panting sound — right away — away? It must be at the very edge of the cliff.'

'There's nothing, dearie,' she said, 'indeed there's nothing.'

'You're deaf — and blind — stand back I tell you, it's close upon us.'

I came round the corner of the lane then, and as I came, I saw him catch her arm and throw her against the hedge — violently, as though the danger he feared were indeed close upon them. I stopped behind the turn of the hedge and stepped back. They had not seen me. Her eyes were on his face, and they held a world of pity, love, agony — his face was set in a mask of terror, and his eyes moved quickly as though they followed down the lane the swift passage of Something — something that neither she nor I could see. Next moment he was cowering, pressing his body into the hedge — his face hidden in his hands, and his whole body trembling so that I could see it, even from where I was a dozen yards away, through the light screen of the overgrown hedge.

'And the smell of it!' — he said, 'do you mean to tell me you can't smell it?'

She had her arms round him.

'Come home, dearie,' she said. 'Come home! It's all your fancy — come home with your old wife that loves you.'

They went home.

Next day I asked her to come to my room to look at the new blue blouse. When I had shown it to her I told her what I had seen and heard yesterday in the lane.

'And now I know,' I said, 'which of you it is that wants care.'

To my amazement she said very eagerly, 'Which?'

'Why, he — of course' — I told her, 'there was nothing there.'

She sat down in the chintz covered armchair by the window, and broke into wild weeping. I stood by her and soothed her as well as I could.

'It's a comfort to know,' she said at last, 'I haven't known what to believe. Many a time, lately, I've wondered whether after all it could be me that was mad, like he said. And there was nothing there? There always *was* nothing there — and it's on him the judgment, not on me. On him. Well, that's something to be thankful for.'

So her tears, I told myself, had been more of relief at her own escape. I looked at her with distaste, and forgot that I had been fond of her. So that her next words cut me like little knives.

'It's bad enough for him as it is,' she said — 'but it's nothing to what it would be for him, if I was really to go off my head and him left to think he'd brought it on me. You see, now I can look after him the same as I've always done. It's only once in the day it comes over him. He couldn't bear it, if it was all the time — like it'll be for me now. It's much better it should be him — I'm better able to bear it than he is.'

I kissed her then and put my arms round her, and said, 'Tell me what it is that frightens him so — and its every day, you say?'

'Yes — ever since. I'll tell you. It's a sort of comfort to speak out. It was a violet coloured car that killed our Bessie. You know our girl that I've told you about. And it's a violet coloured car that he thinks he sees — every day up there in the lane. And he says he hears it, and that he smells the smell of the machinery — the stuff they put in it — you know.'

'Petrol?'

'Yes, and you can *see* he hears it, and you can *see* he sees it. It haunts him, as if it was a ghost. You see, it was he that picked her up after the violet car went over her. It was that that turned him. I only saw her as he carried her in, in his arms — and then he'd covered her face. But he saw her just as they'd left her, lying in the dust ... you could see the place on the road where it happened for days and days.'

'Didn't they come back?'

'Oh yes ... they came back. But Bessie didn't come back. But there was a judgment on them. The very night of the funeral, that violet car went over the cliff — dashed to pieces

— every soul in it. That was the man's widow that drove you home the first night.'

'I wonder she uses a car after that,' I said — I wanted something commonplace to say.

'Oh,' said Mrs Eldridge, 'it's all what you're used to. We don't stop walking because our girl was killed on the road. Motoring comes as natural to them as walking to us. There's my old man calling — poor old dear. He wants me to go out with him.'

She went, all in a hurry, and in her hurry slipped on the stairs and twisted her ankle. It all happened in a minute and it was a bad sprain.

When I had bound it up, and she was on the sofa, she looked at him, standing as if he were undecided, staring out of the window with his cap in his hand. And she looked at me.

'Mr Eldridge mustn't miss his walk,' she said. 'You go with him, my dear. A breath of air will do you good.'

So I went, understanding as well as though he had told me, that he did not want me with him, and that he was afraid to go alone, and that he yet had to go.

We went up the lane in silence. At that corner he stopped suddenly, caught my arm, and dragged me back. His eyes followed something that I could not see. Then he exhaled a held breath, and said, 'I thought I heard a motor coming.' He had found it hard to control his terror, and I saw beads of sweat on his forehead and temples. Then we went back to the house.

The sprain was a bad one. Mrs Eldridge had to rest, and again next day it was I who went with him to the corner of the lane.

This time he could not, or did not try to, conceal what he felt. 'There — listen!' he said. 'Surely you can hear it?'

I heard nothing.

'Stand back,' he cried shrilly, suddenly, and we stood back close against the hedge.

Again the eyes followed something invisible to me, and again the held breath exhaled.

'It will kill me one of these days,' he said, 'and I don't know that I care how soon — if it wasn't for her.'

'Tell me,' I said, full of that importance, that conscious competence, that one feels in the presence of other people's troubles. He looked at me.

'I will tell you, by God,' he said. 'I couldn't tell *her*. Young lady, I've gone so far as wishing myself a Roman, for the sake of a priest to tell it to. But I can tell *you*, without losing my soul more than it's lost already. Did you ever hear tell of a violet car that got smashed up — went over the cliff?'

'Yes,' I said. 'Yes.'

'The man that killed my girl was new to the place. And he hadn't any eyes — or ears — or he'd have known me, seeing we'd been face to face at the inquest. And you'd have thought he'd have stayed at home that one day, with the blinds drawn down. But not he. He was swirling and swivelling all about the country in his cursed violet car, the very time we were burying her. And at dusk — there was a mist coming up — he comes up behind me in this very lane, and I stood back, and he pulls up, and he calls out, with his damned lights full in my face:

"Can you tell me the way to Hexham, my man?" says he.

'I'd have liked to shew him the way to hell. And that was the way for me, not him. I don't know how I came to do it. I didn't mean to do it. I didn't think I was going to — and before I knew anything, I'd said it. "Straight ahead," I said; "keep straight ahead." Then the motor-thing panted, chuckled, and he was off. I ran after him to try to stop him — but what's the use of running after these motor-devils? And he kept straight on. And every day since then, every dear day,

the car comes by, the violet car that nobody can see but me —
and it keeps straight on.'

'You ought to go away,' I said, speaking as I had been trained
to speak. 'You fancy these things. You probably fancied the
whole thing. I don't suppose you ever *did* tell the violet car
to go straight ahead. I expect it was all imagination, and the
shock of your poor daughter's death. You ought to go right
away.'

'I can't,' he said earnestly, 'If I did, someone else would see
the car. You see, somebody *has* to see it every day as long as
I live. If it wasn't me, it would be someone else. And I'm the
only person who *deserves* to see it. I wouldn't like anyone else
to see it — it's too horrible. *It's* much more horrible than you
think,' he added slowly.

I asked him, walking beside him down the quiet lane, what
it was that was so horrible about the violet car. I think I quite
expected him to say that it was splashed with his daughter's
blood … What he did say was, 'It's too horrible to tell you,'
and he shuddered.

I was young then, and youth always thinks it can move
mountains. I persuaded myself that I could cure him of
his delusion by attacking — not the main fort — that is
always, to begin with, impregnable, but one, so to speak, of
the outworks. I set myself to persuade him not to go to that
corner in the lane, at that hour in the afternoon.

'But if I don't, someone else will see it.'

'There'll be nobody there *to* see it,' I said briskly.

'Someone will be there. Mark my words, someone will be
there — and then they'll know.'

'Then I'll be the someone,' I said. 'Come — you stay at
home with your wife, and *I'll* go — and if I see it I'll promise
to tell you, and if I don't — well, then I will be able to go
away with a clear conscience.'

'A clear conscience,' he repeated.

I argued with him in every moment when it was possible to catch him alone. I put all my will and all my energy into my persuasions. Suddenly, like a door that you've been trying to open, and that has resisted every key till the last one, he gave way. Yes — I should go to the lane. And he would not go.

I went.

Being, as I said before, a novice in the writing of stories, I perhaps haven't made you understand that it was quite hard for me to go — that I felt myself at once a coward and a heroine. This business of an imaginary motor that only one poor old farmer could see, probably appears to you quite commonplace and ordinary. It was not so with me. You see, the idea of this thing had dominated my life for weeks and months, had dominated it even before I knew the nature of the domination. It was this that was the fear that I had known to walk with these two people, the fear that shared their bed and board, that lay down and rose up with them. The old man's fear of this and his fear of his fear. And the old man was terribly convincing. When one talked with him, it was quite difficult to believe that he was mad, and that there wasn't, and couldn't be, a mysteriously horrible motor that was visible to him, and invisible to other people. And when he said that, if he were not in the lane, someone else would see it — it was easy to say 'Nonsense,' but to think 'Nonsense' was not so easy, and to *feel* 'Nonsense' quite oddly difficult.

I walked up and down the lane in the dusk, wishing not to wonder what might be the hidden horror in the violet car, I would not let blood into my thoughts. I was not going to be fooled by thought transference, or any of those transcendental follies. I was not going to be hypnotised into seeing things.

I walked up the lane — I had promised him to stand near that corner for five minutes, and I stood there in the deepening dusk, looking up towards the downs and the sea. There were pale stars. Everything was very still. Five minutes is a long time. I held my watch in my hand. Four — four and a half — four and a quarter. Five. I turned instantly. And then I saw that *he* had followed me — he was standing a dozen yards away — and his face was turned from me. It was turned towards a motor car that shot up the lane — It came very swiftly, and before it came to where he was, I knew that it was very horrible. I crushed myself back into the crackling bare hedge, as I should have done to leave room for the passage of a real car — though I knew that this one was not real. It looked real — but I knew it was not.

As it neared him, he started back, then suddenly he cried out. I heard him. 'No, no, no, no — no more, no more,' was what he cried, with that he flung himself down on the road in front of the car, and its great tires passed over him. Then the car shot past me and I saw what the full horror of it was. There was no blood — that was not the horror. The colour of it was, as she had said, violet.

I got to him and got his head up. He was dead. I was quite calm and collected now, and felt that to be so was extremely credible to me. I went to a cottage where a labourer was having tea — he got some men and a hurdle.

When I had told his wife, the first intelligible thing she said was: 'It's better for him. Whatever he did he's paid for now.' So it looks as though she had known — or guessed — more than he thought.

I stayed with her till her death. She did not live long.

You think perhaps that the old man was knocked down and killed by a real motor, which happened to come that way of all ways, at that hour of all hours, and happened to be, of all colours, violet. Well, a real motor leaves its mark on you where it kills you, doesn't it. But when I lifted up that old man's head from the road, there was no mark on him, no blood — no broken bones — his hair was not disordered, nor his dress. I tell you there was not even a speck of mud on him, except where he had touched the road in falling. There were no tyre-marks in the mud.

The motor car that killed him came and went like a shadow. As he threw himself down, it swerved a little so that both its wheels should go over him.

He died, the doctor said, of heart-failure. I am the only person to know that he was killed by a violet car, which, having killed him, went noiselessly away towards the sea. And that car was empty — there was no one in it. It was just a violet car that moved along the lanes swiftly and silently, and was empty.

15 The Marble Child

All over the pavement of the church spread the exaggerated cross-hatching of the old pews' oak, a Smithfield market of intersecting lines such as children made with cards in the old days when kings and knaves had fat legs bulging above their serviceable feet, and queens had skirts to their gowns and were not cut across their royal middles by mirrors reflecting only the bedizened torso of them and the charge — heart, trefoil, or the like — in the right-hand top corner of the oblong that framed them.

The pew had qualities: tall fat hassocks, red cushions, a comparative seclusion, and, in the case of the affluent, red curtains drawn at sermon-time.

The child wearied by the spectacle of a plump divine, in black gown and Geneva bands, thumping the pulpit-cushions in the madness of incomprehensible oratory, surrendered his ears to the noise of intonations which, in his own treble, would have earned the reprimand, 'Naughty temper'. His eyes, however, were, through some oversight of the gods of his universe, still his own. They found their own pasture: not, to be sure, the argent and sable of gown and bands, still less the gules of flushed denunciatory gills.

There is fair pasture in an old church which, when Norman work was broken down, men loved and built again as from the heart, with pillars and arches, that, to their rude time, symbolized all that the heart desires to materialize, in symbolic stone. The fretted tombs where the effigies of warrior and priest lay life-like in dead marble, the fretted canopies that brooded above their rest. Tall pillars like the trunks of the pine woods that smelt so sweet, the marvel of the timbered roof — turned upside down it would be like a ship. And what could be easier than to turn it upside down?

Imagination shrank bashfully from the pulpit already tightly tenanted, but the triforium was plainly and beautifully empty; there one could walk, squeezing happily through the deep thin arches and treading carefully by the unguarded narrow ledge. Only if one played too long in the roof aunts nudged, and urgent whispers insisted that one must not look about like that in church. When this moment came it came always as a crisis foreseen, half-dreaded, half longed-for. After that the child kept his eyes lowered, and looked only at the faded red hassocks that the straw bulged from, and in brief, guarded, intimate moments, at the other child.

The other child was kneeling, always, whether the congregation knelt or stood or sat. Its hands were clasped. Its face was raised, but its back bowed under a weight — the weight of the font, for the other child was of marble and knelt always in the church, Sundays and weekdays. There had been once three marble figures holding up the shallow basin, but two had crumbled or been broken away, and now it seemed that the whole weight of the superimposed marble rested on those slender shoulders.

The child who was not marble was sorry for the other. He must be very tired.

The child who was not marble — his name was Ernest — that child of weary eyes and bored brain, pitied the marble boy while he envied him.

'I suppose he doesn't really feel, if he's stone,' he said. 'That's what they mean by the stony-hearted tyrant. But if he does feel — How jolly it would be if he could come out and sit in my pew, or if I could creep under the font beside him. If he would move a little there would be just room for me.'

The first time that Ernest ever saw the marble child move was on the hottest Sunday in the year. The walk across the fields had been a breathless penance, the ground burned the soles of Ernest's feet as red-hot ploughshares the feet of the saints. The corn was cut, and stood in stiff yellow stooks, and the shadows were very black. The sky was light, except in the west beyond the pine trees, where blue-black clouds were piled.

'Like witches' feather-beds,' said Aunt Harriet, shaking out the folds of her lace shawl.

'Not before the child, dear,' whispered Aunt Emmeline.

Ernest heard her, of course. It was always like that: as soon as anyone spoke about anything interesting, Aunt Emmeline intervened. Ernest walked along very melancholy in his starched frill. The dust had whitened his strapped shoes, and there was a wrinkle in one of his white socks.

'Pull it up, child, pull it up,' said Aunt Jessie; and shielded from the world by the vast silk-veiled crinolines of three full-sized aunts, he pulled it up.

On the way to church, and indeed, in all walks abroad, you held the hand of an aunt; the circumferent crinolines made the holding an arm's-length business, very tiring. Ernest was always glad when, in the porch, the hand was dropped. It was just as the porch was reached that the first lonely roll of thunder broke over the hills.

'I knew it,' said Aunt Jessie, in triumph, 'but you would wear your blue silk.'

There was no more thunder till after the second lesson, which was hardly ever as interesting as the first, Ernest thought. The marble child looked more tired than usual, and Ernest lost himself in a dream-game where both of them got out from prison and played hide-and-seek among the tombstones. Then the thunder cracked deafeningly right over the church. Ernest forgot to stand up, and even the clergyman waited till it died away.

It was a most exciting service, well worth coming to church for, and afterwards people crowded in the wide porch and wondered whether it would clear, and wished they had brought their umbrellas. Some went back and sat in their pews till the servants should have had time to go home and return with umbrellas and cloaks. The more impetuous made clumsy rushes between the showers, bonnets bent, skirts held well up. Many a Sunday dress was ruined that day, many a bonnet fell from best to second-best.

And it was when Aunt Jessie whispered to him to sit still and be a good boy and learn a hymn, that he looked to the marble child with, 'Isn't it a shame?' in his heart and his eyes, and the marble child looked back, 'Never mind, it will soon be over,' and held out its marble hands. Ernest saw them come toward him, reaching well beyond the rim of the basin under which they had always, till now, stayed.

'Oh!' said Ernest, quite out loud, and dropping the hymn-book, held out his hands, or began to hold them out. For before he had done more than sketch the gesture, he remembered that marble does not move and that one must not be silly. All the same, marble *had* moved. Also Ernest had 'spoken out loud' in church. Unspeakable disgrace!

He was taken home in conscious ignominy, treading in all the puddles to distract his mind from his condition.

He was put to bed early, as a punishment, instead of sitting up and learning his catechism under the charge of one of the maids while the aunts went to evening church. This, while terrible to Ernest, was in the nature of a reprieve to the housemaid, who found means to modify her own consequent loneliness. Far-away whisperings and laughings from the back or kitchen windows assured Ernest that the front or polite side of the house was unguarded. He got up, simulated the appearance of the completely dressed, and went down the carpeted stairs, through the rosewood-furnished drawing-room, rose-scented and still as a deathbed, and so out through the French windows to the lawn, where already the beginnings of dew lay softly.

His going out had no definite aim. It was simply an act of rebellion such as, secure from observation, the timid may achieve; a demonstration akin to putting the tongue out behind people's backs.

Having got himself out on the lawn, he made haste to hide in the shrubbery, disheartened by a baffling consciousness of the futility of safe revenges. What is the tongue put out behind the back of the enemy without the applause of some admirer?

The red rays of the setting sun made splendor in the dripping shrubbery.

'I wish I hadn't,' said Ernest.

But it seemed silly to go back now, just to go out and to go back. So he went farther into the shrubbery and got out at the other side where the shrubbery slopes down into the wood, and it was nearly dark there — so nearly that the child felt more alone than ever.

And then quite suddenly he was not alone. Hands parted the hazels and a face he knew looked out from between them.

He knew the face, and yet the child he saw was not any of the children he knew.

'Well,' said the child with the face he knew, 'I've been watching you. What did you come out for?'

'I was put to bed.'

'Do you not like it?'

'Not when it's for punishment.'

'If you'll go back now,' said the strange child, 'I'll come and play with you after you're asleep.'

'You daren't. Suppose the aunts catch you?'

'They won't,' said the child, shaking its head and laughing. 'I'll race you to the house!'

Ernest ran. He won the race. For the other child was not there at all when he reached the house.

'How odd!' he said. But he was tired and there was thunder

again and it was beginning to rain, large spots as big as pennies on the step of the French window. So he went back to bed, too sleepy to worry about the question of where he had seen the child before, and only a little disappointed because his revenge had been so brief and inadequate.

Then he fell asleep and dreamed that the marble child had crept out from under the font, and that he and it were playing hide-and-seek among the pews in the gallery at church. It was a delightful dream and lasted all night, and when he woke he knew that the child he had seen in the wood in yesterday's last light was the marble child from the church.

This did not surprise him as much as it would surprise you: the world where children live is so full of amazing and incredible-looking things that turn out to be quite real. And if Lot's wife could be turned into a pillar of salt, why should not a marble child turn into a real one? It was all quite plain to Ernest, but he did not tell anyone: because he had a feeling that it might not be easy to make it plain to them.

'That child doesn't look quite the thing,' said Aunt Emmeline at breakfast. 'A dose of Gregory's, I think, at eleven.'

Ernest's morning was blighted. Did you ever take Gregory's powder? It is worse than quinine, worse than senna, worse than anything except castor oil.

But Ernest had to take it — in raspberry jam.

'And don't make such faces,' said Aunt Emmeline, rinsing the spoon at the pantry sink. 'You know it's all for your own good.'

As though the thought that it is for one's own good ever kept anyone from making faces!

The aunts were kind in their grown-up crinolined way. But Ernest wanted someone to play with. Every night in his dreams he played with the marble child. And at church on Sunday the marble child still held out its hands, farther than before.

'Come along then,' Ernest said to it, in that voice with which heart speaks to heart; 'come and sit with me behind the red curtains. Come!'

The marble child did not look at him. Its head seemed to be bent farther forward than ever before.

When it came to the second hymn Ernest had an inspiration. All the rest of the churchful, sleepy and suitable, were singing —

> The roseate hues of early dawn,
> The brightness of the day,
> The crimson of the sunset sky,
> How fast they fade away.

Ernest turned his head towards the marble child and softly mouthed — you could hardly call it singing —

> The rosy tews of early dawn,
> The brightness of the day,
> Come out, come out, come out, come out,
> Come out with me and play.

And he pictured the rapture of that moment when the marble child should respond to this appeal, creep out from under the font, and come and sit beside him on the red cushions beyond the red curtains. The aunts would not see, of course. They never saw the things that mattered. No one would see except Ernest. He looked hard at the marble child.

'You must come out,' he said; and again, 'You must come, you must.'

And the marble child did come. It crept out and came to sit by him, holding his hand. It was a cold hand certainly, but it did not feel like marble.

And the next thing he knew, an aunt was shaking him and whispering with fierceness tempered by reverence for the sacred edifice —

'Wake up, Ernest. How can you be so naughty?'

And the marble child was back in its place under the font.

When Ernest looks back on that summer it seems to have thundered every time he went to church. But of course this cannot really have been the case.

But it was certainly a very lowering purple-skied day that saw him stealthily start on the adventure of his little life. He was weary of aunts — they were kind yet just; they told him so and he believed them. But their justice was exactly like other people's nagging, and their kindness he did not want at all. He wanted someone to play with.

'May we walk up to the churchyard?' was a request at first received graciously as showing a serious spirit. But its reiteration was considered morbid, and his walks took the more dusty direction of the County Asylum.

His longing for the only child he knew, the marble child, exacerbated by denial, drove him to rebellion. He would run away. He would live with the marble child in the big church porch; they would eat berries from the wood nearby, just as children did in books, and hide there when people came to church.

So he watched his opportunity and went quietly out through the French window, skirted the side of the house where all the windows were blank because of the old window-tax, took the narrow strip of lawn at a breathless run, and found safe cover among the rhododendrons.

The church-door was locked, of course, but he knew where there was a broken pane in the vestry window, and his eye had marked the lop-sided tombstone underneath it. By climbing upon that and getting a knee in the carved water-spout — He did it, got his hand through, turned the catch of the window, and fell through upon the dusty table of the vestry.

The door was ajar and he passed into the empty church. It seemed very large and gray now that he had it to himself. His feet made a loud echoing noise that was disconcerting. He had meant to call out, 'Here I am!' But in the face of these echoes he could not.

He found the marble child, its head bent more than ever, its hands reaching out quite beyond the edge of the font; and when he was quite close he whispered —

'Here I am — Come and play!'

But his voice trembled a little. The marble child was so plainly marble. And yet it had not always been marble. He was not sure. Yet —

'I *am* sure,' he said. 'You did talk to me in the shrubbery, didn't you?'

But the marble child did not move or speak.

'You did come and hold my hand last Sunday,' he said, a little louder.

And only the empty echoes answered him.

'Come out,' he said then, almost afraid now of the church's insistent silence. 'I've come to live with you altogether. Come out of your marble, do come out!'

He reached up to stroke the marble cheek. A sound thrilled him, a loud everyday sound. The big key turning in the lock of the south door. The aunts!

'Now they'll take me back,' said Ernest; 'you might have come.'

But it was not the aunts. It was the old pew-opener, come to scrub the chancel. She came slowly in with pail and brush; the pail slopped a little water on to the floor close to Ernest as she passed him, not seeing.

Then the marble child moved, turned toward Ernest with speaking lips and eyes that saw.

'You can stay with me forever if you like,' it said, 'but you'll have to see things happen. I have seen things happen.'

'What sort of things?' Ernest asked.

'Terrible things.'

'What things shall I have to see?'

'*She*,' the marble child moved a free arm to point to the old woman on the chancel steps, 'and your aunt who will be here presently, looking for you. Do you hear the thunder? Presently the lightning will strike the church. It won't hurt us, but it will fall on them.'

Ernest remembered in a flash how kind Aunt Emmeline had been when he was ill, how Aunt Jessie had given him his chessmen, and Aunt Harriet had taught him how to make paper rosettes for picture-frames.

'I must go and tell them,' he said.

'If you go, you'll never see me again,' said the marble child, and put its arms round his neck.

'Can't I come back to you when I've told them?' Ernest asked, returning the embrace.

'There will be no coming back,' said the marble child.

'But I want you. I love you best of everybody in the world,' Ernest said.

'I know.'

'I'll stay with you,' said Ernest.

The marble child said nothing.

'But if I don't tell them I shall be the same as a murderer,' Ernest whispered. 'Oh! let me go, and come back to you.'

'I shall not be here.'

'But I must go. I must,' said Ernest, torn between love and duty.

'Yes.'

'And I shan't have you anymore?' the living child urged.

'You'll have me in your heart,' said the marble child — 'that's where I want to be. That's my real home.'

They kissed each other again.

✖

'It was certainly a direct Providence,' Aunt Emmeline used to say in later years to really sympathetic friends, 'that I thought of going up to the church when I did. Otherwise nothing could have saved dear Ernest. He was terrified, quite crazy with fright, poor child, and he rushed out at me from behind our pew shouting, "Come away, come away, auntie, come away!" and dragged me out. Mrs Meadows providentially followed, to see what it was all about, and the next thing was the catastrophe.'

'The church was struck by a thunder-bolt, was it not?' the sympathetic friend asks.

'It was indeed — a deafening crash, my dear — and then the church slowly crumbled before our eyes. The south wall broke like a slice of cake when you break it across — and the noise and the dust! Mrs Meadows never had her hearing again, poor thing, and her mind was a little affected too. I became unconscious, and Ernest — well, it was altogether too much for the child. He lay between life and death for weeks. Shock to the system, the physician said. He had been rather run down before. We had to get a little cousin to come and live with us afterwards. The physicians said that he required young society.'

'It must indeed have been a shock,' says the sympathetic friend, who knows there is more to come.

'His intellect was quite changed, my dear,' Aunt Emmeline resumes; 'on regaining consciousness he demanded the marble child! Cried and raved, my dear, always about the marble child. It appeared he had had fancies about one of the little angels that supported the old font, not the present font, my dear. We presented that as a token of gratitude to Providence for our escape. Of course we checked his fancifulness as well as we could, but it lasted quite a long time.'

'What became of the little marble angel?' the friend inquires as in friendship bound.

'Crushed to powder, dear, in the awful wreck of the church. Not a trace of it could be found. And poor Mrs Meadows! So dreadful those delusions.'

'What form did her delusions take?' the friend, anxious to be done with the old story, hastily asks.

'Well, she always declared that *two* children ran out to warn me and that one of them was very unusual looking. "It wasn't no flesh and blood, ma'am," she used to say in her ungrammatical way; "it was a little angel a-taking care of Master Ernest. It 'ad 'old of 'is 'and. And I say it was 'is garden angel, and its face was as bright as a lily in the sun."'

The friend glances at the India cabinet, and Aunt Emmeline rises and unlocks it.

'Ernest must have been behaving in a very naughty and destructive way in the church — but the physician said he was not quite himself probably, for when they got him home and undressed him they found this in his hand.'

Then the sympathizing friend polishes her glasses and looks, not for the first time, at the relic from the drawer of the India cabinet. It is a white marble finger.

Thus flow the reminiscences of Aunt Emmeline. The memories of Ernest run as this tale runs.

16 The Haunted House

It was by the merest accident that Desmond ever went to the Haunted House. He had been away from England for six years, and the nine months' leave taught him how easily one drops out of one's place.

He had taken rooms at the Greyhound before he found that there was no reason why he should stay in Elmstead rather than in any other of London's dismal outposts. He wrote to all the friends whose addresses he could remember, and settled himself to await their answers.

He wanted someone to talk to, and there was no one. Meantime he lounged on the horsehair sofa with the advertisements, and his pleasant grey eyes followed line after line with intolerable boredom. Then, suddenly, 'Halloa!' he said, and sat up. This is what he read:

A HAUNTED HOUSE — Advertiser is anxious to have phenomena investigated. Any properly accredited investigator will be given full facilities. Address, by letter only, Wildon Prior, 237, Museum Street, London.

'That's rum!' he said. Wildon Prior had been the best wicket-keeper in his club. It wasn't a common name. Anyway, it was worth trying, so he sent off a telegram.

'Wildon Prior, 237, Museum Street, London. May I come to you for a day or two and see the ghost? — WILLIAM DESMOND.'

On returning next day from a stroll there was an orange envelope on the wide Pembroke table in his parlour.

'Delighted — expect you today. Book to Crittenden from Charing Cross. Wire train. — WILDON PRIOR, Ormehurst Rectory, Kent.'

'So that's all right,' said Desmond, and went off to pack his bag and ask in the bar for a time-table. 'Good old Wildon; it will be ripping, seeing him again.'

A curious little omnibus, rather like a bathing-machine, was waiting outside Crittenden Station, and its driver, a swarthy, blunt-faced little man, with liquid eyes, said, 'You a friend of Mr Prior, sir?' shut him up in the bathing-machine, and banged the door on him. It was a very long drive, and less pleasant than it would have been in an open carriage.

The last part of the journey was through a wood; then came a churchyard and a church, and the bathing-machine turned in at a gate under heavy trees and drew up in front of a white house with bare, gaunt windows.

'Cheerful place, upon my soul!' Desmond told himself, as he tumbled out of the back of the bathing-machine.

The driver set his bag on the discoloured doorstep and drove off. Desmond pulled a rusty chain, and a big-throated bell jangled above his head.

Nobody came to the door, and he rang again. Still nobody came, but he heard a window thrown open above the porch. He stepped back on to the gravel and looked up.

A young man with rough hair and pale eyes was looking out. Not Wildon, nothing like Wildon. He did not speak, but he seemed to be making signs; and the signs seemed to mean. 'Go away!'

'I came to see Mr Prior,' said Desmond. Instantly and softly the window closed.

'Is it a lunatic asylum I've come to by chance?' Desmond asked himself, and pulled again at the rusty chain.

Steps sounded inside the house, the sound of boots on stone. Bolts were shot back, door opened, and Desmond, rather hot and a little annoyed, found himself looking into a pair of very dark, friendly eyes, and a very pleasant voice said:

'Mr Desmond, I presume? Do come in and let me apologize.'

The speaker shook him warmly by the hand, and he found himself following down a flagged passage a man of more than mature middle-age, well-dressed, handsome, with an air of competence and alertness which we associate with what is called 'a man of the world'. He opened a door and led the way into a shabby, bookish, leathery room.

'Do sit down, Mr Desmond.'

'This must be the uncle, I suppose,' Desmond thought, as he fitted himself into the shabby, perfect curves of the arm-chair. 'How's Wildon?' he asked, aloud. 'All right, I hope?'

The other looked at him. 'I beg your pardon,' he said, doubtfully.

'I was asking how Wildon is?'

'I am quite well, I thank you,' said the other man, with some formality.

'I beg your pardon' — it was now Desmond's turn to say it — 'I did not realize that your name might be Wildon, too. I meant Wildon Prior.'

'I am Wildon Prior,' said the other, 'and you, I presume, are the expert from the Psychical Society?'

'Good Lord, no!' said Desmond. 'I'm Wildon Prior's friend, and, of course, there must be two Wildon Priors.'

'You sent the telegram? You are Mr Desmond? The Psychical Society were to send an expert, and I thought —'

'I see,' said Desmond, 'and I thought you were Wildon Prior, an old friend of mine — a young man,' he said, and half rose.

'Now, don't,' said Wildon Prior. 'No doubt it's my nephew who is your friend. Did he know you were coming? But of course he didn't. I am wandering. But I'm exceedingly glad to see you. You will stay, will you not? If you can endure to be the guest of an old man. And I will write to Will tonight and ask him to join us.'

'That's most awfully good of you,' Desmond assured him.

'I shall be glad to stay. I was awfully pleased when I saw Wildon's name in the paper, because —' And out came the tale of Elmstead, its loneliness and disappointment.

Mr Prior listened with the kindest interest.

'And you have not found your friends? How sad! But they will write to you. Of course, you left your address?'

'I didn't, by Jove!' said Desmond. 'But I can write. Can I catch the post?'

'Easily,' the elder man assured him. 'Write your letters now. My man shall take them to the post, and then we will have dinner, and I will tell you about the ghost.'

Desmond wrote his letters quickly, Mr Prior just then reappearing.

'Now I'll take you to your room,' he said, gathering the letters in long, white hands. 'You'll like a rest. Dinner at eight.'

The bed-chamber, like the parlour, had a pleasant air of worn luxury and accustomed comfort.

'I hope you will be comfortable,' the host said, with courteous solicitude. And Desmond was quite sure that he would.

Three covers were laid, the swarthy man who had driven Desmond from the station stood behind the host's chair, and a figure came towards Desmond and his host from the shadows beyond the yellow circles of the silver-slicked candles.

'My assistant, Mr Verney,' said the host, and Desmond surrendered his hand to the limp, damp touch of the man who had seemed to say to him, from the window above the porch, 'Go away!' Was Mr Prior perhaps a doctor who received 'paying guests', persons who were, in Desmond's phrase, 'a bit balmy'? But he had said 'assistant'.

'I thought,' said Desmond, hastily, 'you would be a clergyman. The Rectory, you know — I thought Wildon, my friend Wildon, was staying with an uncle who was a clergyman.'

'Oh, no,' said Mr Prior. 'I rent the Rectory. The rector thinks it is damp. The church is disused, too. It is not considered safe, and they can't afford to restore it. Claret to Mr Desmond, Lopez.' And the swarthy, blunt-faced man filled his glass.

'I find this place very convenient for my experiments. I dabble a little in chemistry, Mr Desmond, and Verney here assists me.'

Verney murmured something that sounded like 'only too proud', and subsided.

'We all have our hobbies, and chemistry is mine,' Mr Prior went on. 'Fortunately, I have a little income which enables me to indulge it. Wildon, my nephew, you know, laughs at me, and calls it the science of smells. But it's absorbing, very absorbing.'

After dinner Verney faded away, and Desmond and his host stretched their feet to what Mr Prior called a 'handful of fire', for the evening had grown chill.

'And now,' Desmond said, 'won't you tell me the ghost story?'

The other glanced round the room.

'There isn't really a ghost story at all. It's only that — well, it's never happened to me personally, but it happened to Verney, poor lad, and he's never been quite his own self since.'

Desmond flattered himself on his insight.

'Is mine the haunted room?' he asked.

'It doesn't come to any particular room,' said the other, slowly, 'nor to any particular person.'

'Anyone may happen to see it?'

'No one sees it. It isn't the kind of ghost that's seen or heard.'

'I'm afraid I'm rather stupid, but I don't understand,' said

Desmond, roundly. 'How can it be a ghost, if you neither hear it nor see it?'

'I did not say it was a ghost,' Mr Prior corrected. 'I only say that there is something about this house which is not ordinary. Several of my assistants have had to leave; the thing got on their nerves.'

'What became of the assistants?' asked Desmond.

'Oh, they left, you know; they left,' Prior answered, vaguely. 'One couldn't expect them to sacrifice their health. I sometimes think — village gossip is a deadly thing, Mr Desmond — that perhaps they were prepared to be frightened; that they fancy things. I hope the Psychical Society's expert won't be a neurotic. But even without being a neurotic one might — but you don't believe in ghosts, Mr Desmond. Your Anglo-Saxon common sense forbids it.'

'I'm afraid I'm not exactly Anglo-Saxon,' said Desmond. 'On my father's side I'm pure Celt; though I know I don't do credit to the race.'

'And on your mother's side?' Mr Prior asked, with extraordinary eagerness; an eagerness so sudden and disproportioned to the question that Desmond stared. A faint touch of resentment as suddenly stirred in him, the first spark of antagonism to his host.

'Oh,' he said, lightly, 'I think I must have Chinese blood. I get on so well with the natives in Shanghai, and they tell me I owe my nose to a Red Indian great grandmother.'

'No negro blood, I suppose?' the host asked, with almost discourteous insistence.

'Oh, I wouldn't say that,' Desmond answered. He meant to say it laughing, but he didn't. 'My hair, you know — it's a very stiff curl it's got, and my mother's people were in the West Indies a few generations ago. You're interested in distinctions of race, I take it?'

'Not at all, not at all,' Mr Prior surprisingly assured him;

'but, of course, any details of your family are necessarily interesting to me. I feel,' he added, with another of his winning smiles, 'that you and I are already friends.'

Desmond could not have reasoningly defended the faint quality of dislike that had begun to tinge his first pleasant sense of being welcomed and wished for as a guest.

'You're very kind,' he said; 'it's jolly of you to take in a stranger like this.'

Mr Prior smiled, handed the cigar-box, mixed whisky and soda, and began to talk about the history of the house.

'The foundations are almost certainly thirteenth century. It was a priory, you know. There's a curious tale, by the way, about the man Henry gave it to when he smashed up the monasteries. There was a curse; there seems always to have been a curse —'

The gentle, pleasant, high-bred voice went on. Desmond thought he was listening, but presently he roused himself and dragged his attention back to the words that were being spoken.

'— that made the fifth death ... There is one every hundred years, and always in the same mysterious way.'

Then he found himself on his feet, incredibly sleepy, and heard himself say:

'These old stories are tremendously interesting. Thank you very much. I hope you won't think me very uncivil, but I think I'd rather like to turn in; I feel a bit tired, somehow.'

'But of course, my dear chap.'

Mr Prior saw Desmond to his room.

'Got everything you want? Right. Lock the door if you should feel nervous. Of course, a lock can't keep ghosts out, but I always feel as if it could,' and with another of those pleasant, friendly laughs he was gone.

William Desmond went to bed a strong young man, sleepy indeed beyond his experience of sleepiness, but well and comfortable. He awoke faint and trembling, lying deep in the billows of the feather bed; and lukewarm waves of exhaustion swept through him. Where was he? What had happened? His brain, dizzy and weak at first, refused him any answer. When he remembered, the abrupt spasm of repulsion which he had felt so suddenly and unreasonably the night before came back to him in a hot, breathless flush. He had been drugged, he had been poisoned!

'I must get out of this,' he told himself, and blundered out of bed towards the silken bell-pull that he had noticed the night before hanging near the door.

As he pulled it, the bed and the wardrobe and the room rose up round him and fell on him, and he fainted.

When he next knew anything someone was putting brandy to his lips. He saw Prior, the kindest concern in his face. The assistant, pale and watery-eyed. The swarthy man-servant, stolid, silent, and expressionless. He heard Verney say to Prior:

'You see it was too much — I told you —'

'Hush,' said Prior, 'he's coming to.'

✕

Four days later Desmond, lying on a wicker chair on the lawn, was a little disinclined for exertion, but no longer ill. Nourishing foods and drinks, beef-tea, stimulants, and constant care — these had brought him back to something like his normal state. He wondered at the vague suspicions, vaguely remembered, of that first night; they had all been proved absurd by the unwavering care and kindness of everyone in the Haunted House.

'But what caused it?' he asked his host, for the fiftieth time. 'What made me make such a fool of myself?' And this time Mr Prior did not put him off, as he had always done before by begging him to wait till he was stronger.

'I am afraid, you know,' he said, 'that the ghost really did come to you. I am inclined to revise my opinion of the ghost.'

'But why didn't it come again?'

'I have been with you every night, you know,' his host reminded him. And, indeed, the sufferer had never been left alone since the ringing of his bell on that terrible first morning.

'And now,' Mr Prior went on, 'if you will not think me inhospitable, I think you will be better away from here. You ought to go to the seaside.'

'There haven't been any letters for me, I suppose?' Desmond said, a little wistfully.

'Not one. I suppose you gave the right address? Ormehurst Rectory, Crittenden, Kent?'

'I don't think I put Crittenden,' said Desmond. 'I copied the address from your telegram.' He pulled the pink paper from his pocket.

'Ah, that would account,' said the other.

'You've been most awfully kind all through,' said Desmond, abruptly.

'Nonsense, my boy,' said the elder man, benevolently. 'I only wish Willie had been able to come. He's never written, the rascal! Nothing but the telegram to say he could not come and was writing.'

'I suppose he's having a jolly time somewhere,' said Desmond, enviously; 'but look here — do tell me about the ghost, if there's anything to tell. I'm almost quite well now, and I *should* like to know what it was that made a fool of me like that.'

'Well' — Mr Prior looked round him at the gold and red of dahlias and sunflowers, gay in the September sunshine — 'here, and now, I don't know that it could do any harm. You remember that story of the man who got this place from Henry VIII and the curse? That man's wife is buried in a vault under the church. Well, there were legends, and I confess I was curious to see her tomb. There are iron gates to the vault. Locked, they were. I opened them with an old key — and I couldn't get them to shut again.'

'Yes?' Desmond said.

'You think I might have sent for a locksmith; but the fact is, there is a small crypt to the church, and I have used that crypt as a supplementary laboratory. If I had called anyone in to see to the lock they would have gossiped. I should have been turned out of my laboratory — perhaps out of my house.'

'I see.'

'Now the curious thing is,' Mr Prior went on, lowering his voice, 'that it is only since that grating was opened that this house has been what they call "haunted". It is since then that all these things have happened.'

'What things?'

'People staying here, suddenly ill — just as you were. And the attacks always seem to indicate loss of blood. And —' He hesitated a moment. 'That wound in your throat. I told you you had hurt yourself falling when you rang the bell. But that was not true. What is true is that you had on your throat just the same little white wound that all the others have had. I wish' — he frowned — 'that I could get that vault gate shut again. The key won't turn.'

'I wonder if I could do anything?' Desmond asked, secretly convinced that he *had* hurt his throat in falling, and that his host's story was, as he put it, 'all moonshine'. Still, to put a lock right was but a slight return for all the care and kindness. 'I'm an engineer, you know,' he added, awkwardly, and rose. 'Probably a little oil. Let's have a look at this same lock.'

He followed Mr Prior through the house to the church. A bright, smooth old key turned readily, and they passed into the building, musty and damp, where ivy crawled through the broken windows, and the blue sky seemed to be laid close against the holes in the roof. Another key clicked in the lock of a low door beside what had once been the Lady Chapel, a thick oak door grated back, and Mr Prior stopped a moment to light a candle that waited in its rough iron candlestick on a ledge of the stonework. Then down narrow stairs, chipped a little at the edges and soft with dust. The crypt was Norman, very simply beautiful. At the end of it was a recess, masked with a grating of rusty ironwork.

'They used to think,' said Mr Prior, 'that iron kept off witchcraft. This is the lock,' he went on, holding the candle against the gate, which was ajar.

They went through the gate, because the lock was on the other side. Desmond worked a minute or two with the oil and feather that he had brought. Then with a little wrench the key turned and re-turned.

'I think that's all right,' he said, looking up, kneeling on one knee, with the key still in the lock and his hand on it.

'May I try it?'

Mr Prior took Desmond's place, turned the key, pulled it out, and stood up. Then the key and the candlestick fell rattling on the stone floor, and the old man sprang upon Desmond.

'Now I've got you,' he growled, in the darkness, and Desmond says that his spring and his clutch and his voice were like the spring and the clutch and the growl of a strong savage beast.

Desmond's little strength snapped like a twig at his first bracing of it to resistance. The old man held him as a vice holds. He had got a rope from somewhere. He was tying Desmond's arms.

Desmond hates to know that there in the dark he screamed like a caught hare. Then he remembered that he was a man, and shouted 'Help! Here! Help!'

But a hand was on his mouth, and now a handkerchief was being knotted at the back of his head. He was on the floor, leaning against something. Prior's hands had left him.

'Now,' said Prior's voice, a little breathless, and the match he struck showed Desmond the stone shelves with long things on them — coffins he supposed. 'Now, I'm sorry I had to do it, but science before friendship, my dear Desmond,' he went on, quite courteous and friendly. 'I will explain to you, and you will see that a man of honour could not act otherwise. Of course, you having no friends who know where you are is most convenient. I saw that from the first. Now I'll explain. I didn't expect you to understand by instinct. But no matter. I am, I say it without vanity, the greatest discoverer since Newton. I know how to modify men's natures. I can make men what I choose. It's all done by transfusion of blood. Lopez you know, my man Lopez — I've pumped the blood of dogs into his veins, and he's my slave — like a dog. Verney, he's my slave, too — part dog's blood and partly the blood of people who've come from time to time to investigate the ghost, and partly my own, because I wanted him to be clever enough to help me. And there's a bigger thing behind all this. You'll understand me when I say' — here he became very technical indeed, and used many words that meant nothing to Desmond, whose thought dwelt more and more on his small chance of escape.

To die like a rat in a hole, a rat in a hole! If he could only loosen the handkerchief and shout again!

'Attend, can't you?' said Prior, savagely, and kicked him. 'I beg your pardon, my dear chap,' he went on, suavely, 'but this is important. So you see the elixir of life is really the blood. The blood is the life, you know, and my great discovery is that to make a man immortal, and restore his youth, one only needs blood from the veins of a man who unites in himself blood of the four great races — the four colours, black, white, red, and yellow. Your blood unites these four. I took as much as I dared from you that night. I was the vampire, you know.' He laughed pleasantly. 'But your blood didn't act. The drug I had to give you to induce sleep probably destroyed the vital germs. And, besides, there wasn't enough of it. Now there is going to be enough!'

Desmond had been working his head against the thing behind him, easing the knot of the handkerchief down till it slipped from head to neck. Now he got his mouth free, and said, quickly:

'That was not true what I said about the Chinamen and that. I was joking. My mother's people were all Devon.'

'I don't blame you in the least,' said Prior, quietly. 'I should lie myself in your place.'

And he put back the handkerchief. The candle was now burning clearly from the place where it stood — on a stone coffin. Desmond could see that the long things on the shelves *were* coffins, not all of stone. He wondered what this madman would do with his body when everything was over. The little wound in his throat had broken out again. He could feel the slow trickle of warmth on his neck. He wondered whether he would faint. It felt like it.

'I wish I'd brought you here the first day — it was Verney's doing, my tinkering about with pints and half-pints. Sheer waste — sheer wanton waste!'

Prior stopped and stood looking at him.

Desmond, despairingly conscious of growing physical weakness, caught himself in a real wonder as to whether this might not be a dream — a horrible, insane dream — and he could not wholly dismiss the wonder, because incredible things seemed to be adding themselves to the real horrors of the situation, just as they do in dreams. There seemed to be something stirring in the place — something that wasn't Prior. No — nor Prior's shadow, either. That was black and sprawled big across the arched roof. This was white, and very small and thin. But it stirred, it grew — now it was no longer just a line of white, but a long, narrow, white wedge — and it showed between the coffin on the shelf opposite him and that coffin's lid.

And still Prior stood very still looking down on his prey. All emotion but a dull wonder was now dead in Desmond's weakened senses. In dreams — if one called out, one awoke — but he could not call out. Perhaps if one moved — But before he could bring his enfeebled will to the decision of movement — something else moved. The black lid of the coffin opposite rose slowly — and then suddenly fell, clattering and echoing, and from the coffin rose a form, humbly white and shrouded, and fell on Prior and rolled with him on the floor of the vault in a silent, whirling struggle. The last thing Desmond heard before he fainted in good earnest was the scream Prior uttered as he turned at the crash and saw the white-shrouded body leaping towards him.

'It's all right,' he heard next. And Verney was bending over him with brandy. 'You're quite safe. He's tied up and locked in the laboratory. No. That's all right, too.' For Desmond's eyes had turned towards the lidless coffin. 'That was only me. It was the only way I could think of, to save you. Can you walk now? Let me help you, so. I've opened the grating. Come.'

※

Desmond blinked in the sunlight he had never thought to see again. Here he was, back in his wicker chair. He looked at the sundial on the house. The whole thing had taken less than fifty minutes.

'Tell me,' said he. And Verney told him in short sentences with pauses between.

'I tried to warn you,' he said, 'you remember, in the window. I really believed in his experiments at first — and — he'd found out something about me — and not told. It was when I was very young. God knows I've paid for it. And when you came I'd only just found out what really had happened to the other chaps. That beast Lopez let it out when he was drunk. Inhuman brute! And I had a row with Prior that first night, and he promised me he wouldn't touch you. And then he did.'

'You might have told me.'

'You were in a nice state to be told anything, weren't you? He promised me he'd send you off as soon as you were well enough. And he *had* been good to me. But when I heard him begin about the grating and the key I *knew* — so I just got a sheet and —'

'But why didn't you come out before?'

'I didn't dare. He could have tackled me easily if he had known what he was tackling. He kept moving about. It had to be done suddenly. I counted on just that moment of weakness when he really thought a dead body had come to life to defend you. Now I'm going to harness the horse and drive you to the police-station at Crittenden. And they'll send and lock him up. Everyone knew he was as mad as a hatter, but somebody had to be nearly killed before anyone would lock him up. The law's like that, you know.'

'But you — the police — won't they —'

'It's quite safe,' said Verney, dully. 'Nobody knows but the old man, and now nobody will believe anything he says. No, he never posted your letters, of course, and he never wrote to your friend, and he put off the Psychical man. No, I can't find Lopez; he must know that something's up. He's bolted.'

But he had not. They found him, stubbornly dumb, but moaning a little, crouched against the locked grating of the vault when they came, a prudent half-dozen of them, to take the old man away from the Haunted House. The master was dumb as the man. He would not speak. He has never spoken since.

17 The Pavilion

There was never a moment's doubt in her own mind. So she said afterwards. And everyone agreed that she had concealed her feelings with true womanly discretion. Her friend and confidante, Amelia Davenant, was at any rate completely deceived. Amelia was one of those featureless blondes who seem born to be overlooked. She adored her beautiful friend, and never, from first to last, could see any fault in her, except, perhaps, on the evening when the real things of the story happened. And even in this matter she owned at the time that it was only that her darling Ernestine did not understand.

Ernestine was a prettyish girl with the airs, so irresistible and misleading, of a beauty; most people said that she was beautiful, and she certainly managed, with extraordinary success, to produce the illusion of beauty. Quite a number of plainish girls achieve that effect nowadays. The freedom of modern dress and coiffure and the increasing confidence in herself which the modern girl experiences aid her in fostering the illusion; but in the sixties, when everyone wore much the same sort of bonnet, when your choice in coiffure was limited to bandeaux or ringlets, and the crinoline was your only wear, something very like genius was needed to deceive the world in the matter of your personal charms. Ernestine had that genius; hers was the smiling, ringletted, dark-haired, dark-eyed, sparkling type.

Amelia had a blond bandeau and kind appealing blue eyes, rather too small and rather too dull; her hands and ears were beautiful, and she kept them out of sight as much as possible. In our times the blond hair would have been puffed out to make a frame for the forehead, a little too high; a certain shade of blue and a certain shade of boldness would have made her eyes effective. And the beautiful hands would have learned that flower-like droop of the wrist so justly and so universally admired. But as it was, Amelia was very nearly plain, and in her secret emotional self-communings told herself that she was ugly. It was she who, at the age of fourteen, composed the remarkable poem beginning:

> I know that I am ugly: did I make
> The face that is the laugh and jest of all?

and went on, after disclaiming any personal responsibility for the face, to entreat the kind earth to 'cover it away from mocking eyes', and to 'let the daisies blossom where it lies'.

Amelia did not want to die, and her face was not the laugh and jest, or indeed the special interest, of anyone. All that was poetic license. Amelia had read perhaps a little too much poetry of the type of *'Quand je suis morte, mes amies, plantez un saule au cimetiere'*; but really life was a very good thing to Amelia, especially when she had a new dress and someone paid her a compliment. But she went on writing verses extolling the advantages of The Tomb, and grovelling metrically at the feet of One who was Another's until that summer when she was nineteen and went to stay with Ernestine at Doricourt. Then her Muse took flight, scared, perhaps, by the possibility, suddenly and threateningly presented, of being asked to inspire verse about the real things of life.

At any rate, Amelia ceased to write poetry about the time when she and Ernestine and Ernestine's aunt went on a visit to Doricourt, where Frederick Doricourt lived with his aunt. It was not one of those hurried motor-fed excursions which we have now, and call week-ends, but a long leisurely visit, when all the friends of the static aunt called on the dynamic aunt, and both returned the calls with much state, a big barouche and a pair of fat horses. There were croquet parties and archery parties and little dances, all pleasant informal little gaieties arranged without ceremony among people who lived within driving distance of each other and knew each other's tastes and incomes and family history as well as they knew their own. The habit of importing huge droves of strangers from distant counties for brief harrying raids did not then obtain. There was instead a wide and constant circle of pleasant people and an unflagging stream of gaiety, mild indeed, but delightful to unjaded palates.

And at Doricourt life was delightful even on the days when there was no party. It was perhaps more delightful to Ernestine than to her friend, but even so, the one least pleased was Ernestine's aunt.

'I do think,' she said to the other aunt whose name was Julia — 'I daresay it is not so to you, being accustomed to Mr W Frederick, of course, from his childhood, but I always find gentlemen in the house so unsettling, especially young gentlemen, and when there are young ladies also. One is always on the *qui vive* for excitement.'

'Of course,' said Aunt Julia, with the air of a woman of the world, 'living as you and dear Ernestine do, with only females in the house —'

'We hang up an old coat and hat of my brother's on the hat-stand in the hall,' Aunt Emmeline protested.

'— The presence of gentlemen in the house must be a little unsettling. For myself, I am inured to it. Frederick has so many friends. Mr Thesiger, perhaps, the greatest. I believe him to be a most worthy young man, but peculiar.' She leaned forward across her bright-tinted Berlin woolwork and spoke impressively, the needle with its trailing red poised in air. 'You know, I hope you will not think it indelicate of me to mention such a thing, but dear Frederick — your dear Ernestine would have been in every way so suitable.'

'Would have been?' Aunt Emmeline's tortoiseshell shuttle

ceased its swift movement among the white loops and knots of her tatting.

'Well, my dear,' said the other aunt, a little shortly, 'you must surely have noticed —'

'You don't mean to suggest that Amelia — I thought Mr Thesiger and Amelia —'

'Amelia! I really must say! No, I was alluding to Mr Thesiger's attentions to dear Ernestine. Most marked. In dear Frederick's place I should have found some excuse for shortening Mr Thesiger's visit. But, of course, I cannot interfere. Gentlemen must manage these things for themselves. I only hope that there will be none of that trifling with the most holy affections of others which —'

The less voluble aunt cut in hotly with: 'Ernestine's incapable of anything so unladylike.'

'Just what I was saying,' the other rejoined blandly, got up and drew the blind a little lower, for the afternoon sun was glowing on the rosy wreaths of the drawing-room carpet.

Outside in the sunshine Frederick was doing his best to arrange his own affairs. He had managed to place himself beside Miss Ernestine Meutys on the stone steps of the pavilion, but then, Mr Thesiger lay along the lower step at her feet, a very good position for looking up into her eyes. Amelia was beside him, but then it never seemed to matter whom Amelia sat beside.

They were talking about the pavilion on whose steps they sat, and Amelia, who often asked uninteresting questions, had wondered how old it was. It was Frederick's pavilion after all, and he felt this when his friend took the words out of his mouth and used them on his own account, even though he did give the answer in the form of an appeal.

'The foundations are Tudor, aren't they?' he said. 'Wasn't it an observatory or laboratory or something of that sort in Fat Henry's time?'

'Yes,' said Frederick, 'there was some story about a wizard or an alchemist or something, and it was burned down, and then they rebuilt it in its present style.'

'The Italian style, isn't it?' said Thesiger; 'but you can hardly see what it is now, for the creeper.'

'Virginia creeper, isn't it?' Amelia asked, and Frederick said, 'Yes, Virginia creeper.' Thesiger said it looked more like a South American plant, and Ernestine said Virginia was in South America and that was why. 'I know, because of the war,' she said modestly, and nobody smiled or answered. There were manners in those days.

'There's a ghost story about it surely?' Thesiger began again, looking up at the dark closed doors of the pavilion.

'Not that I ever heard of,' said the pavilion's owner. 'I think the country people invented the tale because there have always been so many rabbits and weasels and things round dead near it. And once a dog, my uncle's favourite spaniel. But of course that's simply because they get entangled in the Virginia creeper — you see how fine and big it is — and can't get out, and die as they do in traps. But the villagers prefer to think it's ghosts.'

'I thought there was a real ghost story,' Thesiger persisted.

Ernestine said, 'A ghost story. How delicious! Do tell it, Mr Doricourt. This is just the place for a ghost story. Out of doors and the sun shining, so that we can't *really* be frightened.'

Doricourt protested again that he knew no story.

'That's because you never read, dear boy,' said Eugene Thesiger. 'That library of yours. There's a delightful book — did you never notice it? — brown tree-calf with your arms on it; the head of the house writes the history of the house as far as he knows it. There's a lot in that book. It began in Tudor times — 1515 to be exact.'

'Queen Elizabeth's time,' Ernestine thought that made it so much more interesting. 'And was the ghost story in that?'

'It isn't exactly a ghost story,' said Thesiger. 'It's only that the pavilion seems to be an unlucky place to sleep in.'

'Haunted?' Frederick asked, and added that he must look up that book.

'Not haunted exactly. Only several people who have slept the night there went on sleeping.'

'Dead, he means,' said Ernestine, and it was left for Amelia to ask:

'Does the book tell anything particular about how the people died? What killed them, or anything?'

'There are suggestions,' said Thesiger, 'but there, it *is* a gloomy subject. I don't know why I started it. Should we have time for a game of croquet before tea, Doricourt?'

⁜

'I wish *you'd* read the book and tell me the stories,' Ernestine said to Frederick, apart, over the croquet balls.

'I will,' he answered fervently; 'you've only to tell me what you want.'

'Or perhaps Mr Thesiger will tell us another time — in the twilight. Since people like twilight for ghosts. Will you, Mr Thesiger?' She spoke over her blue muslin shoulder.

Frederick certainly meant to look up the book, but he delayed till after supper; the half-hour before bed when he and Thesinger put on their braided smoking-jackets and their braided smoking-caps with the long yellow tassels, and smoked the cigars which were, in those days still, more of a luxury than a necessity. Ordinarily, of course, these were smoked out of doors, or in the smoking-room, a stuffy little den littered with boots and guns and yellow-backed railway novels. But tonight Frederick left his friend in that dingy hutch, and went alone to the library, found the book and took it to the circle of light made by the colza lamp.

'I can skim through it in half an hour,' he said, and wound

up the lamp and lighted his second cigar. Then he opened the shutters and windows, so that the room should not smell of smoke in the morning. Those were the days of consideration for the ladies who had not yet learned that a cigarette is not exclusively a male accessory like a beard or a bass voice.

But when, his preparations completed, he opened the book, he was compelled to say 'Pshaw!' Nothing short of this could relieve his feelings. (You know the expression I mean, though of course it isn't pronounced as it's spelt, any more than Featherstonehaugh or St Maur are.)

'Pshaw!' said Frederick, fluttering the pages. His remark was justified. The earlier part of the book was written in the beautiful script of the early sixteenth century, that looks so plain and is so impossible to read, and the later pages, though the handwriting was clear and Italian enough, left Frederick helpless, for the language was Latin, and Frederick's Latin was limited to the particular passages he had 'been through' at his private school. He recognised a word here and there, *mors*, for instance, and *pallidus* and *pavor* and *arcanum*, just as you or I might; but to read the complicated stuff and make sense of it! Frederick said something just a shade stronger than 'Pshaw!' — 'Botheration!' I think it was; replaced the book on the shelf, closed the shutters, and turned out the lamp. He thought he would ask Thesiger to translate the thing, but then again he thought he wouldn't. So he went to bed wishing that he had happened to remember more of the Latin so painfully beaten into the best years of his boyhood.

And the story of the pavilion was, after all, told by Thesiger.

There was a little dance at Doricourt next evening, a carpet dance, they called it. The furniture was pushed back against the walls, and the tightly stretched Axminster carpet was not so bad to dance on as you might suppose. That, you see, was before the days of polished floors and large rugs with loose edges that you can catch your feet in. A carpet was a carpet in those days, well and truly laid, conscientiously exact to the last least recess and fitting the floor like a skin. And on this quite tolerable surface the young people danced very heavily, some ten or twelve couples. The old people did not dance in those days, except sometimes a quadrille of state to 'open the ball'. They played cards in a room provided for the purpose, and in the dancing-room three or four kindly middle-aged ladies were considered to provide ample chaperonage. You were not even expected to report yourself to your chaperon at the conclusion of a dance. It was not like a real ball. And even in those far off days there were conservatories.

It was on the steps of the conservatory, not the steps leading from the dancing-room, but the steps leading to the garden, that the story was told. The four young people were sitting together, the girls' crinolined flounces spreading round them like huge pale roses, the young men correct in their high-shouldered coats and white cravats. Ernestine had been very kind to both the men — a little too kind, perhaps — who can tell? At any rate, there was in their eyes exactly that light which you may imagine in the eyes of rival stags in the mating season. It was Ernestine who asked Frederick for the story, and Thesiger who, at Amelia's suggestion, told it.

'It's quite a number of stories,' he said, 'and yet it's really all the same story. The first man to sleep in the pavilion slept there ten years after it was built. He was a friend of the alchemist or astrologer who built it. He was found dead in the morning. There seemed to have been a struggle. His arms bore the marks of cords. No; they never found any cords. He died from loss of blood. There were curious wounds. That was all the rude leeches of the day could report to the bereaved survivors of the deceased.'

'How funny you are, Mr Thesiger!' said Ernestine, with that celebrated soft, low laugh of hers. When Ernestine was elderly, many people thought her stupid. When she was young, no one seems to have been of this opinion.

'And the next?' asked Amelia.

'The next was sixty years later. It was a visitor that time, too. And he was found dead with just the same marks, and the doctors said the same thing. And so it went on. There have been eight deaths altogether — unexplained deaths. Nobody has slept in it now for over a hundred years. People seem to have a prejudice against the place as a sleeping apartment. I can't think why.'

'Isn't he simply killing?' Ernestine asked Amelia, who said:

'And doesn't anyone know how it happened?' No one answered till Ernestine repeated the question in the form of: 'I suppose it was just accident?'

'It was a curiously recurrent accident,' said Thesiger, and Frederick, who throughout the conversation had said the right things at the right moment, remarked that it did not do to believe all these old legends. Most old families had them, he believed. Frederick had inherited Doricourt from an unknown great-uncle of whom in life he had not so much as heard, but he was very strong on the family tradition. 'I don't attach any importance to these tales myself.'

'Of course not. All the same,' said Thesiger deliberately, 'you wouldn't care to pass a night in that pavilion.'

'No more would you,' was all Frederick found on his lips.

'I admit that I shouldn't enjoy it,' said Eugene, 'but I'll bet you a hundred you don't do it.'

'Done,' said Frederick.

'Oh, Mr Doricourt,' breathed Ernestine, a little shocked at betting 'before ladies'.

'Don't!' said Amelia, to whom, of course, no one paid any attention, 'don't do it!'

You know how, in the midst of flower and leafage, a snake

will suddenly, surprisingly rear a head that threatens? So, amid friendly talk and laughter, a sudden fierce antagonism sometimes looks out and vanishes again, surprising most of all the antagonists. This antagonism spoke in the tones of both men, and after Amelia had said, 'Don't', there was a curiously breathless little silence. Ernestine broke it. 'Oh,' she said, 'I do wonder which of you will win. I should like them both to win, wouldn't you, Amelia? Only I suppose that's not always possible, is it?'

Both gentlemen assured her that in the case of bets it was very rarely possible.

'Then I wish you wouldn't,' said Ernestine. 'You could *both* pass the night there, couldn't you, and be company for each other? I don't think betting for such large sums is quite the thing, do you, Amelia?'

Amelia said 'No, she didn't,' but Eugene had already begun to say:

'Let the bet be off then, if Miss Meutys doesn't like it. That suggestion is invaluable. But the thing itself needn't be off. Look here, Doricourt. I'll stay in the pavilion from one to three and you from three to five. Then honour will be satisfied. How will that do?'

The snake had disappeared.

'Agreed,' said Frederick, 'and we can compare impressions afterwards. That will be quite interesting.'

Then someone came and asked where they had all got to, and they went in and danced some more dances. Ernestine danced twice with Frederick and drank iced sherry and water and they said goodnight and lighted their bedroom candles at the table in the hall.

'I do hope they won't,' Amelia said as the girls sat brushing their hair at the two large white muslin frilled dressing-tables in the room they shared.

'Won't what?' said Ernestine, vigorous with the brush.

'Sleep in that hateful pavilion. I wish you'd ask them not to, Ernestine. They'd mind, if *you* asked them.'

'Of course I will if you like, dear,' said Ernestine cordially. She was always the soul of good nature. 'But I don't think you ought to believe in ghost stories, not really.'

'Why not?'

'Oh, because of the Bible and going to church and all that,' said Ernestine. 'Do you really think Rowland's Macassar has made any difference to my hair?'

'It is just as beautiful as it always was,' said Amelia, twisting up her own little ashen-blond handful. 'What was that?'

'That' was a sound coming from the little dressing-room. There was no light in that room. Amelia went into the little room though Ernestine said, 'Oh, don't! How can you? It might be a ghost or a rat or something,' and as she went she whispered, 'Hush!'

The window of the little room was open and she leaned out of it. The stone sill was cold to her elbows through her print dressing jacket.

Ernestine went on brushing her hair. Amelia heard a movement below the window and listened. 'Tonight will do,' someone said.

'It's too late,' said someone else.

'If you're afraid, it will always be too late or too early,' said someone. And it was Thesiger.

'You know I'm not afraid,' the other one, who was Doricourt, answered hotly.

'An hour for each of us will satisfy honour,' said Thesiger carelessly. 'The girls will expect it. I couldn't sleep. Let's do it now and get it over. Let's see. Oh, damn it!'

A faint click had sounded.

'Dropped my watch. I forgot the chain was loose. It's all right, though; glass not broken even. Well, are you game?'

'Oh, yes, if you insist. Shall I go first, or you?'

'I will,' said Thesiger. 'That's only fair, because I suggested it. I'll stay till half-past one or a quarter to two, and then you come on. See?'

'Oh, all right. I think it's silly, though,' said Frederick.

Then the voices ceased. Amelia went back to the other girl.

'They're going to do it tonight.'

'Are they, dear?' Ernestine was placid as ever. 'Do what?'

'Sleep in that horrible pavilion.'

'How do you know?'

Amelia explained how she knew.

'Whatever can we do?' she added.

'Well, dear, suppose we go to bed,' suggested Ernestine helpfully. 'We shall hear all about it in the morning.'

'But suppose anything happens?'

'What could happen?'

'Oh, *anything*,' said Amelia. 'Oh, I do wish they wouldn't! I shall go down and ask them not to.'

'*Amelia!*' the other girl was at last aroused. 'You *couldn't*. I shouldn't *let* you dream of doing anything so unladylike. What would the gentlemen think of you?'

The question silenced Amelia, but she began to put on her so lately discarded bodice.

'I won't go if you think I oughtn't,' she said.

'Forward and fast, auntie would call it,' said the other. 'I am almost sure she would.'

'But I'll keep dressed. I shan't disturb you. I'll sit in the dressing-room. I *can't* go to sleep while he's running into this awful danger.'

'Which he?' Ernestine's voice was very sharp. 'And there isn't any danger.'

'Yes, there is,' said Amelia sullenly, 'and I mean *them*. Both of them.'

Ernestine said her prayers and got into bed. She had put

her hair in curl-papers which became her like a wreath of white roses.

'I don't think auntie will be pleased,' she said, 'when she hears that you sat up all night watching young gentlemen. Goodnight, dear!'

'Goodnight, darling,' said Amelia. 'I know you don't understand. It's all right.'

She sat in the dark by the dressing-room window. There was no moon, but the starlight lay grey on the dew of the park, and the trees massed themselves in bunches of a darker grey, deepening to black at the roots of them. There was no sound to break the stillness, except the little cracklings of twigs and rustlings of leaves as birds or little night wandering beasts moved in the shadows of the garden, and the sudden creakings that furniture makes if you sit alone with it and listen in the night's silence.

Amelia sat on and listened, listened. The pavilion showed in broken streaks of pale grey against the wood, that seemed to be clinging to it in dark patches. But that, she reminded herself, was only the creeper. She sat there for a very long time, not knowing how long a time it was. For anxiety is a poor chronometer, and the first ten minutes had seemed an hour. She had no watch. Ernestine had — and slept with it under her pillow. The stable clock was out of order; the man had been sent for to see to it. There was nothing to measure time's flight by, and she sat there rigid, straining her ears for a footfall on the grass, straining her eyes to see a figure come out of the dark pavilion and across the dew-grey grass towards the house. And she heard nothing, saw nothing.

Slowly, imperceptibly, the grey of the sleeping trees took on faint dreams of colour. The sky turned faint above the trees, the moon perhaps was coming out. The pavilion grew more clearly visible. It seemed to Amelia that something moved among the leaves that surrounded it, and she looked to see him come out. But he did not come.

'I wish the moon would really shine,' she told herself. And suddenly she knew that the sky was clear and that this growing light was not the moon's cold silver, but the growing light of dawn.

She went quickly into the other room, put her hand under the pillow of Ernestine, and drew out the little watch with the diamond 'E' on it.

'A quarter to three,' she said aloud. Ernestine moved and grunted.

There was no hesitation about Amelia now. Without another thought for the ladylike and the really suitable, she lighted her candle and went quickly down the stairs, paused a moment in the hall, and so out through the front door. She passed along the terrace. The feet of Frederick protruded from the open French window of the smoking-room. She set down her candle on the terrace — it burned clearly enough in that clear air — went up to Frederick as he slept, his head between his shoulders and his hands loosely hanging, and shook him.

'Wake up,' she said. 'Wake up! Something's happened! It's a quarter to three and he's not come back.'

'Who's not what?' Frederick asked sleepily.

'Mr Thesiger. The pavilion.'

'Thesiger? — the — *You*, Miss Davenant? I beg your pardon. I must have dropped off.'

He got up unsteadily, gazing dully at this white apparition still in evening dress with pale hair now no longer wreathed.

'What is it?' he said. 'Is anybody ill?'

Briefly and very urgently Amelia told him what it was, imploring him to go at once and see what had happened. If he had been fully awake, her voice and her eyes would have told him many things.

'He said he'd come back,' he said. 'Hadn't I better wait? You go back to bed, Miss Davenant. If he doesn't come in half an hour —'

'If you don't go this minute,' said Amelia tensely, 'I shall.'

'Oh, well, if you insist,' Frederick said. 'He has simply fallen asleep as I did. Dear Miss Davenant, return to your room, I beg. In the morning when we are all laughing at this false alarm, you will be glad to remember that Mr Thesiger does not know of your anxiety.'

'I hate you,' said Amelia gently, 'and I am going to see what has happened. Come or not, as you like.'

She caught up the silver candlestick and he followed its wavering gleam down the terrace steps and across the grey dewy grass.

Half-way she paused, lifted the hand that had been hidden among her muslin flounces and held it out to him with a big Indian dagger in it.

'I got it out of the hall,' she said. 'If there's any *real* danger. Anything living, I mean. I thought — but I know I couldn't use it. Will you take it?'

He took it, laughing kindly.

'How romantic you are!' he said admiringly and looked at her standing there in the mingled gold and grey of dawn and candlelight. It was as though he had never seen her before.

They reached the steps of the pavilion and stumbled up them. The door was closed but not locked. And Amelia noticed that the trails of creeper had not been disturbed; they grew across the doorway as thick as a man's finger, some of them.

'He must have got in by one of the windows,' Frederick said. 'Your dagger comes in handy, Miss Davenant.'

He slashed at the wet sticky green stuff and put his shoulder to the door. It yielded at a touch and they went in.

The one candle lighted the pavilion hardly at all, and the

dusky light that oozed in through the door and windows helped very little. And the silence was thick and heavy.

'Thesiger!' said Frederick, clearing his throat. 'Thesiger! Hullo! Where are you?'

Thesiger did not say where he was. And then they saw.

There were low seats to the windows, and between the windows low stone benches ran. On one of these something dark, something dark and in places white, confused the outline of the carved stone.

'Thesiger,' said Frederick again in the tone a man uses to a room that he is almost sure is empty. 'Thesiger!'

But Amelia was bending over the bench. She was holding the candle crookedly so that it flared and guttered.

'Is he there?' Frederick asked, following her; 'is that him? Is he asleep?'

'Take the candle,' said Amelia, and he took it obediently. Amelia was touching what lay on the bench. Suddenly she screamed. Just one scream, not very loud. But Frederick remembers just how it sounded. Sometimes he hears it in dreams and wakes moaning, though he is an old man now and his old wife says, 'What is it, dear?' and he says, 'Nothing, my Ernestine, nothing.'

Directly she had screamed she said, 'He's dead,' and fell on her knees by the bench. Frederick saw that she held something in her arms.

'Perhaps he isn't,' she said. 'Fetch someone from the house — brandy — send for a doctor. Oh, go, go, go!'

'I can't leave you here,' said Frederick with thoughtful propriety; 'suppose he revives?'

'He will not revive,' said Amelia dully; 'go, go, go! Do as I tell you. Go! If you don't go,' she added suddenly and amazingly, 'I believe I shall kill you. It's all your doing.'

The astounding sharp injustice of this stung Frederick into action.

'I believe he's only fainted or something,' he said. 'When I've roused the house and everyone has witnessed your emotion you will regret —'

She sprang to her feet and caught the knife from him and raised it, awkwardly, clumsily, but with keen threatening, not to be mistaken or disregarded. Frederick went.

When Frederick came back with the groom and the gardener (he hadn't thought it well to disturb the ladies), the pavilion was filled full of white revealing daylight. On the bench lay a dead man, and kneeling by him a living woman on whose warm breast his cold and heavy head lay pillowed. The dead man's hands were full of the green crushed leaves, and thick twining tendrils were about his wrists and throat. A wave of green seemed to have swept from the open window to the bench where he lay.

The groom and the gardener and the dead man's friend looked and looked.

'Looks like as if he'd got himself entangled in the creeper and lost 'is 'ead,' said the groom, scratching his own.

'How'd the creeper get in, though? That's what I says.' It was the gardener who said it.

'Through the window,' said Doricourt, moistening his lips with his tongue.

'The window was shut, though, when I come by at five yesterday,' said the gardener stubbornly. ''Ow did it get all that way since five?'

They looked at each other voicing, silently, impossible things.

The woman never spoke. She sat there in the white ring of her crinolined dress like a broken white rose. But her arms were round Thesiger and she would not move them.

When the doctor came, he sent for Ernestine, who came flushed and sleepy-eyed and very frightened and shocked.

'You're upset, dear,' she said to her friend, 'and no wonder.

How brave of you to come out with Mr Doricourt to see what happened. But you can't do anything now, dear. Come in and I'll tell them to get you some tea.'

Amelia laughed, looked down at the face on her shoulder, laid the head back on the bench among the drooping green of the creeper, stooped over it, kissed it, and said quite quietly and gently, 'Goodbye, dear, goodbye!' — took Ernestine's arm and went away with her.

The doctor made an examination and gave a death-certificate. 'Heart failure' was his original and brilliant diagnosis. The certificate said nothing, and Frederick said nothing of the creeper that was wound about the dead man's neck, nor of the little white wounds, like little bloodless lips half-open, that they found about the dead man's neck.

'An imaginative or uneducated person,' said the doctor, 'might suppose that the creeper had something to do with his death. But we mustn't encourage superstition. I will assist my man to prepare the body for its last sleep. Then we need not have any chattering women.'

'Can you read Latin?' Frederick asked. The doctor could, and, later, did.

It was the Latin of that brown book with the Doricourt arms on it that Frederick wanted read. And when he and the doctor had been together with the book between them for three hours, they closed it, and looked at each other with shy and doubtful eyes.

'It can't be true,' said Frederick.

'If it is,' said the more cautious doctor, 'you don't want it talked about. I should destroy that book if I were you. And I should root up that creeper and burn it. It is quite evident, from what you tell me, that your friend believed that this creeper was a man-eater, that it fed, just before its flowering time, as the book tells us, at dawn; and that he fully meant that the thing, when it crawled into the pavilion seeking its prey, should find you and not him. It would have been so, I understand, if his watch had not stopped at one o'clock.'

'He dropped it, you know,' said Doricourt like a man in a dream.

'All the cases in this book are the same,' said the doctor, 'the strangling, the white wounds. I have heard of such plants; I never believed.' He shuddered. 'Had your friend any spite against you? Any reason for wanting to get you out of the way?'

Frederick thought of Ernestine, of Thesiger's eyes on Ernestine, of her smile at him over her blue muslin shoulder.

'No,' he said, 'none. None whatever. It must have been an accident. I am sure he did not know. He could not read Latin.' He lied, being, after all, a gentleman, and Ernestine's name being sacred.

'The creeper seems to have been brought here and planted in Henry the Eighth's time. And then the thing began. It seems to have been at its flowering season that it needed the — that, in short, it was dangerous. The little animals and birds found dead near the pavilion — But to move itself all that way, across the floor! The thing must have been almost conscient,' he said with a sincere shudder. 'One would think,' he corrected himself at once, 'that it knew what it was doing, if such a thing were not plainly contrary to the laws of nature.'

'Yes,' said Frederick, 'one would. I think if I can't do anything more I'll go and rest. Somehow all this has given me a turn. Poor Thesiger!'

His last thought before he went to sleep was one of pity.

'Poor Thesiger,' he said, 'how violent and wicked! And what an escape for me! I must never tell Ernestine. And all the time there was Amelia — Ernestine would never have done *that* for *me*.' And on a little pang of regret for the impossible he fell asleep.

Amelia went on living. She was not the sort that dies even

of such a thing as happened to her on that night, when for the first and last time she held her love in her arms and knew him for the murderer he was. It was only the other day that she died, a very old woman. Ernestine, who, beloved and surrounded by children and grandchildren, survived her, spoke her epitaph:

'Poor Amelia,' she said, 'nobody ever looked the same side of the road where she was. There was an indiscretion when she was young. Oh, nothing disgraceful, of course. She was a lady. But people talked. It was the sort of thing that stamps a girl, you know.'

18 The Detective

I

His mind was made up. There should be no looking back, no weakening, no foolish relentings. Civilisation had no place for him in her scheme of things; and he in his turn would show the jade that he was capable of a scheme in which she had no place, she and her pinchbeck meretricious substitutions of stones for bread, serpents for eggs. What exactly it was that had gone wrong does not matter. There was a girl in it perhaps; a friend most likely. Almost certainly money and pride and the old detestation of arithmetic played their part. His mother was now dead, and his father was dead long since. There was no one nearer than a great-uncle to care where he went or what he did; whether he throve or went under, whether he lived or died. Also it was springtime.

His thoughts turned longingly to the pleasant green country, the lush meadows, the blossoming orchards, nesting birds and flowering thorn, and to roads that should wind slowly, pleasantly between these. The remembrance came to him of another spring day when he had played truant, had found four thrushes' nests and a moorhen's, and tried to draw a kingfisher on the back of his Latin prose; had paddled in a mill stream between bright twinkling leaves and the bright twinkling counterfeits in the glassy water, had been caned at school next day, and his mother had cried when he told her. He rememberd how he had said: 'I will be good, oh, mother, I will!' and then added with one of those odd sudden cautions that lined the fluttering garment of his impulsive soul, 'at least, I'll try to be good.'

Well, he had tried. For more than a year he had tried, bearing patiently the heavy yoke of ledger and costs book, the weary life of the office the great-uncle had found for him. There had been a caged bird at the cobbler's in the village at home, that piped sweetly in its prison and laboured to draw up its own drinking water by slow chained thimblefulls. He sometimes thought that he was like that caged bird, straining and straining forever at the horrible machinery which grudgingly yielded to his efforts the little pittance that kept him alive. And all the while the woods and fields and the long white roads were calling, calling.

And now the chief had been more than usually repulsive, and the young man stood at the top of the stairs, smoothing the silk hat that stood for so much, and remembering in detail the unusual repulsiveness of the chief. An error of two and sevenpence in one column, surely a trivial error, and of two hundred pounds in another, quite an obvious error that, and easily rectified, had been the inspiration of the words that sang discordantly to his revolted soul. He suddenly tossed his hat in the air, kicked it as it fell, black and shining, and sent it spinning down the stairs. The office boy clattered out, thin-necked, red-eared, slack mouth well open.

'My hat!' was his unintentionally appropriate idiom.

'Pardon me, *my* hat,' said the young man suavely. But the junior was genuinely shocked.

'I say, Mr Sellinge,' he said solemnly, 'it'll never be the same again, that tile won't. Ironing it won't do it, no, nor yet blocking.'

'Bates,' the young man retorted with at least equal solemnity, 'I shall never wear that hat again. Remove your subservient carcase. I'm going back to tell the chief.'

'About your hat?' the junior asked, breathless, incredulous.

'About my hat,' Sellinge repeated.

The chief looked up a little blankly. Clerks who had had what he was well aware they called the rough side of his tongue rarely returned to risk a second helping. And now this hopeless young incompetent, this irreverent trifler with the columns of the temple of the gods L, S and D, was standing before him, and plainly standing there to speak, not merely to be spoken to.

'Well, Sellinge,' he said, frowning a little, but not too much, lest he should scare away an apology more ample than that with which Sellinge had met the rough side. 'Well, what is it?'

Sellinge, briefly, respectfully, but quite plainly told him what it was. And the chief listened, hardly able to believe his respectable ears.

'And so,' the tale ended, 'I should like to leave at once, please, sir.'

'Do you realise, young man,' the head of the firm asked heavily, 'that you are throwing away your career?'

Sellinge explained what he did realise.

'Your *soul*, did you say?' the portly senior looked at him through gold-rimmed glasses. 'I never heard of such a thing in my life.'

Sellinge waited respectfully, and the head of the house looked suddenly older. The unusual is the disconcerting. The chief was not used to hearing souls mentioned except on Sundays. Yet the boy was the grand-nephew of an old friend, a valued and useful business friend, a man whom it would be awkward for him to offend or annoy. This is the real meaning of friendship in the world of business. So he said: 'Come, come, now, Sellinge; think it over. I've had occasion to complain, but I've not complained unjustly — not unjustly, I think. Your opportunities in this office — what did you say?'

The young man had begun to say, quite politely, what he thought of the office.

'But, God bless my soul!' said the older man, quite flustered by this impossible rebellion. 'What is it you want? Come now,' he said, remembering the usefulness of that eminent great-uncle, and unbending as he remembered, 'if this isn't good enough for you, a respectable solicitor's office and every chance of rising — every chance,' he repeated pensively, oblivious now of all that the rough side had said; 'if this isn't good enough for you, what is? What *would* you like?' he asked, with a pathetic mixture of hopelessness, raillery, and the certitude that his question was unanswerable.

'I should like,' said Sellinge slowly, 'to be a tramp, or a burglar ...'

('Great Heavens!' said the chief.)

'— or a detective. I want to go about and do things. I want ...'

'A detective?' said the chief. 'Have you ever ...'

'No,' said Sellinge, 'but I could.'

'A new Sherlock Holmes, eh?' said the chief, actually smiling.

'Never,' said the clerk firmly, and he frowned. 'May I go now, sir? I've no opening in the burgling or the detective line, so I shall be a tramp, for this summer at least. Perhaps I'll go to Canada. I'm sorry I haven't been a success here. Bates is worth twice my money. He never wavers in his faith. Seven nines are always sixty-three with Bates.'

Again the chief thought of his useful city friend.

'Never mind Bates,' he said. 'Is the door closed? Right. Sit down, if you please, Mr Sellinge. I have something to say to you.'

Sellinge hesitated, looked round at the dusty leather-covered furniture, the worn Turkey carpet, the black, shiny deed-boxes, and the shelves of dull blue and yellow papers. The brown oblong of window framed a strip of blue sky and a strip of the opposite office's dirty brickwork. A small strayed cloud, very white and shining, began to cross the strip of sky.

'It's very kind of you, sir,' said Sellinge, his mind more made up than ever; 'but I wouldn't reconsider my decision for ten times what I've been getting.'

'Sit down,' said the chief again. 'I assure you I do not propose to raise your salary, nor to urge you to reconsider your decision. I merely wish to suggest an alternative — one of your own alternatives,' he added persuasively.

'Oh!' said Sellinge, sitting down abruptly, 'which?'

II

And now behold the dream realised. A young man with bare sun-bleached hair that looks as though it had never known the shiny black symbol of civilisation, boots large and dusty, and on his back the full equipment of an artist in oils; a little too new the outfit, but satisfactory and complete. He goes slowly along through the clean white dust of the roads, and his glance to right and left embraces green field and woodland with the persuasive ardour of a happy lover. The only blot on the fair field of life outspread before him the parting words of the chief.

'It's a very simple job for a would-be detective. Just find out whether the old chap's mad or not. You get on with the lower orders, you tell me. Well, get them to talk to you. And if you find that out, well, there may be a career for you. I've long been dissatisfied with the ordinary enquiry agent. Yes, two pounds a week, and expenses. But in reason. Not first-class, you know.'

This much aloud. To himself he had said: 'A simpleton's useful sometimes, if he's honest. And if he doesn't find out anything we shall be no worse off than we were before, and I shall be able to explain to his uncle that I really gave him exceptional opportunities — exceptional.'

Sellinge also, walking along between the dusty powdered white-flowered hedges, felt that the opportunity was exceptional. All his life people had told him things, and the half-confidences of two people often make up a complete sphere of knowledge, if only the confidant possesses the power of joining the broken halves. This power Sellinge had. He knew many things; the little scandals, the parochial intrigues and intricacies of the village where he was born were clearer to him than to the principal performers. He looked forward pleasantly to the lodging in the village ale-house, and to the slow gossip on the benches by the door.

The village (he was nearing it now) was steep and straggling, displaying its oddly assorted roofs amid a flutter of orchard trees, a carpet of green spaces. The Five Bells stood to the left, its tea-gardens beside it, cool and alluring.

Sellinge entered the dark sandy passage where the faint smell of last night's tobacco and this morning's beer contended with the fresh vigour of a bunch of wallflowers in a blue jug on the ring-marked bar.

Within ten minutes he had engaged his room, a little hot white attic under the roof, and had learned that it was Squire who lived in the big house, and that there was a lot of tales, so there was, but it didn't do to believe all you heard, nor yet more'n half you see, and least said soonest mended, and the house *was* worth looking at, or so people said as took notice of them old ancient tumble-down places. No, it wasn't likely you could get in. Used to be open of a Thursday, the 'ouse and grounds, but been closed to visitors this many year. Also that, for all it looked so near, the house was a good four and a half miles by the road.

'And Squire's mighty good to the people in the village,' the pleasant-faced old landlady behind the bar went on; 'pays good wages, 'e does, and if anyone's in trouble he's always got his hand in his pocket. I don't believe he spends half on himself to what he gives away. It'll be a poor day for Jevington when anything happens to him, sir, you take that from me. No harm in your trying to see the house, sir, but as for seeing him, he never sees no one. Why, listen, '— there was the sound of hoofs and wheels in the road — 'look out, sir, quick!'

Sellinge looked out to see an old-fashioned carriage and pair sweep past, in the carriage a white-haired old man with a white thin face and pale clouded eyes.

'That's him,' said the landlady beside him, ducking as the carriage passed. 'Yes, four and a half miles by the road, sir.'

Harnessed in his trappings of colour-box and easel, the young detective set out. There was about him none of the furtivity of your stage detective. His disguise was perfect, mainly because it was not a disguise. Such disguise as there was hung over his soul, which was pretending to itself that the errand was one of danger and difficulty. The attraction of the detective's career was to him not so much the idea of hunting down criminals as the dramatic attitude of one who goes about the world with a false beard and a makeup box in one hand and his life in the other. To find out the truth about an old gentleman's eccentricities was quite another pair of sleeves, but of these, as yet, our hero perceived neither the cut nor the colour. He had wanted to be a tramp or a detective, and here he was, both. One has to earn one's bread, and what better way than this?

A smooth worn stile prefaced a path almost hidden in grass up for hay, a blaze of red sorrel, buttercups, ox-eyed daisies in the feathery foam of flowered grasses. The wood of the stile was warm to his hand, and the grasses that met over the path powdered his boots with their little seeds.

Then there was a copse, and a rabbit warren, and short crisp grass dry on the chalk it thinly covered. The sun shone hardly in a sky of brass. The wayfarer panted for shade. It showed far ahead like a mirage in a desert, a group of pines, a flat whiteness of pond-water, a little house. One might ask the way at that house, and get — talk.

He fixed his eyes on it and walked on, the leather straps hot on his shoulders, his oak stick-handle hot in his hand. Then suddenly he saw on the hill, pale beyond the pines, someone coming down the path. He knew the magnet that a planted easel is to rustic minds. This might perhaps be, after all, the better way. Never did artist prepare so rapidly the scene that should attract the eye of the rustic gazer, the lingering but inevitable approach of the rustic foot.

In three minutes he was seated on his camp-stool, a canvas before him, his palette half-set. Four minutes saw a good deal of blue on the canvas. Purple, too, at the fifth minute, because the sky had turned that colour in the west, purple and, moreover, a strange threatening tint that called for burnt sienna and mid chrome and a dash of madder. The white advancing figure had disappeared among the pines. He madly squeezed green paint on to the foreground; one must at least have a picture begun. And the sun searched intolerably every bit of him as he sat in the shadeless warren awaiting the passing of the other.

And then, more sudden than an earthquake or the birth of love, a mighty rushing wind fell on him, caught up canvas and easel, even colour-box and oak staff, and whirled them away like leaves in an autumn equinox. His hat went too, not that that mattered, and the virgin sketch book whirled white before a wind that, the papers said next day, travelled at the rate of five-and-fifty miles an hour. The wonderful purple and copper of the west rushed up across the sky, a fierce spatter of rain stung face and hands. He pursued the colour-box, which had lodged in the front entry of a rabbit's house, caught at the canvas, whose face lay closely pressed to a sloe-bush, and ran for the nearest shelter, the house among the pines. In a rain like that one has to run head down or be blinded, and so he did not see till he drew breath in the mouldering rotten porch of it that his shelter was not of those from which hospitality can be asked.

A little lodge it was, long since deserted; walls and ceiling bulging and discoloured with damp, its latticed windows curtained only by the tapestry of the spider, its floors carpeted with old dust and drift of dry pine needles, and on its hearth the nests of long-fledged birds had fallen on the ashes of a fire gone out a very long time ago. A blazing lightning-flash dazzled him as he tried the handle of the door, and the door, hanging by one rusty hinge, yielded to his push as the first shattering peal of thunder clattered and cracked overhead. So a shelter it was, though the wind drove the rain almost horizontally through the broken window and across the room. He reached through the casement, and at the cost of a soaked coat-sleeve pulled to a faded green shutter, and made this fast. Then he explored the upper rooms. Holes in the thatch had let through the weather, and the drop, drop of the water that wears away stone had worn away the boards of the floor, so that they bent dangerously to his tread. The half-way landing of the little crooked staircase seemed the dryest place. He sat down there with his back against the wall and listened to the cracking and blundering of the thunder, watched through the skylight the lightning shoot out of the clouds, rapid and menacing as the tongue from the mouth of a snake.

No man who is not a dreamer chooses as a symbolic rite the kicking of a tall black hat down the stairs of the office he has elected to desert. Sellinge, audience at first to the glorious orchestra, fell from hearing to a waking dream, and the waking dream merged in a dreamless sleep.

When he awoke he knew at once that he was not alone in the little forgotten house. A tramp perhaps, a trespasser almost certainly. He had not had time to move under this thought before the other overpowered it. It was *he* who was the tramp, the trespasser. The other might be the local police. Have you ever tried to explain anything to the police in a rural district? It would be better to lie quietly, holding one's breath, and so, perhaps, escape an interview that could not be to his advantage, and might, in view of the end he pursued, be absolutely the deuce-and-all.

So he lay quietly, listening. To almost nothing. The other person, whoever it was, moved hardly at all; or perhaps the movements were drowned in the mutter of the thunder and the lashing of the rain, for Sellinge had not slept out the storm. But its violence had lessened while he slept, and presently the great thunders died away in slow sulky mutterings, and the fierce rain settled to a steady patter on the thatch and a slow drip, drip from the holes in the roof to the rotting boards below. And the dusk was falling; shadows were setting up their tents in the corners of the stairs and of the attic whose floor was on a level with his eyes. And below, through the patter of the rain, he could hear soft movements. How soft, his strained ears hardly knew till the abrupt contrast of a step on the earth without reminded him of the values of the ordinary noises that human beings make when they move.

The step on the hearth outside was heavy and plashy in the wet mould; the touch on the broken door was harsh, and harshly the creaking one hinge responded. The footsteps on the boarded floor of the lower room were loud and echoing. Those other sounds had been as the half-heard murmur of summer woods in the ears of one half asleep. This was definite, undeniable as the sound of London traffic.

Suddenly all sounds ceased for a moment, and in that moment Sellinge found time to wish that he had never found this shelter. The wildest, wettest, stormiest weather out under the sky seemed better than this little darkening house which he shared with these two others. For there were two. He knew it even before the man began to speak. But he had not known till then that the other, the softly moving first-comer, was a woman, and when he knew it, he felt, in a thrill of impotent resentment, the shame of his situation and the impossibility of escaping from it. He was an eavesdropper. He had not, somehow, thought of eavesdropping as incidental to the detective career. And there was nothing he could do to make things better which would not, inevitably, make them worse. To declare himself now would be to multiply a thousandfold everything which he desired to minimise. Because the first words that came to him from the two below were love-words, low, passionate, and tender, in the voice of a man. He could not hear the answer of the woman, but there are ways of answering which cannot be overheard.

'Stay just as you are,' he heard the man's voice again, 'and let me stay here at your feet and worship you.'

And again: 'Oh, my love, my love, even to see you like this! It's all so different from what we used to think it would be; but it's heaven compared with everything else in the world.'

Sellinge supposed that the woman answered, though he caught no words, for the man went on:

'Yes, I know it's hard for you to come, and you come so seldom. And even when you're not here, I know you understand. But life's very long and cold, dear. They talk about death being cold. It's life that's the cold thing, Anna.'

Then the voice sank to a murmur, cherishing, caressing, hardly articulate, and the shadows deepened, deepened inside the house. But outside it grew lighter because the moon had risen and the clouds and the rain had swept away, and sunset and moonrise were mingling in the clear sky.

'Not yet; you will not send me away yet?' he heard. 'Oh, my love, such a little time, and all the rest of life without you! Ah! let me stay beside you a little while!'

The passion and the longing of the voice thrilled the listener to an answering passion of pity. He himself had read of love, thought of it, dreamed of it; but he had never heard it speak; he had not known that its voice could be like this.

A faint whispering sound came to him; the woman's answer,

he thought, but so low was it that it was lost even as it reached him in the whisper of a wet ivy-branch at the window. He raised himself gently and crept on hands and knees to the window of the upper room. His movements made no sound that could have been heard below. He felt happier there, looking out on the clear, cold, wedded lights, and also he was as far as he could be, in the limits of that house, from those two poor lovers.

Yet still he heard the last words of the man, vibrant with the agony of a death-parting.

'Yes, yes, I will go.' Then, 'Oh, my dear, dear love; goodbye, goodbye!'

The sound of footsteps on the floor below, the broken hinged door was opened and closed again from without; he heard its iron latch click into place. He looked from the window. The last indiscretion of sight was nothing to the indiscretions of hearing that had gone before, and he wanted to see this man to whom all his soul had gone out in sympathy and pity. He had not supposed that he could ever be so sorry for anyone.

He looked to see a young man bowed under a weight of sorrow, and he saw an old man bowed with the weight of years. Silver-white was the hair in the moonlight, thin and stooping the shoulders, feeble the footsteps, and tremulous the hand that closed the gate of the little enclosure that had been a garden. The figure of a sad old man went away alone through the shadows of the pine-trees.

And it was the figure of the old man who had driven by the Five Bells in the old-fashioned carriage, the figure of the man he had come down to watch, to spy upon. Well, he had spied, and he had found out — what?

He did not wait for anyone else to unlatch that closed door and come out into the moonlight below the window. He thinks now that he knew even then that no one else would come out. He went down the stairs in the darkness, careless of the sound of his feet on the creaking boards. He lighted a match and held it up and looked round the little bare room with its one shuttered window and its one door, close latched. And there was no one there, no one at all. The room was as empty and cold as any last year's nest.

He got out very quickly and got away, not stopping to shut door or gate nor to pick up the colour-box and canvas from the foot of the stairs where he had left them. He went very quickly back to the Five Bells, and he was very glad of the lights and the talk and the smell and sight and sound of living men and women.

It was next day that he asked his questions; this time of the round-faced daughter of the house.

'No,' she told him, 'Squire wasn't married,' and 'Yes, there was a sort of story.'

He pressed for the story, and presently got it.

'It ain't nothing much. Only they say when Squire was a young man there was some carryings on with the gamekeeper's daughter up at the lodge. Happen you noticed it, sir, an old tumble-down place in the pine woods.'

Yes, he had happened to notice it.

'Nobody knows the rights of it now,' the girl told him; 'all them as was in it's under the daisies this long time, except Squire. But he went away and there was some mishap; he got thrown from his horse and didn't come home when expected, and the girl she was found drownded in the pond nigh where she used to live. And Squire he waren't never the same man. They say he hangs about round the old lodge to this day when it's full moon. And they do say ... But there, I dunno, it's all silly talk, and I hope you won't take no notice of anything I've said. One gets talking.'

Caution, late born, was now strong in her, and he could not get any more.

'Do you remember the girl's name?' he asked at last, finding all assaults vain against the young woman's caution.

'Why, I wasn't born nor yet thought of,' she told him, and laughed and called along the fresh sanded passage: 'Mother, what was that girl's name, you know, the one up at the lodge that ...'

'Ssh!' came back the mother's voice; 'you keep a still tongue, Lily; it's all silly talk.'

'All right, mother, but what *was* her name?'

'Anna,' came the voice along the fresh sanded passage.

✕

'Dear sir,' ran Sellinge's report, written the next day.

'I have made enquiries and find no ground for supposing the gentleman in question to be otherwise than of sound mind. He is much respected in the village and very kind to the poor. I remain here awaiting your instructions.'

While he remained there awaiting the instructions he explored the neighbourhood, but he found nothing of much interest except the grave on the north side of the churchyard, a grave marked by no stone, but covered anew every day with fresh flowers. It had been so covered every day, the sexton told him, for fifty years.

'A long time, fifty years,' said the man, 'a long time, sir. A lawyer in London, he pays for the flowers, but they do say ...'

'Yes,' said Sellinge quickly, 'but then people say all sorts of things, don't they?'

'Some on 'em's true though,' said the sexton.

Notes on the stories

BY KATE MACDONALD

1 Man-Size in Marble

good colours: good quality paints.

Liberty's: the fashionable new department store off Oxford Circus where William Morris fabrics and art nouveau decorations could be bought.

do for us: to come in daily to clean and cook as needed.

little magazine stories: Edith Nesbit earned her living writing stories for story magazines.

Monthly Marplot: an invented magazine name.

rise in her screw: she wants a pay rise.

reticulated windows: tall windows divided into vertical bars, topped with a network of circles; a style of structural decoration typical of the early fourteenth century in English churches.

blackleading: the standard method of cleaning a cast-iron kitchen range, by polishing or painting it with a paste of black lead and white spirit, and then buffing it up when dried. It is notoriously messy and hard work.

Rubinstein: probably the prolific Russian pianist and composer Anton Rubinstein (1829–1894) of whom it was remarked that he composed enough for three.

cavendish: a treated tobacco with a sweet taste and a strong smell.

Arcadian: from Arcady, a mythological place of harmony, joy and peace.

vesta: an early form of match.

2 John Charrington's Wedding

got the mitten: archaic saying meaning that he has been rejected.

Gladstone: Gladstone bag, a large carryall.

3 Uncle Abraham's Romance

Ob. **1723**: Latin, obiit, she died.

4 The Ebony Frame

unconsidered pars: freelance journalists would submit paragraphs for newspaper publication, paid at a penny a word, and as paragraphs they were often too short to be remembered by the reading public.

after long grief and pain: from the opening of the second part of *Maud* by Alfred, Lord Tennyson.

6 Hurst of Hurstcote

Schools: the exams at Oxford University.

threw the handkerchief: a contemptuous saying for a proposal of marriage where one party is of higher estate, thus the other has to bend to pick up the metaphorical handkerchief offered.

8 The Haunted Inheritance

Tempus fugit manet amor: Latin, Time flies, love remains.

brakes: carriages.

9 The Power of Darkness

Musée Grevin: Paris waxworks museum founded in 1882.

Loie Fuller: celebrated American dancer who pioneered a theatrical dance using large pleated and billowing silks and innovative lighting.

coulisses: French, backstage, the life behind the scenes in a theatre.

Fashoda: a town now in Sudan, which became in 1898 a strategic point for railway access to the rest of central and southern Africa disputed by France and Britain, in which Kitchener, for the British, persuaded the French commander to stand down and relinquish French claims to the area.

Madame de Lamballe: a confidante of Marie-Antoinette, murdered in 1792 during the French Revolution.

Deianira: from Classical Greek myth, she was the wife of Hercules and his murderer.

10 The Shadow

second extra: the second of the extra dances put on at the end of a ball.

sacque: a distinctive eighteenth-century fashion of informal ladies' dress, suggesting that they're talking about a ghost.

Cleopatra's Needle: very large Pharaonic-era stone column with squared-off corners brought from Egypt and erected on the Victoria Embankment in central London in 1877.

salt cellars: referring to the hollow at the base of the girl's throat, showing how thin she is.

the gas suddenly glared higher: use of early gas supplies in a house affected different rooms. When the men had finished playing billiards, and turned out the gas, the release of that pressure back to the supply made other lights still in use burn brighter.

post-chaise: a two- or four-horse coach for hire, which would be ridden 'post', ie one set of horses would draw it at high speed to the next coaching inn or post-house, where the coachman would change horses and carry on with the journey.

encaustic tiles: colourful patterned tiles made using a medieval technique repopularised after the Victorian Gothic revival in architecture and design.

cypress, aucuba: these are both thick, light-obscuring evergreen shrubs.

inapropos: the inappropriate.

12 Number 17

commercial: commercial traveller, a salesman.

travelled in: he was a salesman for a brand of children's underclothing, and travelled from town to town to get orders for this from shops.

13 In the Dark

all-wooler: along with alternative Edwardian lifestyle choices such as vegetarianism and teetotalism, wearing all-wool clothing was advocated as a particularly healthy choice, but also considered by the mainstream to be unnecessarily virtuous.

the Albany: exclusive and expensive sets of apartments just off Piccadilly, indicating that the narrator has very good connections and money to match.

Exhibition: The *Exposition des primitifs flamands à Bruges* was held from June to October 1902, and was groundbreaking for art collection and research into early Netherlandish art. It drew immense crowds.

14 The Violet Car

rep: a tough and plain furnishing fabric.

15 The Marble Child

kings and knaves: a description of the traditional playing card.

plump divine: a stout vicar.

Geneva bands: the plain white strips of starched linen at the collar worn by a Protestant minister of religion.

argent and sable, gules: names for colours from heraldry. Argent is silver or white, sable is black, gules is red.

fretted: complex edging patterns in stone.

triforium: an upper gallery in a church, above the nave or a side chapel, sometimes with its own balcony or walkway around the three closed sides.

you would wear your blue silk: silk does not tolerate being splashed with water, as the splashmarks remain, spoiling the garment.

Lot's wife: one of the more fantastical stories from the Old Testament that a child's imagination would retain (Genesis 19).

window-tax: the Act to tax the number of windows in a house was brought in in England in 1696 and repealed in 1851. Existing houses that already had more windows than their owners wanted to pay tax on had some of the windows bricked up, and newer houses were built with the window spaces already filled in with the building stone, leaving the impression of a symmetrical arrangement of spaces.

17 The Pavilion

Quand je suis morte: From the poem 'Lucie' by Alfred de Musset;
'When I am dead, my friends, plant a willow in the churchyard',
a very Romantic sentiment.

qui vive: Latin, the sentry's challenge of 'Who goes there',
transmuted to a slang term for being on the lookout.

tatting: the craft of making edgings and decorative trimmings
out of thread, rather like lace-making.

18 The Detective

pinchbeck: an alloy of copper and zinc that closely resembles
gold; its inventor's name became a byword for something that
was cheap or valueless.

stones for bread: from Luke 11:11–13, a parable about the
generosity of fathers, but the narrator here has mangled the story
slightly in his passion.

tile: slang for a top hat.

the gods L, S and D: pounds, shillings and pence, which the narrator,
a reluctant and not very good accountant, has to wrestle with.

ducking: curtseying.

The Living Stone
Stories of Uncanny Sculpture,
1858–1943
Edited by Henry Bartholomew

The Living Stone

Stories of Uncanny Sculpture, 1858–1943

Edited by Henry Bartholomew

A fearful anthology of forgotten stories to persuade you that a stone hand has been placed on your shoulder when you least expect it, or that something heavy is scraping its way up the stairs. Well-known authors of the uncanny and mistresses of supernatural short stories to frighten the heart into some loud thumpings.

Authors include:

Sabine Baring-Gould, E F Benson, Nellie K Blissett, Bernard Capes, James Causey, Robert W Chambers, N Dennett, W W Fenn, Hazel Heald, H P Lovecraft, Arthur Machen, W C Morrow, Oliver Onions, E R Punshon, Eleanor Scott, Clark Ashton Smith, and Edith Wharton.

Strange Relics

Stories of Archaeology and the Supernatural, 1895–1954

Edited by Amara Thornton & Katy Soar

Strange Relics

Stories of Archaeology and the Supernatural, 1895–1954

Edited by Amara Thornton and Katy Soar

A new anthology of twelve classic short stories combining the supernatural and archaeology. Never before have so many relics from the past caused such delicious and intriguing shivers down the spine. From a Neolithic rite to Egyptian religion to Roman remains to medieval masonry to some uncanny ceramic tiles in a perfectly ordinary American sun lounge, the relics in these stories are, frankly, horrible.

Stories include:

'The Ape', by E F Benson, 'Roman Remains', by Algernon Blackwood, 'Ho! The Merry Masons', by John Buchan, 'Through the Veil', by Arthur Conan Doyle, 'View From A Hill', M R James, 'Curse of the Stillborn', by Margery Lawrence, 'Whitewash', by Rose Macaulay, 'The Shining Pyramid', by Arthur Machen, 'Cracks of Time', by Dorothy Quick and 'The Cure', by Eleanor Scott.

From the Abyss

Weird Fiction, 1907–1945

By D K Broster

D K Broster

From the Abyss

Weird Fiction, 1907–1945

Edited by Melissa Edmundson

D K Broster was one of the great British historical novelists of the twentieth century, but her Weird fiction has long been forgotten. She wrote some of the most impressive supernatural short stories to be published between the wars. Melissa Edmundson, editor of Handheld's *Women's Weird*, has curated a selection of Broster's best and most terrifying work. Stories in *From the Abyss* include these tales of particular archaeological and architectural interest:

- 'The Window', in which a deserted chateau exacts revenge when one particular window is opened.
- 'The Pavement', in which the protectress of a Roman mosaic cannot bear to let it go.
- 'Clairvoyance', in which the spirit of a vengeful Japanese swordmaster enters an adolescent girl.
- 'The Pestering', in which a cursed hidden treasure draws its victim across centuries to find it.
- 'The Taste of Pomegranates' draws two young women into the palaeolithic past.